I0739399

KAREN M. DILLON

THE
IMMORTAL
SOULS

MAGIC & CHAOS
BOOK ONE

THE IMMORTAL SOULS

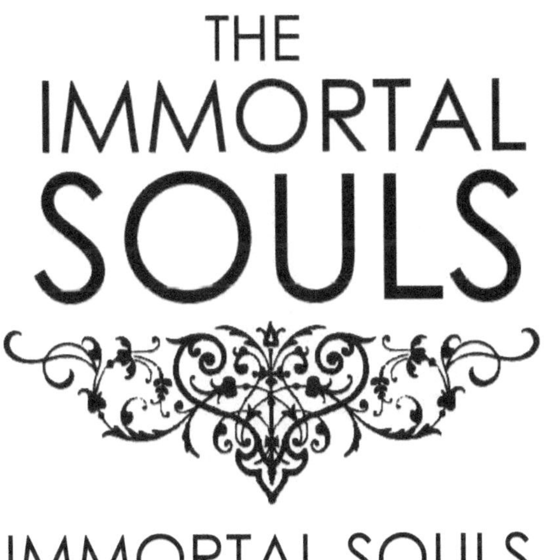

IMMORTAL SOULS

For M. Donnelly...

... the first person to suggest I publish this

PROLOGUE

1300 YEARS AGO...

Atropos stood with her sisters in the back of the grand hall, watching in mournful silence as the Witches and Demons arrived.

Shadows danced in gleeful anticipation, their presence darkening the aura of the room, making the air thick and hard to breathe, their very presence a taint which poisoned all they touched.

Things were not right and had not been for quite some time.

But recently, something had changed.

What had started out as simple acts of selfishness, strongly worded arguments and minor fights for freedom had turned into all out acts of war and brutality.

The current display being the most depraved.

Atropos looked on as three women strolled into the hall. All with white hair, white skin and white eyes.

They called themselves the Elder Witches.

Although their years did not show on their faces, they were three of the oldest Witches alive.

The sisters had just recently taken control of the Witches' Kingdom and had organised these public executions as a display of power. And to show *Her* that they no longer abided by Her laws.

The sound of metal chains dragging across stone floors echoed throughout the hall.

All present turned to face the door where two guards walked in, both gripping the arms of a semi-conscious girl.

Her head was down, her long golden hair—matted with dirt and blood—was loose and obscured most of her face from view. Her clothes were torn and filthy, her pale skin covered with dark purple bruises, making obvious the abuse she had suffered at the hands of her captors.

Her feet barely touched the ground as they moved her; it appeared as though she was so limp that the guards were carrying most of her weight.

It was easy to sense—with the dimness that weighed on the girl's usually bright, vibrant aura—that the Elder Witches had somehow managed to bind her Powers, knowing that if she were to have access to her Magic she could have easily brought an end to every being present with no more than a flick of her wrist.

The guards brought the small girl to the centre of the hall where a wooden stake awaited her. One of the men held her upright, keeping her back pressed against the wood, as the other tied ropes around her to hold her in place.

As they let her go, her body slumped forward slightly. She was so weak and powerless that she would barely notice what was happening until the pain became too much for her to bear.

Atropos felt a cold rage swarm through her veins, causing her stomach to turn with revulsion at what she was witnessing.

Making her more furious with herself for not having enough Power to stop it.

The girl was no more than an innocent victim, caught in the middle of a war.

She gripped her ancient scissors so tightly it almost sliced through her hand.

Atropos felt a soft brush against the fingers that gripped the scissors. She looked down to find a hand holding onto hers. "Do not stain the scissors with your blood," whispered Clotho. Atropos looked at her sister, seeing in her eyes the same guilt and sadness that she felt within herself.

She turned towards Lachesis who was staring straight ahead with unseeing eyes. "This isn't right," Atropos mumbled, fearing the repercussions if anyone else should hear her objection to these murders.

"There's nothing to be done," Lachesis said. Her voice cold and unfeeling. "Fate has been sealed. The prophecy has been written."

A shiver ran down Atropos' spine, making her stomach feel sick. She turned to find the source of her discomfort . . . and there *he* was.

The cloaked figure in the corner of the room.

A faceless evil shrouded in darkness with shadows seeping out of every pore.

The cause of all of the chaos, all of the bloodshed, was him.

There was a crash from outside the hall. A murmur of confusion swept through the crowd.

Atropos looked towards the door where she saw two more guards dragging with them a man who was struggling with all his strength to escape. His wrists were bound with chains, his face bloody and bruised.

Another innocent soul that had been sentenced to death.

"Don't!" he cried out as he looked up and saw the girl tied

to the stake. He attempted to run forward but was pulled back by the guards who were keeping him chained. "Don't hurt her! *Please!* She's done nothing to you!"

"Why has he not been spelled into silence?" asked one of the Elder Witches, the first time any of them had made a sound since entering the room.

The guards looked to one another, trying to decide which of them should answer. After a momentary pause the one to the left answered, "He spat the potion out. We couldn't get him to keep it down."

The Elder Witch stared at the guard for a moment, appearing personally insulted by his incompetence. She turned to look at the man who was still struggling for his freedom. She sighed in boredom and waved her hand in his direction, sending out a current of energy which subdued the man, causing him to fall into unconsciousness.

"Bring the others in quickly!" ordered the Elder Witch in impatience.

The guards tied the now unconscious man to a second stake as more of the Elder Witches' guards came into the room. Each pair with their own semi-conscious person.

In total there were thirteen stakes and thirteen victims. Each one innocent of any crime.

The room filled with an orange glow and a wave of heat surged through the hall as the fires were started.

Atropos turned her face away, not wanting the image of the burning bodies to be forever seared into her mind. She took a breath to calm her shaking hands and began cutting threads.

CHAPTER 1

Sam stood on the dewy grass of her backyard and turned her face upwards. She breathed in a gulp of the cold fresh air and watched as the grey sky of Abrams Place gave way to a sheet of darker grey.

The sun was setting invisibly again, the same way it had risen this morning. As she watched colourless swirls float through the already dull sky, she wished that she could see the colours of the sunset.

Especially now, considering it would have been the last time she would see them.

Sam closed her eyes and let the raindrops wet her eyelashes and run down her face, using the droplets of rain as a substitute for her tears.

Given Sam's life, crying would have been something good, especially after everything that had happened.

Tears are supposed to be a way of evacuating your soul of the unnecessary clutter of feelings that would do you no good to hold onto. When you can't cry your feelings out of your body, it's for one reason.

You're broken.

Sam believed that her inability to cry was some sort of punishment. Some people may think that not being able to cry would be great; if you can't cry you must be happy all the time.

Those people are wrong.

If you can't cry your bad feelings out it leaves them trapped inside your body. Slowly filling you up with nothing but pain and there's not a thing you can do to make it stop. The tears that can't come out drown you on the inside until eventually you can't feel anything at all.

Sad things don't seem sad.

Happy things don't seem happy.

Even things that should piss you off leave you feeling nothing.

Sam's inability to cry made everything seem futile. She was empty of every feeling but guilt.

One of the many curses that she had been plagued with.

For Sam death was an option. An option that she had thought about more times than any rational person should.

But she couldn't help those thoughts, which floated through her mind like a dark cloud, every time another person died because she was too stubborn to just let herself die.

She couldn't help thinking that this time she would just end it all. Who knew how many people she could save by just doing it.

So do it, she told herself. *It will be easy, painless.* Sam looked at the potion she held in her hand, a quick and simple solution. All she had to do was drink.

Sam brought the vial to her lips. The liquid smelled of raspberries. She had made herself a sweet poison, one that would be easy to swallow and would have painless effects.

She would fall asleep, her pulse would slow, as would her breath, until they both ceased entirely.

It will be easy, she told herself and closed her eyes.

She parted her lips to drink the potion, when the vial flew out of her hand and into a tree on the other end of the backyard. Sam opened her eyes and watched as the vial smashed into dozens of sparkling shards, sending the potion inside splashing out like tiny droplets of raspberry rain.

"Did you really think I was going to let you go through with that?" Jack asked rhetorically as he materialised next to her.

Sam was tall for a girl, about five ten in height. Which meant that most people were either the same height as her, significantly smaller, or only slightly taller.

But Jack, he was a lot taller than her, larger in both height and general size which made him practically giant for a man. He had blonde hair, a few shades darker than hers, unusually blue eyes and tanned skin covered in the blood-coloured marks of a Hunter. He looked to be somewhere in his mid to late twenties, but Sam had no idea what age he really was, or anything about him really.

All she knew was that he had been a Hunter, he was Scottish, he was dead, he was a Ghost and for some unfathomable reason he — of all the dead people in the universe — had been assigned to protect her from everyone in the world who wished her harm.

Jack wasn't the sort of person to volunteer information about himself — all of the things she knew where things she had learned through observation — and whenever Sam asked him a question, he'd respond vaguely with a non-answer and if she pushed he would go on about 'the rules' insisting that there were some things he was forbidden to speak out loud.

He'd been with her for so long now though that the answers she had once needed no longer seemed important. Through the years they'd known each other she'd learned the important things.

Like the fact that he loved her beyond all comprehension and that he was fully committed to keeping Sam safe and alive.

And a lot of the time he was more committed to those goals than she was.

He was her ghostly guardian, protecting her from beyond the grave. He had been keeping her safe for her whole life, and right now she could see the worry plain on his face.

"The world would be better off without me," she mumbled. "If I had done it sooner then everyone would still be alive."

"No they wouldn't," Jack said surely. "People die because it's their time to go. It has nothing to do with you."

Sam sighed. There was no point arguing with Jack, as there was no way he could every really understand and she didn't really feel like explaining.

"Whatever," she grumbled as she turned her back to him and walked inside.

The moment the back door closed behind her, she heard a bang coming from the living room. For a moment Sam just stood there. She looked behind her to see where Jack was, her immediate thought being that he has to be the one making noises. But he was standing outside, the same place he had been when she came inside. She could see him through the kitchen window. He stood with his back to her looking up at the sky, or perhaps at something he could see and she could not.

Bang.

Sam looked towards the door in confusion and slowly walked out of the kitchen and through the hallway.

Bang.

She reached the doorway to the living room just in time to see a book fall from the shelves to the floor where two other books were lying. Jack appeared beside her. She turned to him. "Did you do that?" she asked accusingly.

"Go to the library," Jack said while staring straight ahead, his eyes seeming slightly unfocused as he spoke. "They're due back today."

Sam stormed into the living room and picked the books up off the floor. Opening the cover on the first one to check the date stamp inside. Jack was right. She studied the books in confusion. "Didn't I take these back two weeks ago?"

He looked to her and shrugged, his expression seeming just as confused as hers. "Obviously not."

CHAPTER 2

$\mathcal{S}$am walked through the library's wrought iron gates which squealed piercingly as they opened.

The library was the oldest building in town. From the outside it looked like an old Gothic church. It was made of a grey stone and had a steeple on top with a clock that had been added back in sixteen-twelve. It had arched windows and a giant arched door that was about ten feet tall and six feet wide.

People from outside of town often mistook the library for the church. But the town's only church wasn't built until eighteen-oh-six when the first outsiders moved in and began to question the town's lack of religious establishment.

Sam walked towards the large doors with Jack strolling along behind her. She checked the clock on the library's steeple; it was just about to turn six. She paused at the door for just a moment and swiftly turned her gaze behind, glaring out at the small empty road beyond the gates. Without having to look, she was fully aware that Jack was watching her; she could feel his eyes glaring into her from where he stood.

"What is it?" he asked.

It was July, but despite the fact that it was summer the sky was a dull murky grey, the sort of colour it turned when the rain had stopped, but the clouds had not yet dissipated and behind them the sun burned as it set, tinting the grey clouds brown with its glow.

But there was nothing unusual about the weather, or the fact that the streets surrounding the library were empty in summertime, which was why it was strange that, despite the vacant street, and the overall normality of the world as it seemed right now, Sam couldn't help the stirring within her that made her feel as though there *was* something to be seen from where she now stood.

Yet no matter how long she stared, all her eyes saw was the normality and her brain told her there was nothing to be seen, despite a small voice within her screaming to the contrary.

With a sigh, she shook her head in response to Jack's question and pushed the heavy wooden doors open.

The inside of the library, as always, was warm and welcoming and held the scent of books, both old and new.

She walked inside, her boots making a slight click on the white marble floors. Slowly she made her way towards the librarian's desk where Michelle — the librarian — slept with her head resting atop a pile of books.

Sam tapped lightly on her shoulder in a feeble attempt to wake the sleeping woman. Michelle sighed in her sleep, but didn't rouse.

Grumbling her annoyance, Sam cleared her throat and tapped Michelle's shoulder again, this time not as lightly as before. "Michelle," she called. "Michelle, wake up."

Still there was no response.

Sam looked to Jack questioningly, though he just stared at

Michelle in confusion and said, "Heavy sleeper?"

She placed a hand on Michelle's shoulder once more, but instead of tapping lightly as she had before, she got a firm grip and shook her roughly, feeling her heart thump a little faster when there was no response from the slumbering woman.

Before Sam had a chance to speak or do anything else, Jack's hand shot out and he placed his fingers on Michelle's throat, feeling around to ensure that she was in fact still breathing.

He paused for a moment as he waited to feel her pulse, his lips pressed together tightly. After a few seconds he moved his hand away and looked to Sam. "She's alive," he said. "But I'm damn sure no one sleeps *that* soundly . . . Maybe you should have a check, see if there's something going on with her. I'm gonna have a wander around, see if there's anything suspicious lurking."

Sam nodded in agreement, though she wasn't sure that there would be anything suspicious to be found.

At least not anything suspicious in the category that Jack was thinking.

With instincts to outmatch a psychic, Sam would have been able to sense any kind of supernatural presence the moment she walked through the door. Which is why she was sure, without having to cast her senses outwards and actually check, that there was nothing for Jack to find.

Again, that niggling voice in the back of her head refuted the claims of her Powers and tried to convince her there was something more.

Sam pulled the strap of her bag from her shoulder and let it fall to the floor with a thud, moving around to the side of the desk where there was a section that lifted upwards to allow people to pass through.

Sam moved the desk upward only slightly then immediately froze as her skin began to tingle. She looked down at her hand, which was holding onto the desk, only noticing the carvings beneath her fingers when she forced herself to look closer.

She pushed the hatch open completely and gazed at them, able to tell just by looking that they were runes of some description. But no matter how hard she concentrated, her brain was unable to decipher what they could possibly mean.

"Jack!" she called.

It took less than a second for him to manifest himself beside her.

"Look at this," she said without taking her eyes off the markings. "Do you recognise them?"

"No," he replied casually, not sounding worried or curious in the slightest. "If they have Power you should be able to read them. If you can't read them then they're just doodles."

Sam shook her head. "No, they don't feel right."

Jack laughed a little. "Remember when I told you you were too paranoid? Well, you're doing it again. You *know* if they were Magic in any way you'd be able to read them."

Sam let a sigh. "Maybe you're right," she replied, though she still couldn't shake the feeling that there was something more going on.

She threw the hatch open completely and it fell right into the top of the desk, hitting into it with a loud bang.

Just as Sam was about to step behind the desk, Michelle's eyes shot open and Sam paused where she was.

"Huh? . . ." Michelle mumbled as she looked up from her desk and blinked in a daze. She was looking around to gather her surroundings when her eyes settled on Sam. "Oh . . . sorry Sam."

Sam watched Michelle for a moment, subtly checking for any outward signs of damage. From what Sam could tell, she seemed to be okay now.

She allowed her eyes to wander in the direction of the hatch on the desk, wondering what those symbols were.

What they said.

They were runes she had never seen before, and they stirred within her a strange feeling of not only déjà vu, but of dread.

There was something not quite right here, and Sam needed to know what it was. She had thought about asking Michelle, but when she looked at the woman sitting there smiling obliviously, gently dabbing at her eyes with her index fingers, fastidiously fixing her eye make-up to make it appear as though she had never even been unconscious, she couldn't make herself do it.

Couldn't make the words come out, because somewhere in the back of her mind she felt that there was a possibility that whatever was going on, Michelle could be a part of it. Or if not a part of it, then in some very serious danger.

With a forced smile, Sam moved back towards the front of the desk, took the books out of her bag and placed them on to the table. "I just came to return these."

Michelle ran the books past the scanner one at a time.

"So, where's Jessie?" Sam asked in an attempt to make casual conversation. "I haven't seen her in few days."

Michelle rolled her eyes and sighed. "Jessie took the summer off, so I have to work her shift as well as mine. I swear, I feel like I haven't slept in forever," she said as she frowned at the computer screen. "It says you brought these back two weeks ago."

"Really?" Sam asked with a sideways glance at Jack, who was pretending he hadn't done anything by avoiding eye contact and watching the ceiling as if it was the most interesting thing he'd ever seen. "That *is* weird."

"Yeah," Michelle agreed. "There must be something up with the computers." She tapped the top of the computer screen. "Stupid machine," she mumbled. "Must be broken."

"Mmhm . . . so, Jessie's gone for a while then?"

"Yeah," Michelle nodded.

"You wouldn't happen to want a temporary substitute?"

CHAPTER 3

*J*amie had been Turned almost two centuries ago, but it wasn't until that evening that he actually came up with a proper plan to find out more about what he was.

He had spent most of his undead life travelling the world, relentlessly searching for another Vampire to guide him. To teach him all the things he felt he should know. All of the things that the Sire who abandoned him should have stuck around to tell him.

Over the years he had managed to figure out most of his strengths for himself, but he was too scared to attempt to figure out his weaknesses.

And not knowing one's weaknesses was a weakness in itself.

The fact that he was a Vampire and yet found it impossible to find even a trace of another one had always made Jamie feel perplexed and more than a little useless. What good was being a Vampire if he couldn't even use his hunting and tracking skills to find something that, for him, should be so blatantly simple?

What made Jamie feel even more useless was that after almost two centuries of searching, it wasn't until this evening that he had thought of something that was such a simple idea it made him feel like an imbecile for not thinking of it sooner.

Research.

He walked out of his bedroom and down the stairs to the living room, where he proceeded to think of how and where he could find some useful information about Vampires, like for example, where they might be found.

Given the decade that it was, the internet was the obvious first choice. Jamie turned his head to the corner of the living room where his computer sat. He had never used it for research before, the sole purpose of the device was to provide him with entertainment during sleepless days, and of course, to give him access to eBay, where he made money by selling some of the more useless things he had acquired over the years.

Before he had even taken a step towards the computer, Jamie dismissed the idea of doing research online.

Although the internet did give people access to anything and everything they wanted, Jamie knew from previous experience, that in order to find what you were looking for you'd have to spend hours upon hours sifting through all of the junk first.

Jamie paced the floor, the room filled with nothing but the sound of his shoes hitting off the hard wood. He looked around as he thought, hoping that something in the room would inspire him with a useful idea.

His eyes shifted past the sofa, the TV, the stacks of DVD's and games that lay around it, the kitchen door, the computer, the staircase, and then they settled upon something that made him feel as though he should be kicked and beaten to death for his idiocy.

Books!

He had always known that the simplest idea was, more often than not, the one that worked best. So why would he think of using the internet before he thought of using books?

Jamie grabbed his jacket from the coat hanger next to the door.

For the first time since he had moved to this town, he would pay a visit to the local library.

CHAPTER 4

"Really?" Michelle asked as her face broke into the largest smile Sam had ever seen. "Because I've been working double shifts for a week now and I think I might die if I have to go on."

Sam laughed a little. "Yeah, I mean it. I need a summer job, you need the help. So I guess it works out okay for everyone?"

Michelle placed a hand on her chest and let a relieved sigh, giving Sam another overly large smile. "Thank you, I one hundred percent accept."

"Awesome. When do I start?"

Michelle's smile of joy quickly became tinted with guilt and apprehension. "Would I be pushing my luck if I asked you to start right now?"

Sam smiled internally, glad that she would get her chance to investigate so soon and wouldn't have to have one or two sleepless nights obsessing over what was going on ... that would have been especially annoying if it turned out there was nothing to find.

On the outside Sam shrugged and smiled her most polite smile. "I didn't have any other plans tonight, so now works fine for me."

Michelle practically jumped over the desk when she reached across and pulled Sam in for a hug. The desk between them making it awkward and slightly painful for both.

"Come on back here," Michelle said and ushered Sam behind the desk, watching her as though she were the bravest and shiniest of all the white knights.

With a smile, Sam obeyed.

"Okay," Michelle said, then began instructing Sam on all she needed to know. "The computer system is pretty basic. The only program you need opens automatically, but just in case you switch it off by accident I'll just write the password down here."

She held up a pink Post-It, then stuck it to the computer screen. "If anyone is taking books out you scan their card through first, then the books. If they don't have a card just type their name and details into the computer. And if they're returning books you just scan them through."

Michelle picked one of the books up off the return cart, and held it to the side so Sam could see the labels on its spine. "The books have specific places on the shelves. They're categorised by genre, and—"

Sam held up her hands to stop Michelle's speech before it went on much longer. "Michelle, I've read most of the books in this place, I know how they're organised and where they all go. You don't need to explain it."

Michelle smiled. "Right," she said. "Sorry." She opened one of the drawers in the desk and pulled out a set of keys. "These are Jessie's keys. You lock up at—"

"Midnight," Sam finished. "I know."

"You have to unplug the computer and switch off all the lights. Then just lock the doors. Any questions before I leave?"

"Yeah," Sam said and shrugged her jacket off, folding it over the back of the chair. "Does this mean I'm allowed to use the staff bathroom, because I need to pee and those other ones are kinda gross."

"Sure." Michelle laughed and pointed to the door behind the desk. "Staff bathroom is back there."

Sam walked past her, through the door behind the desk. Beyond it was a short narrow hallway with yellow walls. There were two doors, one to the left and one to the right. Sam spent perhaps a second looking at each one before she reached out and placed her hand on the doorknob of the door to the left.

She turned the handle, and tried to push it open but a hand wrapped around her wrist, stopping her from moving forward.

Sam looked at Michelle curiously. Her expression seemed frightened. "Not that one," she said quickly, her voice panicked. "Never that one."

Sam raised an eyebrow in confusion. Slowly, she let her hand fall away from the doorknob; the moment her hand fell Michelle released her grasp on Sam's wrist.

Michelle let a breath as she relaxed a little. "Sorry," she said. "That's the basement. We've been having some ... *problems* down there, so for safety we keep the door locked at *all* times."

Strange, Sam thought while she nodded her understanding.

"I'll wait until you're finished." Michelle stood in front of the basement door, almost if she were guarding it.

The thought that stuck with Sam as she walked into the bathroom was, why did Michelle feel the need to guard the door?

And more importantly, was she doing it to keep Sam out or was she trying to keep something in?

When Jamie reached the library, he could only sense one person.

The librarian.

She was a woman who looked as though she were in her forties, with light mousy brown hair cut just a little shorter than her shoulders. Jamie made sure to keep tabs on her mind while he was there.

Not that he was threatened by her, he just had a habit of keeping tabs on the humans around him. Knowing his surrounding always made him feel more comfortable.

The librarian greeted him with a smile and a nod. He politely returned her gesture before heading into the labyrinth of shelves.

The library was an extremely large building. It had a huge desk and behind it was a doorway where the librarian was standing.

There were five computers by the back wall, all lined up with dividers separating each one. Several tables and chairs were laid out for the library users, and there were five steps with a railing which divided the lower half from the part where all the books lay.

Up the steps there were about twenty rows of shelves that stretched from ceiling to floor, covered on either side with books. Each shelf had a ladder that could be moved from either end to retrieve books from the higher shelves.

It was, all together, quite impressive.

Jamie had considered asking the librarian for some assistance in finding what he needed, but he thought he'd try himself first. He went hunting around the shelves for a while, wandering through the labyrinth, glancing from one side to the other, his eyes skimming over all of the book titles. But he found nothing.

None of them seemed like they would be any help. Jamie sighed, regretting his decision to come here in the first place.

At the time books had seemed like the best way to find out things quickly, but he hadn't accounted for the fact that he had no idea where to start, or even what books would hold the information he was looking for. Not to mention the fact that he wasn't even sure if there even *were* any books in existence which would contain any truthful information on Vampires. And the best place to find any information that could answer his questions would be online.

Jamie's head shot up and he looked in the direction of the librarian's desk; though he couldn't see it from where he was within the shelves.

Suddenly aware that there was silence.

The librarian was gone.

The library was empty.

He looked up at the ceiling, the lights were still on, and he hadn't heard the doors lock, although he hadn't really been paying close enough attention to hear it if they had.

She had seen him walk into the library and she hadn't seen him walk back out. Surely she wouldn't have left him here alone.

Jamie swiftly made his way through the labyrinth, moving past all of the shelves and back out to the railings by the staircase.

As soon as the desk came into view he froze, suddenly finding himself unable to move.

In the place of the librarian sat a young girl, who was holding a book in her hand studying its cover. She must have been sixteen, maybe seventeen, but she didn't look much older. The girl was beautiful in a dreamlike way, by that he meant that she was so beautiful she hardly seemed real.

She was tall for a female and beautifully proportioned with lightly tanned skin and pale blonde hair which had shimmers of gold sweeping through it.

However, the girl's looks — stunning as they were — weren't what had Jamie frozen in place, but the fact that he felt he *knew* her. Though from where, he hadn't quite figured out.

Jamie couldn't help but stare; he found it impossible to look away. *Why couldn't I sense her presence earlier?* he asked himself as he watched her curiously.

He concentrated all of his Power and his thoughts on her. Allowing the energy to build inside him before he slowly let it spread, encasing her in a wave of psychic energy. He let his mind reach out and search for hers; it took him close to five minutes to find anything. When he eventually did catch something, it wasn't her thoughts, but Jamie's psychic mind was now consciously aware of her presence.

It was strange that he hadn't sensed her earlier. Usually he could sense anyone or anything within a mile's radius, and usually he could do that with little to no effort whatsoever.

He tried harder in an attempt to gain some insight as to who she was, and how she had been able to shield her presence from him. He pushed his mind out further, reaching out to hers and calling her thoughts to him.

Breaking into someone's mind was ordinarily a simple task, but for some reason tonight it was proving to be quite difficult.

He stared at her, hoping that this would make his Powers more effective, his eyes squinted in concentration.

She sat there reading while Jamie tried with all his will to break his way into her mind. Something seemed to be blocking his way through, so he pushed harder. The girl dropped her book, suddenly moving her hand to her head. After a moment she moved both her hands to her temples, closed her eyes and massaged them with her fingertips.

Jamie felt his eyes go wide as he watched her with fascination.

She could feel him.

She shouldn't have been able to sense what he was doing.

But she did.

Even though he knew he was pushing her mind so hard he was causing her discomfort, Jamie didn't back down, he kept on probing, until he finally broke through. He looked at her expression. She appeared to be in a state of serious concentration. Jamie focused just as hard to try keep his hold on her thoughts.

Within her mind there were no words, and no matter how hard he tried he couldn't make out any clear images. Everything was a jumble, almost as if her brain was purposely causing her thoughts to scatter to keep him from knowing what was in there.

Her lips moved and it looked as though she mumbled something under her breath. Jamie didn't hear what she said; too preoccupied in his attempt at deciphering the words in her mind. But before he had a chance to get a clear image, he was pushed out.

The girl's hands were still on her head, massaging the temples like she was trying to rid herself of a headache.

Probably my fault, Jamie thought. Once again he tried again to work his way back in. For only a second feeling as though he almost had it, but there was something stronger than him blocking his powers.

And then he lost all sense of her completely.

When his senses scanned the room, they found nothing.

No trace of any other living being.

If he hadn't been looking at her right then, he would never have believed she was real. Yet there she was, sitting behind the library desk where she had picked up her book and continued reading where she'd left off before he had so rudely interrupted.

All living creatures have a will of their own, which made breaking into their thoughts an effort, but not impossible. No matter how strong a person's will, it was never strong enough. There was *always* a way in if you wanted to find it.

But this girl . . .

She had the ability to not only keep him out of her thoughts, but to fight him off if he managed to break in. And not only that but she could keep herself shielded.

She had the ability to be invisible, which was something that he had never come across before.

She was an anomaly.

A beautiful anomaly, and it was because of this that Jamie found himself wanting to know her. Which was unusual because he had never, in his life, felt the urge to know a person.

But she evoked that feeling in him, along with a few others.

"Hey Sam." Jamie snapped himself out of his reverie to look at the dark haired girl who had just entered and was now walking towards the librarian's desk.

Sam? Jamie wracked his brain for a moment, searching through his memories, trying to place that name with her face.

But there were no thoughts that came to his mind, no memories of her at all. Which made the fact that he recognised her all the more irksome.

"Hey Elle," Sam replied with a polite smile.

"I didn't know you worked here," Elle said. Jamie gave her a scrupulous look and scanned her thoughts to confirm his suspicions.

This girl's mind was alarmingly simple to read, usually a human had at least one wall to break through. This girl, however, had none.

Jamie found what he was looking for within a matter of seconds, confirming what he had thought.

She was lying.

Elle had known Sam was working here and had come specifically to see her.

"I just started today," Sam replied. "Like, about ten minutes ago actually."

"Uh huh . . . So, how've you been? I feel like we haven't talked in ages," Elle said in an attempt to start a conversation with Sam. Though the way she had spoken made it appear, even to someone who was not currently inside her head, that she had an ulterior motive for wanting to know.

Within the girl—Elle's mind, there was no clear image on what the ulterior motive might have been, but within her he could sense a very strong need to know about Sam. What she had been up to recently, what she was doing right now, what her plans for the next day may have been.

Jamie shook his head and with a roll of his eyes wondered why it was that some people found the need to be *that* nosey.

"That's because we haven't. And I'm fine," Sam replied as if she knew the agenda behind the question, making the answer sound as convincing as possible.

"Are you sure?" Elle pushed in an attempt to gain some usable information.

"I'm sure. Is there something you need help with?" Sam asked, distracting the girl by making a quick change of subject.

"Oh, yeah. I have to do a history study on the Renaissance in Europe, so I figured I'd do it now so I won't have to do it later. But I know nothing at all about it."

Without a word Sam got up from her chair and walked out from behind the desk. "Okay, follow me." She wandered into the labyrinth of bookshelves. Stopping at a shelf that was close enough for Jamie to still see her, though he was sure from the lack of attention she had paid him that from where he was she still could not see him. Sam searched the shelves for a moment, then pulled out a book and handed it to Elle.

Elle looked at the book incredulously, turning it from front to back. She gazed up at Sam. "Are you sure this is the right one?" she asked. "You didn't even check it."

Sam stared at her blankly for a moment. Then took the book out of Elle's hands and held it on its side so that Elle could see what was written on the spine. "It's called 'The Renaissance in Europe', I think we can safely assume it's about the Renaissance . . . in Europe."

Elle took the book out of Sam's hands and ran her fingers over the words on the spine. "The Renaissance in Europe could be the name of a novel," Elle stated, then looked at Sam and asked for a second time, "Are you sure it's the right one?"

"Are you serious?" Sam asked, as if she really couldn't believe what Elle was saying. Jamie tried not to laugh at Elle's lack of intelligence. Unsure as to whether or not she was actually as idiotic as she feigned to be or if she was simply stalling for time to come up with another lie, or way to get the information she wanted from Sam.

Elle nodded, indicating that she was indeed serious. Sam pointed to a label on the shelf. "We're in the history section," she stated.

"Things get put in wrong places all the time."

Sam stared at Elle for a moment, as if assessing her sincerity. Then she took the book out of her hands, opened it and read, "The Renaissance is a period in European history from about the 14th to 16th centuries regarded as marking the end of the Middle Ages and featuring major cultural and artistic change including the decline of Gothic architecture, the revival of classical culture, the beginnings of modern science, and geographical exploration—" Sam looked up from the book. "Are you convinced that it's about the Renaissance yet, or do I need to read the whole thing?" she asked mockingly. "You know, just in case they put the wrong pages at the start."

Jamie tried to suppress his laughter. Elle snatched the book out of Sam's hands. "There's no need to be so nasty," she said, then turned and walked away from the shelves back to the librarian's desk.

Sam sighed tiredly and followed her.

CHAPTER 6

The first time Sam noticed the guy standing behind the railing by the books was about five minutes after Elle left. She was surprised to find him watching her and making no effort to hide it. When her eyes caught his, his expression turned to one of surprise; he ran his hand through his hair as though he was flustered by the fact that he had just been noticed, but he didn't look away.

With the lack of other people being present, Sam came to the conclusion that he must have been the one who had attempted to push into her mind earlier. Sam studied him—trying to do it inconspicuously—as she wondered who he was, and more importantly who he worked for.

He was about six foot tall, give or take. With raven black hair which was an extreme contrast to the pallor of his skin, which practically glowed in his all black outfit. He was youngish, maybe slightly older than her. And she supposed he was moderately attractive.

Sam didn't recognise him at all, which was the first thing to arouse her suspicions.

Abrams Place was a fairly small town. It was large enough for someone to get lost, but small enough for them to be found quite quickly.

It was also small enough for everybody to know everybody else. Usually, when Sam came across people she didn't know, bad things happened.

The second thing that fuelled her suspicion was his wardrobe choice. All black was the colour palette of the Underworld Demons that hunted her.

Could he be one of them, or did he just have an affinity for the colour?

The first two reasons to find this guy suspicious wouldn't mean much to Sam if it wasn't for the fact that he was staring at her and making no effort to hide it. It was almost as though he wanted her to know that he was watching.

<Is he one of them?> Sam thought to Jack, who was also watching the guy cautiously. Obviously, she wasn't the only one who found him suspicious.

"I don't know," Jack whispered, despite the fact that the guy wouldn't be able to hear him. Generally Sam was the only one who could see Jack, unless he felt like making himself visible to everyone. "But he's staring at you like it's nobody's business."

Sam resisted the urge to roll her eyes, or give any indication that she was having a mental conversation with someone. *<Can you find out if he is one of them, please?>*

"Can't you just break into his mind?"

<I feel wrong when I do that> Sam said.

Jack let a sigh and shook his head. "He started it . . . just *do* it."

Sam didn't think about the fact that she was intruding into someone's private thoughts; instead she focused on the fact that she was only doing to him what he had done to her earlier.

She reclined in her chair and pretended to be reading her book, while concentrating really hard on hearing his thoughts. In her mind she focused on his energy, then pictured a vault door. She imagined turning all of the locks and opening the door to the vault. And pictured that inside the vault lay his thoughts and secrets.

Jamie.

That was his name.

He wasn't from outside of town; he had lived here for quite a while. Sam got a picture of a house surrounded by trees. She didn't recognise it, but then she'd never spent that much time wandering through the forests. He was at the library because he was looking for information on —

His thoughts stopped there. He had somehow managed to push her out of his head.

Jack looked to Sam expectantly. "Well? Is he one of them?" he asked.

<I don't know> she said mentally. <I think he pushed me out>

Jack gave the guy an uneasy look. "I'll go wander around Limbo for a while and see what my sources have to say about him."

<Thanks>

"You got your dagger?" he asked.

Sam frowned as she looked to her bag which lay on the floor by her feet, safely tucked beneath her desk. <Yes> Sam thought. <Not that I ever need it>

"I know you don't need it Sam," Jack said. "I just want you to have a back-up plan for if the Magic fails."

My Magic never *fails,* Sam thought to herself as Jack disappeared.

*

Jamie stood at the railing after managing to rid himself of a sudden headache. He stared at Sam, unable to look away, or walk away, or even go talk to her.

He just stared. Overcome with a sense of anxiety and desire rolled into one.

Sam met his gaze and stared him in the eyes. Hers were a perfect shade of indigo-blue, which burned brightly as though there was a fire raging within them. She glared at him, the expression she wore on her face causing her to look far tougher than her soft features should allow.

Stop staring at her you fool! his head yelled at him when he didn't look away. He *wanted* to look away. He felt like a fool just staring at her openly. After a moment, she turned her head away from him, appearing to be annoyed and slightly confused by his attention. She was probably thinking there was something wrong with him. Who stares at someone so blatantly and makes no effort to turn away when caught staring?

Those would be his thoughts if the situation were reversed.

Jamie closed his eyes for a moment as he gathered all the courage he could, took a deep breath to help keep himself calm, and began walking up to the desk where she sat.

She looked even more beautiful up close. And as he drew nearer he found himself overcome by the same feeling of desire and anxiety, only stronger than before; his fingers twitched nervously by his sides.

As he moved closer he could pick up the scent of her shampoo, mixed with the scent of her deodorant and perfume, and her own delicious fragrance. It was so appealing; *everything* about her was so appealing.

She looked so soft.

With hair like strands of golden silk, skin as perfectly smooth as the petals on a magnolia blossom and lips with curves his fingers longed to trace.

And above all else, the familiarity of every one of her features. He felt that if he were to close his eyes, he would still be able to trace her every outline.

It took all the restraint Jamie had not to reach out his hand to her. He may not have had the self control to keep his eyes off, but he had enough brains to keep his hands to himself. He didn't want to scare her or have her call the police on him, which was how it would have ended if he had allowed his hand to reach out as it ached to.

Jamie shoved his hands into the front pockets of his jacket, just in case.

And then he was at the desk, less than half a foot away from her. "Excuse me," he said, trying to keep his voice controlled. Sam put her book down and looked into his eyes. A sudden smile formed on her lips, as if with that one glance into his eyes she could see every one of his secrets.

CHAPTER 7

Sam smiled as Jamie stood on the other side of the desk eyeing her, anxiously waiting for her to speak. *Vampire,* she thought. It was so obvious now that she could see him up close. His aura was what gave him away. It was a mesh of many different energies, from many different blood donors.

"Need some help?" Sam asked, while wondering what a Vampire would be doing at the library. But then, if he could read why *wouldn't* he go to the library?

Briefly she wondered if he'd been sent by Aleczander to check on her, but then she thought that if he had, he wouldn't have been watching her as he had been. He simply would have walked up to her and stated his purpose.

Jamie flashed a shaky smile, exposing more teeth than he should have. Although Sam knew his canines weren't at their full extent, they were still obviously longer than any human's should be. "Yes, actually. There is something I need help with," he said, a slight nervous hint to his voice.

Sam wondered what he was so nervous about. Was he planning to try to feed off her or something? *Not likely*, she thought. His Vampire strength would be no match for the kind of Magic she possessed. One move in the wrong direction and he was gone.

Sam was nobody's victim.

She watched him unwaveringly, waiting for him to finish speaking.

He just stood there.

Staring.

"Uh, am I supposed to guess the rest of that sentence or are you going to tell me what it is you need help with?"

He smiled. "Sorry," he mumbled and ran his hand through his hair again. "I've been through all of the shelves and I can't find any of the books I'm looking for."

Sam noticed that he spoke with an accent. English, slightly diluted, which would mean he had to be over a century old at least. "Okay, well what books are you looking for?" she asked, knowing that she could find any book quite easily.

Jamie took a moment to think about it, then sighed. "I'm not really sure."

She felt her eyebrows pinch together as she looked at him in confusion. Was he serious, or was this a joke? "I'm no detective," Sam said slowly. "But if you're not sure what you're looking for, that's probably why you can't find it." He laughed a little. "What's the subject?" she asked, trying to narrow down the search.

"The subject of what?"

Sam rolled her eyes. *Why is everyone so stupid today?* "Of the books you're looking for," she said, her voice tinged with the irritation she felt. "What subject are they on? What are they about?"

Jamie placed his hands on the desk and lightly tapped his

fingers on the edge. He stared at his hands as if they would hold the answer to her question. "I'm not sure if I should tell you or not, you might think I'm weird."

Sam looked Jamie over sceptically, now thinking that his shiftiness had been for other reasons. "If you're looking for porn, you're in the wrong place."

Jamie's head shot up and he looked at her, his eyes wide with shock, his hands went still. "What?" He spoke slowly, as if taking a moment for his mind to process what she'd just said to him. "No," he said and shook his head. "No, I'm not looking for . . . porn." Jamie appeared a little embarrassed, his lips twitched as though he were trying not to laugh. "Why would you even think that?"

"You're acting suspiciously," Sam stated frankly.

"I am?" he asked, his expression surprised, as though he hadn't realised how shifty his behaviour had been.

"Yes."

"Oh." Jamie rested his arms on the desk and leaned forward a bit, bending slightly so that he was closer to her eye level. The more Sam spoke to him, the braver he seemed to be getting.

One wrong move, Sam thought.

"I don't mean to be suspicious," he said and smiled slowly, appearing more amused than he should have been. "I'm sorry if I've frightened you."

Sam knew exactly what he was trying to do with the way he was watching her and the tone he was using to speak. He was trying to be charming and mixing that with some slight Vampire influencing tricks. Not that she could be affected by the psychic Powers of a Vampire. The fact that he was trying was amusing though, and she wondered if he knew what or who she was, or if he believed her to be an easily malleable human.

She couldn't help smiling; this conversation was the most

entertainment she'd had in a while. "I've seen plenty of suspicious people," Sam stated. "I'm not frightened of you and stop looking at me like that."

"Like what?" Jamie asked, his tone sounding deceptively innocent, but Sam could tell by the artful smile on his lips that he knew exactly what she was talking about.

Sam stood, placed both of her hands on the desk and leaned slightly forward, looking straight into his ice-blue eyes, their faces barely three inches apart. She looked at him the same way he had been looking at her. "Like this," she said slowly.

Jamie licked his lips and breathed in. Sam knew that Vampires didn't necessarily need to breathe, the only reason he would be inhaling would be to pick up her scent.

One wrong move.

"So," Sam said, staying in his personal space, not that he seemed to object to her closeness. "You can either tell me what books you're looking for, or you can leave." She sat back in her seat and folded her arms across her chest.

Jamie let his eyes wander down to just above where she had her arms folded. *Unbelievable,* Sam thought, *what the fuck is wrong with this guy?* He looked back at her face and smiled. "This is a public library," he stated. "You can't make me leave."

Sam smiled to herself. "You'd be surprised at what I can do."

CHAPTER 8

*J*amie smiled; this was the most scintillating banter he had ever shared with a near stranger. *Just tell her,* he thought to himself, *if she finds it strange you can just influence her to think it's not strange at all.*

Jamie frowned internally at that thought. *No influencing,* he ordered his brain. Usually he relied on his skills in mind manipulation to do just about anything that involved humans. He used it to shield himself from them when he didn't feel like being seen. He used it to make women follow him home, then used it to make them forget everything that happened once they got there.

But he wanted all of Sam's thoughts to be her own, and all of her actions to be done of her own volition. If she thought him strange for what he was looking for, let her. Maybe she'd think that strange was good.

Jamie looked at Sam, who was seated in her chair watching him with her arms folded, patiently waiting for him to speak.

"I'm looking for books on Vampires," he said with a sigh, and watched her face for a reaction.

Her expression remained neutral. "Mythology or fiction?" she asked, almost as if it were an automatic response that she hadn't given much thought to. Jamie was a little surprised and a little disappointed. She didn't seem to care about what he was reading at all. For a while he'd thought maybe all of the banter had been her way of flirting with him, *Apparently not.*

"I'm not sure what you mean by that," Jamie said. Lying in an attempt to prolong their conversation.

Sam looked at him as if he were a complete moron and sighed. "Mythology, as in the myths, the legends, the folklore on Vampires, and fiction, as in stories that people make up about them."

Jamie took his time answering, then said, "Could you explain that a little more?"

Sam looked at him, the corner of her lips twitching in a momentary smile. "Seriously?" she asked. Jamie nodded. "You know what mythology and fiction mean," she said with a sigh of boredom.

Jamie innocently shook his head. "The meaning of the words, yes. But when it comes to library classification it could mean something different entirely."

Sam gave him an unconvinced look, then she shook her head a little and said, "Fiction, make-believe stories with Vampire characters that are written by people. People, human beings as a collective." Jamie tried not to laugh, *Was she going to define every word in that sentence?* "Mythology," she continued. "Myths, legends and folklore on Vampires. Vampires, *annoying* bloodsuckers who are allergic to sunlight." Sam looked at Jamie and smiled brazenly. "But I'm sure you knew that already."

Jamie gave her a confused look and tried to hide his fear.

How could she know? "Uh . . . " Jamie had to think a little before speaking. *Deny it!* his brain screamed at him. "I don't know what you mean," he said slowly.

Sam smiled in amusement. "What?" she asked innocently. "You've never heard of Dracula?"

Jamie laughed a little and relaxed. Of course she didn't know. How could she? "Right," he said. "Dracula, of course I have. I read the book when—" Jamie stopped himself from speaking. He had almost said, 'when it was first published.' He took a quick second to think. Sam watched him as she waited for him to finish his sentence. She was smiling as if she could hear his thoughts frantically trying to find some words. Eventually he said, " . . . When I saw the film."

"Which one?" Sam asked. "There's millions of them, Nosferatu," she counted them out on her hands, "Dracula 1931, Dracula 1958, Bram Stoker's Dracula, Dracula 2000 —"

"Uh . . . " Jamie ran his hand through his hair as he wondered why she was asking. Was the one he'd watched really that important? "1931," he answered slowly.

Sam smiled as if that was the answer she had expected, then she laughed a little. Jamie looked at her in confusion, why was that funny? "That one's hilarious," she said when she'd stopped laughing. "Old horror films are so bad they're funny."

Jamie smiled. "Yeah, I suppose they are."

"By the way," she said with a patronising tone. "Dracula is a book of Vampire fiction. I know that may be a little confusing." She batted her eyelashes innocently. "For *you* at least, because like most Vampire fiction it is based upon the myths."

Jamie raised an eyebrow and held back a smile. "Are you mocking me?"

"Yes," Sam admitted shamelessly. She smiled widely. "If you're going to act stupid, you're going to get mocked."

"How was I acting stupid?"

"By pretending you don't know the difference between a fiction novel and a book of mythology," she said. "Speaking of which, you never answered."

"Right," Jamie said, remembering why he had come here in the first place. He exhaled and ran his hand through his hair. "I suppose I would be looking for the mythology."

"Finally," Sam said, and sighed dramatically before standing. She walked out from behind the desk and peered over her shoulder at him. "This way," she said, using her hand to indicate forwards.

Jamie followed her up the steps into the labyrinth of books, to one of the shelves near the back. Sam looked around the assortment of books, mumbling their names to herself, until her eyes settled on one of the shelves near the top. She moved over to the corner and pulled one of the ladders along the shelves to where Jamie was standing. "Stand back," she said.

"Do you want me to get it?" Jamie asked.

She stared at him for a moment, her expression seeming amused. "How are you supposed to get it, when you don't know what books you're getting?" Sam asked rhetorically. Jamie didn't reply. Instead he took a step back to make room for Sam to climb the ladder.

She climbed to a shelf near the top and pulled a heavy looking, red leather-bound book off the shelf. "Catch," she said as she dropped the book. Jamie caught it before it hit the ground. Sam let herself slide down the ladder and landed gracefully on her feet.

"It looks really old," Jamie observed.

The leather the book was bound in looked worn and the colour was slightly faded. He opened it on a random page. Inside all of the words were hand written in faded brown ink. All of the illustrations were hand drawn. The pages were yellowed, the edges frayed. Jamie gently touched the page, lightly rubbing his fingers along the side, careful not to touch the lettering; it didn't feel like paper, and it didn't smell like it either.

"Calfskin," Sam said, when she noticed Jamie examining the book. "It's about six hundred years old. A manuscript written in ye olde ancient times."

Ye olde ancient times? Can she even hear herself speak? Jamie tried not to laugh.

"So *pre-historic* it's not allowed leave the library, so you'll have to read here. And no turning down page corners, or underlining or sticky notes inside the book."

"That's perfectly fine with me," Jamie said, and followed Sam through the maze of books. He had been planning to read here anyway. "If it's so pre-historic, should you really have dropped it twenty feet?"

"I was assuming you had good reflexes. And besides, your job was catching, so if it had gotten damaged in the fall it would have been *your* fault not mine . . . 'cause you would have been the one to let it hit the floor, not me."

Jamie laughed a little. "Wow . . . thanks."

"You're welcome." Sam stopped at a shelf near the stairs and pulled another book down. She placed it on top of the one Jamie was carrying. "Here you go."

Jamie looked at the other book she had given him. It was a dictionary. "Middle English to Modern English," he read aloud. "What's this for?"

"It's written in Middle English, so some of the words are spelled weird and some words meant different things back then. It's just in case you get confused." She smiled. "And considering the fact that you're an idiot, you probably get confused pretty easily."

Jamie pursed his lips, not knowing whether to feel insulted and frown, or to feel flattered by her attention and smile.

"Everyone's an idiot sometimes," he mumbled.

Sam walked back to the librarian's desk and sat down in her chair. Jamie placed his books on the desk closest to Sam and sat facing her, making it easy for him to stare at her a little less obviously.

Sam picked a book up off the desk, the same one she had been looking at earlier, and flicked through a few pages before she started reading.

Jamie carefully opened the manuscript to the first page, the pages were so old they felt like they might crumble if he didn't handle them with care. He spent perhaps a second looking at the text before peering up at Sam.

Jamie stared at her book curiously, wondering how—from the many thousands, if not millions of books—that one had managed to gain her attention. He glanced at the miniscule text on the back cover, skimming through the words. From what he could gather it was some kind of fantasy novel about a game and a shadow world.

So she likes the supernatural . . . good to know, he thought as he smiled to himself, quickly turning away to look down at the manuscript so as not to be caught staring and smiling at her while she wasn't paying attention.

After reading through the first two pages of the manuscript, he paused when he realised that he had never introduced himself.

When he looked up at her she was still reading her book, not paying him any attention. Jamie frowned, only through his disappointment realising that he'd been hoping to catch her spying on him.

He cleared his throat to get her attention. Sam peered over the top of her book looking in his direction. Jamie smiled. "My name is Jamie, by the way. Jamie Williams."

Sam let a slight, almost inaudible laugh. *What's so funny about my name?* he thought. "Samantha Jacobs," she said. "But everyone calls me Sam."

CHAPTER 9

The only noise breaking the silence was the continual turning of pages. For the rest of the night no one had entered the library, leaving Sam to spend the entire night reading while pretending she couldn't see the Vampire watching her, while in the back of her mind wishing she really couldn't see the Vampire.

Because his presence meant that she couldn't spend the night investigating every crevice of the building for something suspicious that would give her some insight into what those runes were.

Meaning that she had a sleepless night of wondering to look forward to, which would be followed by a morning and afternoon of anticipation while she awaited another chance to check out the building.

"We're closing in ten minutes," Sam announced, not bothering to look up as she did. She hit the spacebar on the computer multiple times, getting rid of the screen saver so she could legally steal the book she'd been reading. She typed her card information into the computer then ran the book past the scanner. This one was coming home with her. After she managed to get the program to close, which took so long it made her think the computer was so old it was probably made in the Stone Age, she shut down the computer and turned off the main switch.

Sam looked up as she heard a chair scraping against the tiled floor, Jamie stood and closed the book he'd been 'reading' all night.

"You can leave that up here." Sam pointed to her desk, she would put it back in its place tomorrow night, that was if Michelle didn't put it back first.

"Have you ever read this book?" Jamie asked, placing it on the librarian's desk.

Sam looked at the cover of it. The library had two really old books on Vampire mythology. A few years ago she had read through all of the mythology books the library had to offer, so that she could laugh at all of the things they'd gotten wrong. "Uh, is it the one where Vampire is spelled, V-A-M-P-Y-R?" Jamie nodded. "Yeah, I've read it."

"How accurate do you think the information in here is?"

Sam smiled. "I'd say about ten *maybe* fifteen percent accurate."

"That's not a lot," Jamie said with a frown. "I thought you said there was a difference between myth and fiction."

"There is," Sam stated. "Myths are stories based on facts. Like exaggerated truths. And fiction refers to stories based on myths, so even more exaggerated than the myths are."

"And your guess is that about ten or fifteen percent of this book is fact and the other ninety or eighty-five percent is fiction?"

Sam nodded. "Pretty much. It's tricky to try get accurate

information from myths, legends and folklore, because they're different in different places, so you'll never really know which place has more truths. What the people who write these books do is listen to all of the stories in all of the different places and make up their own myths from the pieces of information that overlap in all of the stories. But then all you end up with is a small part of a big story."

Jamie sighed. "So I'm not going to find anything useful in a book," he said sadly. Sam felt a little sorry for him. She knew how difficult it was to be something different, but to have no idea what being 'different' entailed. "How would I find accurate information on Vampires?" Jamie mumbled to himself.

It was loud enough for Sam to hear, so she answered him. "Find a Vampire and ask lots of questions."

Jamie laughed a little. "And how would I find a Vampire?"

Sam thought for a moment, trying to think of a way to give Jamie some helpful information on finding a Vampire without letting him know that she herself wasn't human. "Maybe you should stop thinking about *how* to find a Vampire."

Jamie looked at her curiously. "Are you saying I should give up my search?" he asked. Then after a moment's pause in which he seemed to have realised what he'd just said, he smiled and jokingly added, "How can I ever become Van Helsing if I do that?"

Vampires were usually extremely careful about what they said, they made sure to act as regular as possible when around anyone they thought was human, so if there was a trophy for 'Most Obvious Vampire' Jamie would be a definite winner. Sam had spent maybe twenty minutes in total talking to him and he naturally came across as a Vampire, with his attempts at normality being an afterthought. She smiled and shook her head. "Start thinking more about *where* you would be likely to find one."

Jamie looked at her for a moment, he clucked his tongue as he considered what she had said. "And where would I be likely to find a Vampire?"

"Have you ever tried a Blood-Bar?"

"What's a Blood-Bar?"

"It's exactly what the name says it is. It's a place where Vampire wannabe's go to dance to heavy metal music, get it on and drink blood. What better place to search for a Vampire than a place where they serve blood?"

Jamie's expression grew sceptical. "Is that a real thing?"

Sam nodded. "Yep."

He looked Sam up and down, wearing the same sceptical expression. "And how would *you* know of a place like *that*?"

"I have a friend who visits one frequently. It's underground and very exclusive. But I can get the address for you if you want."

"If it's very exclusive how am I supposed to get in?"

"Because you'll know where it is," Sam stated. "Anyone who doesn't have an invitation wouldn't have the address." *And the security guard will sense that you're a Vampire,* Sam added in her head.

Jamie smiled. "Would you go with me?"

Sam sighed internally, she knew he would try to ask her out before the night was over. "No," Sam said simply. Going to a Blood-Bar with a Vampire wasn't exactly her idea of a fun night.

"Why not?" Jamie asked smiling suggestively. "Don't you want to go dance to some heavy metal, get it on and drink some blood?"

Sam laughed. "If I do all of that during the summer, I'll have nothing to do at Halloween."

"Well, the offer stands if you change your mind."

Sam took her jacket off the back of the chair and pulled it on while simultaneously putting the book into her bag. "Thanks," she said. "But Blood-Bars aren't really my thing." Sam walked out from behind the desk. Jamie stood and watched her as she walked away. She paused and looked over her shoulder at him when she realised he wasn't following. "Are you coming or are you planning to sleep here tonight?"

Jamie smiled slightly as he pushed himself away from the desk. "Can't wait to get rid of me," he said sarcastically and walked past Sam out the library doors.

Sam switched off the lights.

A chill went through her body as she looked around the darkened library. Without the lights it looked terrifying. The lack of windows made the room pitch black, though Sam was sure she could see shadows moving in the darkness. Her instincts took over for a moment, causing her to slam the door shut and lock it quickly, so that nothing had a chance to step out of the darkness.

Sam stood at the door for a moment, one hand on the handle, the other gripping the key tightly. She let a sigh of relief before pulling the keys out of the door. She turned around to find Jamie watching her, his expression half confused, half concerned.

"Everything alright?" he asked.

Sam tightened her hands into fists, not sure why they were shaking, or why the darkness had caused her heart to race with panic. She looked at Jamie and forced a smile. "Yeah, everything's fine." Her eyes drifted towards the library doors.

"It's okay, you know?" he said. When Sam looked at him in confusion he gave her a kind smile and elaborated, "To be afraid of the dark." He put his hands into the pockets of his jeans and shrugged his shoulders. "Everyone's got something they don't like."

"I'm not usually," Sam explained. "I don't mind the dark, it's just, it felt like . . . I don't know, I just thought . . . "

"Thought what?"

Sam shook her head and laughed. "Nothing . . . I'm just tired I guess. It was nothing."

Sam stood there for a few minutes, just staring at the door, pushing at it with her senses, trying to feel if there was a presence behind it.

There was nothing.

She really must have imagined the whole thing.

But then she remembered the runes, and the feeling she'd had earlier that there was something to be seen that she just couldn't focus on.

"So, what is your thing?" Jamie asked, after standing with her in silence for countless moments.

"What?" When she turned around he was still standing in the same place he had been when she'd turned her back to him.

Still with his hands in his pockets.

Still watching her.

"You said that Blood-Bars aren't your thing. So what is your thing?"

Sam sighed and thought, *getting people killed.* She looked at Jamie, he was probably in danger right now just for the crime of talking to her. Although it wasn't as if she could tell him that. She shrugged. "The usual boring things."

"Is that all your going to tell me?" Jamie asked as if he had been expecting her to divulge every minor detail of what she liked to do.

"Yep," Sam said and started walking away.

"Hey, Sam!" Jamie called. She turned around to look at him. "Uh, do you want a lift home?" he asked, and pointed to the only car in the parking lot, indicating that it was his.

Sam raised an eyebrow. "Are you *insane*?" she asked. He

gave her a confused look. "I don't ride home with strangers. What if you're a serial killer?"

Jamie smiled and raised his left hand, placing his right one over his heart. "I hereby promise that I am most definitely not a serial killer."

"That's *exactly* what a serial killer would say."

Jamie laughed. "We were in an empty library all night," he stated. "Don't you think if I was a serial killer you would be dead, or at the very least, kidnapped by now?"

Sam gave him a sceptical look. "Not unless you were trying to lull me into a false sense of security before you killed me."

Jamie thought about that for a minute, then shook his head. "That's just ridiculous, I'm not a serial killer."

"I watch pretty much every crime drama on television," Sam stated. "I *know* how serial killers work and I'm not falling for your act."

"When was the last time anyone in this town died of anything other than natural causes?" Jamie asked. All of the police reports said natural causes, but Sam knew better than that. *People get murdered in this town more often than anyone realises.* "When did this conversation go wrong?" he asked rhetorically while laughing. "I only asked if you wanted a lift home."

Sam smiled. "I wasn't serious," she said. "Thanks for the offer, but I still don't ride home with strangers."

"You sure?"

"Yeah, I only live about ten minutes away so it's not like I'm travelling for miles or anything."

Jamie shrugged. Sam thought that he looked a little disappointed, but it was difficult to tell with the lack of light. "Well, bye, I guess."

"Bye," Sam said and turned to walk away.

"Maybe I'll see you again sometime?" he called after her.

Sam smiled to herself. "Maybe," she said without looking back.

CHAPTER 10

*J*amie looked at the car he had pointed to earlier. *Why did I say it was mine?* he wondered. He had just been hoping to spend more time with Sam and had blurted the first thing he thought of. *I guess I'm lucky she said no, otherwise I would have had to steal that car, and then teach myself how to drive in five seconds.*

Jamie laughed at his own idiocy and started walking the same way Sam had. He could see her right ahead of him, walking at a casual pace, unaware that she was being followed.

When he stretched his senses and could hear the hum of music. She had headphones on. How could she block her senses with noise while walking down vacant streets in the middle of the night? Did she not know how dangerous that could be? What if someone were to sneak up and attack her? She'd never see it coming because she was shutting herself off from her surroundings.

Jamie felt himself frown as he realised she would be walking alone at this hour every night. And sure . . . she would be safe tonight, but what about tomorrow night? Or the night after that?

Sam turned and walked up the driveway to a two storey detached house. She took her keys out of her pocket, opened the door and walked inside, using her foot to kick the door closed behind her. Jamie stood in the shadows down the end of the driveway.

He didn't hear her speak, which he found a little strange. *Wouldn't she announce that she's home to whoever was inside? Perhaps everyone's asleep*, he thought. He stretched his senses to see how many people were in the house.

Jamie felt an anxiousness in the pit of his stomach when he sensed only Sam. *Surely she doesn't live alone?*

A light in one of the upstairs windows flicked on. Sam came into his view, she walked over to the window, looking out for a moment. Jamie prayed she didn't look at him. What would he do if she saw him?

Jamie stood where he was. <I am just a shadow> he thought and sent his thought out into the air. He hadn't wanted to use any of his mind manipulations on her, but he didn't want her to catch him outside her house even more.

Jamie saw what looked like a smile play on the corner of Sam's lips, almost as if she'd heard his thought. Though that would have been impossible, Sam was human, wasn't she? She closed the curtains without looking at Jamie once. He sighed with relief at not being caught. A few minutes later the light went off.

Jamie stood outside her house for about an hour, just staring at the brick walls and the darkened windows, stretching his senses as far as he could just so he could hear her heart beating as she fell asleep.

What are you doing? he asked himself, taking a step back as he suddenly realised where he was and what he was doing. *You can't follow a girl home and just stand outside her house in the dark. What will people think if they see you?*

He shook his head, then turned and began the journey home, the whole way telling himself that the only reason he had followed her home was because it was dark and he didn't want her walking alone. He just wanted to make sure she got home safely.

Jamie told himself this over and over again, all the while knowing it was a lie.

CHAPTER 11

Aleczander and Evangeline were the other two of Sam's Guardians. In total there were three left standing.

Aleczander.

Evangeline.

Jack.

Not that she had really relied on anyone but Jack for the past few years.

In the beginning there had been seven. Including her adoptive parents Gabrielle and Anthony Jacobs, and then her grandparents, Joan and Henry Foster.

All of whom were now dead.

Sam picked the phone up out of the holder and dialled Aleczander's number. The phone had barely started ringing before it was answered. "Hello?"

Sam sighed internally at the sound of the woman's voice on the other end of the line; she had been hoping to get

Aleczander. "Hi Evangeline, it's —"

"Sam!" Evangeline interrupted. "We haven't heard from you in *ages*. How've you been?"

"I'm fine. How are you?" Sam asked, forcing herself to make polite conversation so that she didn't seem completely uncaring.

"Good, good," she said. "Everything's great."

There was a moment of silence, then Sam asked, "Is Aleczander there?"

Evangeline sighed dramatically. "And here I thought you called to talk to me," she said. Sam rolled her eyes. It wasn't that she disliked Evangeline, it was just that she was the kind of person who always seemed to be in a perpetual good mood, always enthusiastic and on the bright side about *everything*. Which sometimes made talking to her for prolonged periods of time extremely irritating for any person who didn't think that the whole world was made of marshmallow fluff and rainbows.

"I actually just called because I need an address," Sam explained, in an attempt to make Evangeline not feel totally rejected.

"Oh," she said and took a second before saying, "He's in a meeting right now . . . "

Sam thought for a moment, she *had* called for Aleczander, but the odds were if he had the information she was looking for, Evangeline would too. "You wouldn't happen to know the address of a Blood-Bar close to here, would you?"

"I would happen to know," she said simply.

Sam waited for a few seconds, expecting Evangeline to fill the silence by actually giving her the information she'd asked for. When she didn't Sam sighed and asked, "Where?"

"I'm not giving you the address of a Blood-Bar!" Evangeline said, laughing. "You could get yourself killed there Sam. Not every Vampire in the world likes to follow the rules and some of them are dangerous. If they see a pretty girl like you walking into a place like that they'll assume you're consenting to having your blood drained. And then a dangerous Vampire will be walking around filled to his fangs with Magic."

"I don't want to go to a Blood-Bar. The address is for a Vampire I met yesterday," Sam explained. "He was abandoned by his Sire and doesn't know a lot about his situation. He was looking for another Vampire to try explain the do's and don'ts."

"And he told you all of this?" Evangeline asked sceptically.

"No," Sam admitted. "He came into the library yesterday looking for books on Vampire mythology. But he kept looking at me so I assumed he was up to something shifty and I read his thoughts and memories. He doesn't know who I am or what I can do. I didn't tell him anything. But, I dunno, I feel kinda sorry for him so I suggested he try looking for information at a Blood-Bar."

"Why would you suggest a Blood-Bar? Why didn't you just give him this number?"

Sam let a breath of frustration. "Because then he'd wonder how exactly I knew other Vampires and I'd rather not drag every stranger I meet into the middle of all of my crap."

Evangeline laughed a little. "Right," she said. "Sorry, that's understandable I suppose."

"So can I have the address or not?"

"Sure, just give me a second." Sam could hear papers rustling on the other end of the phone. Which presumably was the sound of Evangeline searching for an address book. "There's a few around the area," she said when the noise had stopped. "Mmmm . . . maybe this one," she mumbled to herself. "It's one of the more reputable, less dodgy people. I think Claudio actually goes to this one frequently, so that would be good." Evangeline seemed pleased with her decision. Sam could feel her smiling on the other end of the line. "Okay, two towns over there's a good one. If you tell him to walk to the centre of town where there's small park with a playground. If he walks past on the side of the playground he'll be on the main street, forward on for ten minutes until he finds an old hotel, it should be all boarded up and pretty derelict on the outside. Go down the alley to the far left of the building and he can get in through the emergency exit. This is Nick's bar, he's good people and should be able to direct him to wherever he wants to go. And if he goes there on a Thursday he'll find Claudio."

Sam scribbled all of that down on a piece of paper so that she could remember it all later, when she was sure she'd run into the Vampire again.

CHAPTER 12

$\mathscr{J}$ack arrived at Sam's house just as she opened the front door wearing her jacket. She smiled a genuine smile, which was something that Jack hadn't seen her do in almost two years. *Who knew that a job would make her so happy,* he thought, *maybe I should have gotten her one ages ago.*

"You sure did take your time."

"Not my fault," Jack replied, raising his hands defensively. "Death has a time difference."

She shrugged and closed the door, stepping out onto the porch. "It was a waste of a journey," she said. A kid riding by on a bike stopped to stare at her. She gave the kid an angry glare and he looked away. "Would you mind corporealising so I don't look like a crazy person?"

Jack de-materialised, then re-materialised, doing it inside the house so that the neighbours wouldn't see him appearing out of nowhere. When he was corporeal, he opened the door and stepped outside. Sam started walking, Jack beside her.

"Don't you want to know what I found out about him?" Jack asked, not wanting the day he spent wandering through Limbo then travelling to Athens to be a complete waste of time.

"Vampire," Sam stated.

Jack's shoulders sagged with disappointment. "And you couldn't have figured that out *before* I left?" Although the fact that the guy was a Vampire wasn't the only thing Jack had found out about him, it was pretty much the only thing he was able to tell Sam at this time. He had to keep everything else to himself until the time was right.

At least that's what *they* told him. If all of the rules had been made by Jack, then there probably wouldn't be any rules. As far as he was concerned, secrets didn't keep anyone safe.

"He wasn't close enough," said Sam. "I didn't find out until about ten minutes after you left. They should invent phones that work between dimensions."

"Did you know his name is —"

"Jamie," Sam finished. That wasn't what Jack was going to say, but he had been told that the Vampire answered to two names. "Yeah, he told me."

"Do you know he was in the library —"

"Studying Vampire mythology, hoping it would help him find another Vampire to explain what being a Vampire means," Sam interrupted again then laughed a little. "I *know*."

"Well do you know that's because —"

"His Sire abandoned him."

"How would you know that?" Jack yelled, not hiding his annoyance at the wasted journey. "You said he pushed you out of his head."

"Well, he spent the whole night hitting on me." Jack wasn't surprised by the fact the Vampire had been flirtatious with Sam, she was a naturally beautiful girl. She had an otherworldly aura that drew people's attention. And, when she wasn't in one of her more brooding moods, she was quite good company. Boys her age, and those somewhat older, often paid attention to her. Not that she ever returned their affections or advances.

Which was why Jack had to hide his surprise when he noticed that Sam's hair had a slight curl to it today, she had enough make up on that it looked like she'd made an effort but not so much as to make her look like she was trying too hard, and she was wearing a skirt. Jack couldn't remember the last time Sam had worn a skirt. It had to have been over two years ago. Sam chewed her lip for a moment as she stared up at the clouds while they walked, Jack smiled fondly at her.

At least she's happy, he thought.

"He's a complete idiot," she continued, shaking her head slightly. "He gave away a dangerous amount of information. He's like, the worst Vampire *ever* . . . and I peeked at his memories to fill in the gaps."

Jack was more than a little annoyed by the fact that Sam seemed to already know all of the information he was allowed to give her, but at least the time alone had been good for her.

Perhaps he should start leaving her alone more often.

"Did he seem familiar to you in any way?" Jack asked, knowing it was one of the things he couldn't tell her about, but wanting her to know just the same. She had a right to, and he felt like he couldn't know and *not* tell her, there were already too many things he had to keep to himself. *To hell with those bitches,* he thought, *they can't tell me what to do.*

Sam's nose scrunched up a little as she thought, she seemed confused by his question. "Um . . . Not really. I don't think I've ever met him before." She tilted her head at Jack. "Why?"

Consequences my ass, Jack thought as he smiled. "Because I —"
A stabbing sensation shot right through Jack. He cried out in pain and doubled over, his body feeling like it was being

ripped apart from the inside.

"What's wrong?" Sam asked, her voice tinged with concern, she reached forward to place her hand on his shoulder, but stopped before she touched him.

Jack took a few deep breaths to calm the pain. <Consider this your warning Hunter> Jack smiled bitterly at the sound of Lachesis's voice in his head.

"Nothing," he said as the pain evaporated. He looked at Sam and smiled, trying his best to ease her worry, he let a small laugh. "I was just about to tell you a secret is all."

CHAPTER 13

$\mathcal{S}$am walked through the library doors just as the clock struck six. Michelle was sitting at the desk, her head buried in a magazine. Once again the library was vacant of visitors, as it usually was after five during the summer.

"Hey Sam," Michelle said as Sam approached the desk. She spent a moment looking in Jack's direction, seeming slightly uncomfortable in his presence. After a moment she smiled at him. "Jack," she said with a nod.

Jack returned her smile, but didn't speak to her. He didn't really talk much to other people, which Sam didn't understand because he never stopped talking when it was just the two of them. Jack walked away from the desk and over to the bookshelves, still in his corporeal form.

"Hi," Sam replied and smiled. Today she was in a mood that made smiling feel easy, it was strange because of how long it had been since she'd felt that way, but she was exuding happy gestures as if it was something she did regularly and not something she usually had to force. "I can see it's *very* busy today."

Michelle smiled and looked around. "I *know*," she said with the same sarcastic tone Sam had used. "We'll have no books left for tomorrow." Sam laughed a little. Michelle closed her magazine. "People hardly ever come here this late during the summer. Did anyone come here yesterday?" she asked.

Sam gave her a small smile, "Yeah, you know Elle came in because you told her I was here."

Michelle just gazed at Sam for a moment, dumbfounded. "I didn't—"

"Well then you told Hayley and Hayley sent her to check up on me." She held up a hand to keep Michelle from interrupting. "I *know* you did, because she came in specifically to see me the moment I started, and made up some bullshit excuse about having to do a history report."

"How do you know she doesn't really have a history report?" Michelle asked defensively.

Sam smiled to herself. Elle had left the library yesterday believing she was an amazing liar and deserved an unrealistic amount of awards for her 'acting' skills. But she wasn't very bright when it came to making a plan. "We're in the same history class."

Michelle laughed a little bitterly and shook her head. "I didn't send anyone to check up on you, but I did let Hayley know you working here. She is your legal guardian after all." Sam wanted to say something snide in response to that statement, but before she had a chance to, Michelle asked, "Anyone else?"

"Yeah." Sam thought about Jamie for a moment. Vampires were the type of creatures that liked to keep their existence known only to other non-humans.

Michelle was technically a human.

Though she was a member of the town's coven, she wasn't a born Witch, she was just a practicing one. Sam debated whether or not it would be okay to reveal his existence. She sighed, deciding there was no point in not telling her since she probably already knew he was here. "Did you know there's a Vampire living in town?" she asked.

Michelle's eyes widened. "He was here?" She sounded panicked. Making Sam think that Michelle had obviously never come into contact with an actual Vampire before.

"So you did know."

Michelle looked around the library as if she expected Jamie to be hiding behind one of the bookshelves, waiting to jump out and drain her. "He didn't try to hurt you, did he?" Michelle placed her hands on Sam's shoulders, frantically pulling at the collar of her t-shirt and flicking her hair away from her shoulder. "You're okay?"

Sam didn't back away while Michelle inspected her for bite marks, instead she just rolled her eyes, her lips quirked in an amused smile. "*Please*, he's harmless."

"Vampires can make themselves appear harmless when really—"

"*Calm down*," Sam said, placing a hand on Michelle's shoulder. "I've met lots of Vampires. I know how to tell the harmless ones from the dangerous ones. The one that was here was harmless."

Michelle let a breath and shook her head. "That's not what Hayley said."

Again with Hayley ... the constant repetition of her name made Sam's blood boil and her hands clench into fists.

"Well she's wrong," Sam said through gritted teeth. "Hayley has *never* met a Vampire before *in her life*. She wouldn't know one if he or she were standing right in front of her with its damn fangs on display."

"Bu—"

"Michelle," Sam interrupted, putting her hand up to stop her from speaking. "I was *raised* by Vampires, I think I'd know better than Hayley on this, okay?"

Michelle turned her head to the side slightly, a gesture that made her appear slightly younger than she actually was. "The Jacobs' weren't Vampires."

Sam rolled her eyes. "I lived with Vampires for the first few years of my life," she clarified. "I know Vampires, most of them are harmless, well . . . to me." Sam smiled and added, "They only eat humans."

Michelle gave Sam an unimpressed look as she grabbed her jacket off the back of the chair and put it on. "Speaking of Hayley, are you coming to the coven meeting tonight? We could close the library now, I don't think anyone would mind."

Sam gave Michelle a sideways glance. "When have I ever gone to a coven meeting?" she asked rhetorically.

The answer was never.

"You should," Michelle stated. "Hayley knows a lot about Magic and the supernatural. Maybe you could learn something from her."

"*Please*," Sam scoffed. "I have more knowledge of Magic in the fingernail on my baby finger than Hayley has in her entire brain."

"Why do you hate her so much?" Michelle asked. "After everything she's done for you Sam, you should be grateful. Without Hayley you'd be in a foster home on the other side of the country."

Sam sighed.

Technically Michelle *did* have a point. When her grandfather had died a year ago and the social worker had come to take Sam away, Hayley offered to be Sam's foster mother. And she *was* grateful for that, but she also knew that Hayley's main reason for agreeing to be Sam's legal guardian was to have some kind of claim on Sam and her Power.

"I don't *hate* her," she explained. "I just . . . I don't trust her."

Michelle sighed. "I wish you would. She's not so bad once you get to know her." She walked away. "See you tomorrow," she called over her shoulder.

"Bye," Sam mumbled.

CHAPTER 14

$\mathcal{S}$am was sitting at the librarian's desk, reading the second book in the trilogy she had started yesterday.

"This was the first real book I ever read," Jack's voice sounded suddenly as he walked out from among the shelves holding an old, worn copy of 'Salem's Lot' by Stephen King.

"What age were you when you read it?" Sam asked, thinking that maybe she could guess the year he died.

"Twelve," he answered while flicking through the pages.

Sam was a little surprised. "You read horror at twelve?"

Jack smiled. "I lived horror since the day I was born." He pointed to himself. "Hunter, remember?"

"So you never got a choice about being a Hunter? You were born into it."

"I did get a choice," he stated. "Everyone gets a choice. But when you've spent twenty one years studying the supernatural, and training in fighting skills and hunting skills, you tend to stick with what you know. The odd few choose to do other things. More normal things, like a lawyer or a doctor or a shop manager or something. But, the families never approve of that . . . they usually get disowned. It's quite sad."

"So you *chose* to be a Hunter?" Sam asked in shock. She couldn't understand why anyone would choose to be a Hunter unless they were a murderous psychopath. But Sam knew Jack and he didn't seem like the type of person who enjoyed hunting and killing things. Sometimes human things.

"Yes," Jack said simply, then made a face. "Kind of," he sighed. "I never did the ritual, like the other Hunters did. The immortality ritual. You know, slower to age and difficult to kill."

"Why?" Sam asked. She knew of those spells, everyone did. It was a 'just in case I need to live through something I know will be fatal' kind of spell. However, there weren't a lot of creatures out there with the Power to cast it. Only the strong could achieve immortality through Magic.

Sam was one of those creatures which could become immortal if she chose to; though it was something she knew that she would never do.

"I guess I always kind of wanted to do something else. I don't know what. I just didn't want to fully commit myself to being a Hunter. I wanted to have the option of leaving." Jack scratched his head. "I guess, looking back on it, I probably should have done the ritual." He smiled sadly. "If I had . . . " He let his sentence drift off, then shook his head. He held the book up and looked at Sam. "I'm taking this on your card." Then he turned and sat in the chair closest to where he'd been standing.

Sam put down her book for a moment and typed Salem's Lot into the computer. She looked through the information file on the book, it was published in nineteen-seventy-five. If Jack had been twelve when he read it, assuming it also came out the year he was twelve, then died when he was in his mid-twenties, he would have died sometime in the late eighties. Sam sighed. *Math,* she thought tiredly. "When did you die?" she asked bluntly, deciding it would be easier than attempting to do calculations in her head.

"Three days after you were born," he replied without looking up at her.

Sam stared at Jack, slightly stunned by his sudden openness. "*How* did you die?" she asked slowly. Hoping he wouldn't notice she was taking advantage of the situation.

Jack smiled as if he knew exactly what she was doing. "Sam." He gave her the warning tone and the matching look.

"What?" Sam asked innocently.

"You know what."

Sam looked around the vacant library and sighed. Thinking that right now, while the building was empty would be the perfect time for her to go looking around.

She turned to look over her shoulder where the door to the basement was. Clearly that would be the most obvious place for her to begin her search as Michelle had been so adamant that she not go in there.

But then again, the first time she'd gotten the feeling that there was something not quite right with this place, had been as she stood by the front door.

So perhaps the best thing to do would be to check around the exterior to see just how strange it felt on the outside.

Decided in her plan, Sam stood and declared to Jack, "I'm going to wander around outside the building to check for any more markings like the ones on the desk."

Jack stayed seated as she walked past him and continued reading his book. Without looking up at her he said, "Okay . . . scream if you see any monsters."

Sam rolled her eyes and opened the door, peering outside

before she left, just to check that there was nobody on their way in, or walking around the general area.

Again, the street surrounding the library was just as empty as it had been the day before. Sam stepped outside and took a deep breath of the fresh air, closing her eyes as she did so. She stood by the door and stretched out her senses, casting a psychic net around the building in an attempt to find anything that didn't belong.

The building was still, it's aura even, nothing inside or out seeming even a little out of place.

With a frown, Sam opened her eyes.

She *knew* she wasn't going crazy, which meant she was *sure* there was something to be found.

With a sigh she moved away from the front door and began walking by the wall, making her way round the building. As she moved she paid extra close attention to every brick she passed, staring at them for more than a few seconds each, hoping that somewhere, there would be etchings like the ones under the desk inside.

By the time she had come back to the door where she had started she had found absolutely nothing.

For a moment, Sam just stood there, taking some time to just think.

There was something there, she knew it, even though she couldn't really feel it. She moved a step closer to the door, standing in the exact same place she had before and looked around. Gazing up at the stone arch above her head, then over her shoulder at the street beyond the gates, then back at the wooden door.

As she looked at the door her memories returned to the night previous, where she had slammed it shut and locked it in panic, thinking that there were shadows moving within and more than that, that there was *something* watching her from those vary shadows.

She furrowed her brow in confusion and frustration, wondering how she could have seen such clear evil the night before and yet now there was nothing.

The only difference between now and then was that the Vampire wasn't with her.

Momentarily she wondered if perhaps the Vampire was the cause. Had he managed to get inside her head and plant images in there in there just to mess with her?

No likely.

Even if he could find a way inside her mind without her noticing, Sam was immune to Vampire mind tricks.

The only other thing she could think of that was different between now and then was that it had been night time before.

Perhaps that was it.

Maybe whatever was hiding within the walls of the building only made itself known at night.

With a whole new theory to test, Sam walked back into the library and walked back to her desk.

Picking up her book and reading as she waited for the sun to set.

CHAPTER 15

The town's coven was an eclectic mix of people, mostly women, though occasionally there were some males who would attend a meeting.

Michelle had read books on Wicca when she was younger, so when she had first discovered the existence of this coven she had assumed that she had a pretty good idea of what to expect.

But what she expected was not even close to what she found upon her arrival.

The coven in this town was older—far older—than any other documented outside settlement in the country. They had been in the town for over a millennia. Their primary function, the function for which they were founded, was to act as the gatekeepers and protectors of the kingdom.

The floating island that now resided offshore, completely invisible to all but the few who were permitted entrance beyond its gates. And only those who were one hundred percent pure born Witch were permitted that privilege.

Which meant that mere converts—such as one of their younger members whose father was a Warlock, or Michelle who was mostly human but with some minor magical abilities—and all others with similar lineages would never be granted that privilege.

Either way, it didn't strictly matter as the Elder Witches were no longer in the habit of opening the doors.

Acting as gatekeepers had been the original function of the coven. Its current purpose remained a mystery to most of its members.

Even Michelle, who had been a part of this coven for over a decade, was still not entirely sure of their purpose. In previous years they had all gathered and spent some time discussing their individual dreams and desires, and then worked together to pool their strength and Power in order to help each other to reach their desired goals.

Although the coven did not advertise their presence in the town, they did not hide it either. The women who were members ranged from the elderly to the young and all were there for one reason or another.

Though in recent years, they spent most of their meetings discussing Sam. In one way or another all of the members of the coven would have some interaction with Sam, and therefore between them they would have a complete report on her activities.

Michelle liked to think that they were monitoring Sam in order to keep her protected. It was no secret that she had many enemies who wished her harm. But Michelle didn't wish harm to anyone, especially not Sam who as far as she was concerned was nothing more than a child.

She wasn't entirely sure why they were required to monitor Sam, or where their weekly reports ended up once they had been compiled. Those were questions she never asked, because when it came right down to it, she wasn't entirely sure she really wanted an answer.

Michelle looked up as the door closed with a bang, Hayley stood by it, one hand on the wooden door, the other turning the key locking everyone inside.

"Alright then," Hayley said with a smile. "Let's get started."

CHAPTER 16

oth Sam and Jack were reading in silence when a hispanic boy with brown hair walked into the library. The second Sam saw him she wished she had time to chant an invisibility spell. Because if she were invisible she wouldn't have to deal with *him . . . again.*

"Hey Sam," he said hesitantly as he approached the librarian's desk. "I heard you were working here."

"Only 'til the end of the summer," Sam said.

She hated talking to Scott.

It wasn't just hard for her; she could tell it was difficult for him too. Which is why she wished he would just stop trying to be friends with her. It would be better for them both if he would just move on to something better. Scott stood there chewing his lower lip, staring at his shoes, his hair falling in front of his face. Sam took a breath. "Something you needed?" she asked, and hoped it was books.

It had been two years since she'd broken up with Scott, just after her grandmother was killed. Scott still wasn't over it, and if Sam were being honest, neither was she. The only reason she had broken up with him then was because she wanted to keep him safe, and the only way she could think of doing that was to stay away from him.

"No," he said, and looked at her. "Not really. I just wanted to see you." Sam let her eyes wander in Jack's direction; he had his back to the librarian's desk and was politely pretending he couldn't hear anything. She looked back at Scott.

"I'm going on vacation tomorrow," he said. "For a month." Sam nodded along but wasn't sure why he was telling her. "I'll be gone for your birthday, so I wanted to give you this now."

Oh no, Sam thought as Scott placed a gift on the librarian's desk. She sighed. He did this every year. On her birthday and on Christmas and even one year on Valentine's day. He didn't seem to understand the meaning of 'we're not together anymore'. Scott smiled. "I've gotta go now," he said and walked away without giving Sam time to respond.

"Wait," she called after him. He continued walking away and out the library doors, acting as though he hadn't heard her speak.

Sam let an exasperated sigh. She grabbed the gift off the desk, jumped up out of her chair and followed Scott. Jack stayed where he was, paying no attention to her. She threw the doors open and stepped outside. "Scott, wait!" she called.

He froze at the gate and slowly turned around to face her. Sam ran to where he was standing. She held the gift out to him. "I can't accept this," she said.

Scott kept his hands by his sides, refusing to take it back. "Sure you can," he said. "It's a gift."

"You shouldn't be buying me gifts," Sam said. "We're not together and I don't want you to get the wrong idea or anything."

Scott took the gift back and immediately got *that* look on his face again. The same one he always got when they had this conversation. The one that made Sam feel like she was breaking his heart all over again. "So, what?" he asked and shrugged. "Does that mean we can't even be friends?" Sam didn't answer. They couldn't be anything anymore. "Did I ever do anything to make you hate me?"

Sam sighed. "No," she said. "You're like the nicest person in the world." *Which made breaking up with you so hard*, she added in her head. *It was necessary*, Sam told herself. *It had to be done.*

Scott held the gift out. "Then take it," he said. "It's a friend gift, it doesn't mean anything."

Sam struggled to decide. Scott looked at her and smiled, his brown eyes wide and hopeful as they stared into hers. Sam forced a smile and took the gift out of his hand. "Thanks," she said.

Scott appeared relieved that she had taken the gift. "Would I be pushing it if I asked for a hug?" he said and opened his arms.

Sam knew she shouldn't, it might give him ideas. But she really wanted that hug, so she shook her thoughts away and wrapped her arms around him. Scott held her tightly and Sam held on just as tight. He pressed his head against hers, his chin resting on her shoulder. "I miss you," he whispered into her hair.

Sam missed him too, but she didn't say that. Instead she just held on tighter. After a while she muttered, "I should go back inside."

Scott hesitated before letting her go. "Yeah," he said and smiled. "And I should probably go home."

Sam smiled. "Have fun on vacation," she said and started walking away.

"I'll see you at school," Scott said and walked out the library gates.

Sam headed back towards the building. She tore the wrapping paper open and looked at the gift inside.

She pursed her lips and held back a smile as she shook her head. *Doesn't mean anything,* she thought, *what a liar.* Sam walked through the library doors, then cursed to herself as the power went out and the room was plunged into complete darkness.

CHAPTER 17

$\mathcal{S}$am hurried into the darkened library. The bang of the closing door echoed in the silence. "Jack!" she called, her voice tinged with panic as her mind was flooded with memories of last night.

"What happened?" he asked.

Sam could make out a shadowy Jack shaped blob on a chair at one of the desks. "I think the power went," she said, as she took a step in his direction. "Did anyone else walk in while I was out?"

"No."

"Okay," Sam said. She concentrated her energy and sent it out to the room. The lights flickered pathetically before finally switching on. Although the light was dimmer than it should have been because the bulbs were being powered by Sam's Magic rather than electricity. "Do you know where the main switch is?" she asked.

Sam walked behind the librarian's desk and looked around

pushing books and magazines and cables out of the way in the search of something that looked like a fuse box.

"They usually have those in the basement, or outside by the wires and things," he said. "Do you want me to go down and check?"

"It's fine," she sighed. Sam took the keys Michelle had given her out of her jacket pocket, and used them to open the door behind the desk. "I'll do it."

Jack stood up. "I'll go outside, check the perimeter, see if it's out there." Sam nodded, then walked through the door into the narrow hallway, going straight for the door on the left.

The basement door.

Sam looked at it for a moment, remembering how adamant Michelle had been that she not set foot in the basement. Sam reached forward, key in hand, but before she had a chance to unlock the door, it clicked, then opened on its own.

Nervously chewing her lip, Sam looked back towards the main part of the library as the sinking feeling in her stomach and the dryness in her mouth told her that she shouldn't go down alone.

Jack was nowhere to be seen so he must have been outside. She knew that she should wait for him to return before going into the basement, but even if she did, Jack wasn't allowed to really intervene. All he could do was yell, 'Look out, behind you'.

Sam took a breath as she pushed the door all the way open and stepped onto the first creaky step leading down to the basement.

The first thing she noticed was that it was dark.

Not dark in the average basement way, but dark in the 'you've just walked into a black–hole' sort of way. Shivers ran down her spine as she ventured further into the darkness.

Something felt very wrong here.

Sam sent more Magic out into the air to try make some form of light in the room. Glittering beams of purple Magic latched onto the bare light bulb that hung from the ceiling in the centre of the basement. The Magic burrowed its way inside the bulb, lending it power so it could illuminate the room.

The bulb flickered a little, then slowly began to switch itself on. Sam smiled to herself as the basement lit up in a pale orange glow, but jumped as she saw something move in her peripheral vision. Before the light had a chance to reach its brightest, allowing her to see what was moving, something that appeared to be a shadow jumped on the bulb and sucked all of the light from it.

Sam looked on as the room was once again plunged into darkness.

Fuck it, Sam thought. She allowed her energy to build up in the palms of her hands, feeling the electrical surge run through her veins as her Power manifested, then—with a flick of her wrist—she sent glittering raindrops of Magic into the air. The room filled with pink and purple lights that hovered in the air above her. With a steady source of light, the room looked less terrifying, but Sam had the same feeling she had when it was dark.

The feeling of wrong.

Of dread.

Of fear.

And fear was one of those things that Sam didn't generally feel.

On the far end of the room she saw a little metal box on the wall. She ran to it, prised it open, then flicked the main switch. The lights immediately switched back on and Sam's Magic lights dissipated.

"Sam?" A voice sounded from behind her.

Without wasting a moment in thought, Sam struck out at the

person behind her. She tripped him up; he landed with a thump on the ground. Sam placed a knee on his chest to keep him there.

"What are you doing down here?" Sam asked accusingly. Curiosity was no excuse for wandering in dangerous places.

Dangerous? Sam asked herself. *When did basements make the list of dangerous things to stay away from?*

Jamie stared up at her in astonishment, as if he couldn't believe what had just happened. "Uh, I was upstairs, and no one was there . . . and the door was opened . . . and—" Jamie looked at the ceiling, his brow furrowed in confusion. "Did you see that?" Sam ignored him. Instead she looked around the room and realised that's exactly what this place was.

Dangerous.

That was the first time she noticed that there was a cluster of darkness in every corner of the room, and the more she watched it the more it seemed to be building up in size.

Building for what? Sam wondered, and there it was again.

Fear.

Suddenly the thought struck her, *They're not shadows at all.* Sam stood, quickly scrambling to her feet. "Get up," she ordered. Her voice sounding shrill and panicked.

"What? What's—"

"Get up now!" Sam cried. The shadows were building in every corner of the room, seeping from the spaces between each brick on the wall, edging around the room.

Blocking off the exits.

"Go!" Sam said and pointed at the staircase.

Jamie got to his feet and walked almost hesitantly towards the staircase. Sam moved behind him and gave him a shove to quicken his pace. "Go!" she said again. Jamie obeyed and jogged up the stairs. As they reached the top of the staircase Sam sent a ball of light into the room. It exploded noiselessly, but it seemed to scare the shadows enough to send them scurrying back to their corners.

"What was that?" Jamie asked and turned around just as Sam slammed the basement door shut.

"What was what?" Sam asked. She held her breath for a few seconds in an attempt to calm her racing pulse.

"Did you not see that?" he asked. Sam locked the basement, and holding her hands close to her stomach so her actions couldn't be seen, used her fingers to draw invisible symbols in the air, casting a quick barrier spell over it. Whatever was in there would not be getting out any time soon.

"See what?" Sam asked and turned to face him.

He appeared more confused than Sam had ever seen another person look. "Was that . . . was that lightning?" he asked, looking around the narrow hallway as if trying to find a logical explanation for what he'd witnessed. There were no windows, which just seemed to confuse him more.

Sam shrugged in an attempt at nonchalance. "Do I look like the weather man?" she asked rhetorically. "I didn't see anything." Sam walked out of the room to the librarian's desk. Jack was back at the table. He looked at her questioningly.

<I'll explain later> Sam thought to him.

Jack turned away from her and went back to reading his book.

"You're not allowed be back there," Sam said to Jamie, who was still in shock and standing in the back room. Jamie slowly stepped out, then around from behind the librarian's desk. He stood in front of the desk and just stared at Sam, as if assessing her. She felt a push inside her head. Without too much effort she blocked him from reading her thoughts, just as she had yesterday. Though this only seemed to add to his confusion. "You alright?" Sam asked.

Slowly Jamie nodded.

Sam reached into her pocket and pulled out the folded slip of paper she had written the directions to the Blood-Bar on. She held it out to him. "This is for you," she said.

Jamie looked at the paper in her hand, then at her. "What is it?" he asked.

"The address you asked for yesterday."

Slowly, Jamie reached his hand out to take the paper from Sam.

One touch, his fingertips against the palm of her hand, and Jamie fell to the floor and was unconscious within seconds.

CHAPTER 18

amie felt a surge of Power shoot through his body, momentarily paralysing him and causing him to fall to the floor. He instinctually closed his eyes against the pain, and tried as best he could to pull his strength together so he could push himself to his feet.

"What did you do that for?" he heard a man ask. Jamie felt his body tense at the sound of another person's voice. When he had come into the library he hadn't seen anyone, or felt anyone's presence. The entire place had seemed deserted. It's why, when he saw the open door, he'd gone through it, hoping he'd find Sam.

But he didn't fully understand what he'd found.

He heard light footsteps approach him. "He saw me use Magic," Sam said. *Magic,* he thought, *but, that's impossible.* "I have to wipe his memory."

"You don't *have* to Sam," the man said. "You could just explain everything to him, and then you'd have another ally."

Sam placed her hands on either side of Jamie's head. Warmth radiated from her fingertips and seeped through his skin, causing his body to relax at her touch. "Another ally who will just be killed," she replied. Her voice seemed cold and detached.

"Do whatever you want." The man sighed and mumbled, "You always do."

Something pushed inside his head. A Power stronger than anything he'd ever sensed before moved within his mind. Searching through his memories with alarming ease. Jamie tried to build walls in his mind, in an attempt to shield himself, but his efforts were futile. Whatever was within his head pushed through his defences before he had even finished creating them.

It searched through his memories.

More specifically, his memories of the past fifteen minutes.

He felt the memories being pulled from his mind and he didn't fight it. Instead he put all of his energy into staying perfectly still, unsure as to what he would, or could do to help himself out of this situation.

Was it Sam who was doing this?

He couldn't believe that it was.

Last night he had spent hours looking at her, watching her, observing her. And although he was unable to sense her presence and was unable to enter her mind, she still registered as human. She *looked* human and she acted human and he was sure she wasn't a Vampire. So what else could she be?

After a few moments of Sam attempting to remove his memories, he felt new pictures being formed inside his mind. Images replacing those that had just been stolen from him.

He saw himself enter the library and walk over to the desk where Sam was sitting, reading a book different to the one she had been reading yesterday. He'd struck up a conversation with her, in which he'd suggested that they spend some time together. She declined. He pushed. She told him she wasn't interested. He'd been offended. They argued. She told him to leave.

The scene repeated in his head again and again until it was burned onto his memory as if it belonged.

He felt Sam take her hands off him. And for a moment he just lay there, his cheek pressed against the cold marble floor, fully aware of what had just happened and knowing that Sam had to have been the one responsible for it. But not understanding how she was capable of doing something like that.

<Get up> he heard Sam's voice in his head. Another thing which he *knew* she shouldn't be capable of doing.

Jamie paused for a moment, before he complied with her command, not sure what else he could do.

He pushed himself off the floor, and stood facing Sam who was standing behind the desk in the exact same place she had been when he'd first hit the floor.

She folded her arms across her chest. He looked at her, his head tilted slightly in confusion. She was in the *exact* same place. It made him wonder if he had imagined everything that had just happened.

"You should leave," Sam said, her tone completely neutral, not giving any insight into her emotions or thoughts.

For a moment Jamie just stood there staring at her. She *looked* human. *Everything* about her looked human.

Though everything about him seemed human too, and he wasn't. And she worked the night shift, so perhaps . . .

He felt his hand rise slightly as he reached out towards her. He stopped himself before he touched her, remembering how she had attempted to manipulate him into believing she didn't want him anywhere near her.

Sam watched him steadily, her eyes not leaving his for even a moment. Her lips were set in a harsh line, indicative of her anger, contradicting the feeling he saw in her eyes. Which were filled with an immense sadness and held a strange familiarity. One which he was still unable to place. He didn't know how, but he *knew* those eyes.

Jamie let his arm fall to his side. Then, turning sharply, he walked out of the library. Deciding to give Sam exactly what she wished for.

For now at least.

CHAPTER 19

$\mathcal{S}$am watched Jamie as he walked out the door, her shoulders relaxed and she let a sigh as she heard the heavy thud of the door closing.

"What the fuck happened?" Jack asked. He was standing right next to her now, looking at her with an expression that was somewhere between concern and anger.

Sam chewed her lip as her eyes wandered to the room behind her. "There's something down there," she said without looking at him. She just stared at the door, reaching out to it with her psychic senses, trying to get a clear read on whatever was in there.

"What do you mean? What's down there?"

Sam clenched and unclenched her hands, trying to stop them from shaking. She'd had to deal with everything so fast that she hadn't had time to calm down yet. Her pulse was still racing, her nerves still felt frayed, she still felt scared.

"I don't know," she answered, turning her head so she could

see him. He was watching her intently, almost as if her face would hold some vital piece of information that would help him figure out what had happened.

"It looked like . . . " Sam let her sentence trail off, not wanting to say it out loud, knowing in her mind how crazy it sounded.

"Like what?"

Sam sighed and shook her head. "I'm sure it was nothing." She let a nervous laugh. "I'm probably just tired or something."

"Sam." Jack's tone was serious. "*Tell* me what you saw."

Sam shrugged, glancing at the basement door that was now sealed with a protection spell that would keep things from getting out . . . but it wouldn't keep people from going in.

She remembered Michelle, and how freaked she'd been when Sam had tried to go down there yesterday. Did she know there was something down there? Did she know what it was? Did she realise it was evil?

And if so, then why hadn't she warned Sam that there was something potentially dangerous lurking in the shadows right behind her?

It was unlikely that Michelle, if she did know there was something down there, fully understood the level of its Power and the extent of its evil.

She let another sigh. "It looked like a shadow," she said, meeting Jack's eyes. He nodded his head as if she were making perfect sense, but she could tell that he didn't understand what she meant, or what she was describing. As far as Sam was aware there was nothing in the supernatural world that took the appearance of a shadow. Not one that looked like *that* anyway. "Not like a shape though . . . more like, I don't know . . . like mist or something. Black fog. And it came in through the walls and it attacked the lights and made it dark. I had to use Magic to light the room and scare it away, but . . . "

"But?"

"It adjusted to the light and came at me. And . . . " She chewed her lip nervously, looking at Jack from under her eyelashes before she told him what she should have told him when he first got back. "It wasn't the first time I saw it. You weren't here," she spoke quickly, before Jack had a chance to get angry that she hadn't told him right away. "And by the time you got back I just kinda convinced myself that I imagined it."

"Right." Jack slapped his hand on the desk and jumped over it, landing with more grace than a man his size should logically have. He stepped into the hallway behind the desk and stood outside the basement door. "Unlock it." He pointed at the door, stepping up to it as if he wasn't even slightly scared.

The thing down there wasn't physical, Jack wasn't physical, so the chances were that the thing in the basement could hurt Jack in some way. Maybe even kill him for good.

Sam shook her head. "You could die."

Jack smiled. "Sam . . . Been there, done that. I'd have gotten you a postcard but there's never any good ones."

"No." Sam folded her arms across her chest, letting him know that she meant it.

"One way barrier," he said. "I'm going in, I just wanted you to unlock it so I could get back out." Then without waiting for Sam to reply, he stepped through the wood.

Sam rushed to the door, throwing it open so fast it made a loud crash as it slammed into the wall. Jack stood on the other side of the door grinning at her. "Why Sam, I never knew how much you cared." He wiped away a pretend tear and sniffled. "It makes me so warm and fuzzy on the inside."

Sam scowled at him. "You suck."

He just laughed.

Sam sighed and removed the barrier spell, following Jack

down the stairs where he found the light switch and flicked the lights on. Sam stayed close behind him as he walked into the centre of the room and looked around. She saw his shoulders drop, as if he was disappointed when nothing happened.

Sam furrowed her brow in frustration as she looked around. Everything felt normal.

There were no dark patches, no shadows.

The air didn't feel tainted.

She didn't feel irrationally scared.

"I swear, it was here!"

"I believe you," Jack stated. Sam looked at his face, his expression seemed troubled and confused. As if he didn't know what was going on, and wasn't sure what to make of what Sam had told him.

"What do you think it was?" she asked, as they headed towards the stairs.

Jack shrugged. "I don't know . . . could have been someone playing mind games with you. Maybe your Vampire isn't as nice as we thought and he likes to mess with people's heads."

"It wasn't him," Sam said surely. "First off, I'm immune to Vampire mind tricks. Secondly, I was in his head and he was freaked out when he saw my Magic."

Jack shrugged again and sighed. "I don't know then. I don't know what it could have been. Maybe it was just some bad energy or something."

"Maybe," Sam said, nodding her head in agreement, while the sinking feeling in the pit of her stomach told her that what she saw was more than just some bad energy. What she saw . . . what she *felt* was something with a consciousness.

It was something that could think.

It was something that could feel.

It was angry.

It was *evil*.

CHAPTER 20

Michelle walked into the library slowly, the creak of the door echoing loudly in the empty room.

She'd worked at the library for over ten years. And in all of the ten years that she'd worked there she'd never felt as disturbed by the aura of the building as she had in these past few weeks. The room in the daytime was never the same as it was at night. And perhaps that was why she had never before noticed the voiceless whispers and the faceless shadows that seemed to haunt every crevice of the old building.

Since Jessie had taken the summer off and she'd been forced, for the first time in all the years she'd worked there, to work the night shift, she found that she had become terrified of not only being there alone, but of being there alone at night.

She switched the lights on and ventured in further, shaking off her fear as she repeatedly told herself that it was all in her head. These mantras had become a part of her daily routine, something she had to tell herself so that her legs would allow her to walk to the desk instead of forcing her to turn and run back home as they so desperately wanted to.

It was only when she got to her desk that she felt it.

The strong sense of Magic in the air.

She furrowed her brow and walked behind the desk. Only moving towards the residue of Power because she knew that the Magic she felt was Sam's. Although she and Sam weren't friends, given their age gap there were no social events that would cause them to ever hang out together, the younger girl had spent enough time in the library over the past few years that the sense of her Power had become a familiar thing to anyone in the town with a sixth sense strong enough to feel it.

This particular Magic was not leftover from some spell that Sam may have been casting the night previous, but was still actively working away at whatever it was she had formed it to do.

Slowly, Michelle turned to look behind her, gazing at the door to the basement where she felt the Magic was originating from.

On some level she was glad to have the extra protection of the barricades at her back, but then there was the small part of her that was completely overwhelmed by fear at the realisation that she had been right, there was something in the library that she should be afraid of.

And it was something so terrible that instead of using all of the Magic she was gifted with to kill it, Sam had only locked it away.

She didn't know what was more terrifying.

The thought that there was a monster lurking in the shadows, or the thought that this monster was something stronger than Sam.

CHAPTER 21

$\mathcal{I}$t was the morning of the twenty-sixth and the sun had yet to rise when Jack left for Freya's house. The Moirai had pretty much given him a play-by-play of everything that would happen over the next few months. They told him everything he had to do up 'til the day he was supposed to bring Sam to Athens to see the Moirai for herself.

And they had assured him that before next summer came, his work for them would be finished. He would be free and they would grant him the one thing he wished for. To live again. And he would finally get to tell Sam all the things he'd been waiting so many years to tell her.

But for today, he was supposed to go to Freya and get an amulet from her. The one that had belonged to every female in Sam's family going right back a few thousand years to when it had been Freya's.

When Sam's mother had been killed, the Moirai had given the amulet back to Freya and told her it would find its way to

Sam when the time was right.

Jack felt that the Moirai should have told Freya what they really meant. Because what they *really* meant was, when the time was right for Sam to receive the amulet, they'd send Jack to go get it from her so he could bring it to Sam.

Jack had to use his ghostly Powers to materialise on Hunter land, near the house he used to live in and the house that his family still resided in. But he wasn't allowed to see them, because that was against the goddamn rules. From there he had to corporealise, then walk a few miles to the river that separated his family's property from Valkyrie territory. After that he had to cross the river, and walk another few miles through fields and forests to Freya's house.

Because of the barrier spells that surrounded the Valkyrie's territory, Jack couldn't just materialise at the house. He had to walk all the way there in his corporeal form and get sore legs and feet.

Because the fucking bitches that called themselves the Moirai didn't believe in the post office.

The branches of the trees began to thrash violently as Jack's anger manifested itself in the nature around him.

As a Hunter his emotions had always been quite volatile, and as a Ghost they were much worse. Mostly because if he didn't control his feelings, they would manifest around him, like they were now. Infecting nature and anyone close enough to feel it.

Jack took a breath to calm himself; every time he thought of the Moirai and all of the shit they put him through it made him so angry he could barely contain it.

He continued walking through the green fields of the Valkyrie's territory towards the old brick house. The front door swung open before Jack had even reached it.

The woman standing on the other side was well built, just slightly shorter than Jack, which meant she was incredibly tall for a woman. But then, the Valkyries were built like warriors. She glared at Jack, her dark eyes watching him in a way that if he were living would have incited an extreme discomfort.

"What are you doing here *Hunter*?" Brynhild asked, her tone making it sound as though Jack's very existence had ruined not only her entire day but her entire life.

"Actually, it's *Ghost*," Jack corrected. "I haven't been a Hunter in years, and I'm here to see Freya."

"Who says she wants to see you?" she asked rhetorically. "Why would she? You're the reason Serenity was killed."

Serenity was one of Freya's descendants, and Sam's birth mother. Jack physically flinched at the mention of her name. It was a low blow bringing that up. "He's also the reason that Samantha is alive," Freya said from across the room. Brynhild turned around, as if just noticing Freya's presence for the first time. "Let him in."

Brynhild begrudgingly stepped aside, keeping her eyes on Jack as he walked through the doors, past Brynhild, into the room where Freya was standing.

She turned and led the way to the living room, seated herself on an armchair and directed for Jack to do the same. He took a seat on the sofa across from her. "Is she okay?" Freya asked, wasting no time with small talk. "Is it time yet?"

"No," Jack said. "The Moirai sent me to get the amulet."

"Oh," Freya mumbled, folding and unfolding her hands in her lap. Jack could see the disappointment in her expression even though she tried to hide it.

Freya looked a lot like Sam, and a lot like Serenity. Her skin was slightly darker than Sam's, her hair was also about two shades darker and her eyes were a more vibrant shade of purple. But other than that they looked very much alike. If you were to put them side by side you would be able to see quite clearly that they were from the same family.

Even though Jack had spent all of his Hunter years living just across the river from Freya, he had never really known her. When he was younger he just thought of her as the woman who lived in this house. After a while he started to notice that she wasn't simply a woman, she was actually quite a powerful Witch.

But it wasn't until the last few months of his life that he had learned the truth about what Freya, and everyone related to her, really was.

And he couldn't understand why someone with such an immense amount of Power—someone *that* far up on the food chain—would hide herself away, acting as though she were powerless instead of doing what she could to stop the war that had been started because of what she had created.

"Before next summer," Jack said. Freya looked to him curiously. "That's what they said. You'll meet her before next summer."

Freya sighed, nodding her head. "That's not so long." She stood up and walked out of the room. A few moments later she came back in, holding a silver chain with a clear tear shaped stone on the end. "I always thought she'd come here to get it herself," Freya said as she handed the amulet to Jack. "It needs a drop of her blood to be activated, it won't respond otherwise."

"Right." Jack put the amulet into his pocket.

"So," Freya said and sat down, carefully folding her hands on her lap. "Tell me all about her."

CHAPTER 22

*I*t was eleven o'clock before Jack made it back to Sam's house. Not that she even noticed he'd gone, since she was still sleeping when he arrived. She lay curled up in the middle of her bed wrapped in the duvet. "Sam," he called. She stirred a little at the sound of his voice. "Sam. Sam. Sam."

"What?" she mumbled without opening her eyes.

"Sam," he called again. It was his firmly held belief that she wasn't awake until she opened her eyes. "Sam. Sam."

"What?" she asked again. More agitatedly than before.

Jack paused for a moment. "Sam. Sa —"

Sam opened her eyes. "WHAT?"

"Wake up," Jack said. Sam groaned and pushed herself into a sitting position, rubbing her eyes with her hands, smudging the remnants of yesterday's make-up, creating dark circles under her eyes.

"Why?" she whined.

"I have a present for you." Sam looked at him questioningly, probably confused because he had never given her a gift before, with the exception of the stuffed toy he had bought her when she was a baby. Jack pulled the amulet from his pocket and handed it to her.

She took it from him and studied it for a moment, turning it around in her hands so she could see it from the back and the front. "Thanks," she said with a smile. "I don't really wear jewellery though."

"It's an amulet. You need to put a drop of your blood on it to activate it," Jack explained as he took a seat on the edge of Sam's bed. "It was your mother's."

"It was?" Sam asked, as she examined it closely, as if she would find some clue to her past within it. Jack nodded. "Where'd you get it?"

"I can't tell you that, not yet."

Sam sighed and rolled her eyes. "Of course," she grumbled, her voice tinged with resentment. "Did *you* have it or did you get it off someone else?"

"Someone else," Jack stated, trying not to be hurt by the obvious accusation in her question.

"Who—"

"No," Jack interrupted. "You know the rules."

"But if you know people who knew my parents, they probably know all about me too, so *they* could tell me things—"

Jack shook his head. "No," he repeated. "You know that there are certain things you're not allowed to know. Not yet."

Sam sighed. "Well if I can't find out yet, when can I find out?"

"Soon."

"How soon?"

"*Soon*," he repeated.

"Well *soon* isn't soon enough!"

"Everything will happen as and when it's supposed to

happen," he tried to explain, but Jack could see the doubt on Sam's face. "Just trust me," he sighed. She looked at him sadly, with her big indigo eyes. "Have I ever let you down before?"

"No," Sam mumbled.

Jack corporealised, then wrapped his arms around her and squeezed her tightly. Hoping the gesture would offer her some comfort or make her feel like she wasn't as alone as she thought she was. "Then just trust me." Sam hesitated before returning his hug. "If I could tell you everything right now, I would."

He let her go. She sighed and rubbed her eyes with the back of her hand. "Life sucks."

Jack said nothing in reply. His stomach clenched with the sympathy he felt for her; her life was so much tougher than it should be. Though he was proud of all of the things she could do and all of the things that she would accomplish, he couldn't help wishing that the burdens that came with the amount of Power she had didn't have to fall on her shoulders.

Nobody her age should have to worry about whether or not they were going to live to see tomorrow.

Jack shook away his thoughts. "It's your birthday," he said resolutely and stood. "And you are *not* going to lie around all day and do nothing."

Sam sulked. "But that was my plan."

"Well you can change your plan. Because I'm not going to let you stay home all day doing nothing."

"I won't be doing nothing *all day*," Sam corrected. "I have to go to the library at six."

"And you have more than six hours 'til then, so what do you want to do?"

"Lie around and do nothing," Sam said, then lay back down and pulled the duvet over her head.

"No." Jack glared at the duvet momentarily, willing it to move; it flew off the bed and onto the floor.

Sam dragged herself into a sitting position. "Why not?" she whined.

"Because I said so," Jack said sternly. "Why don't you call Madison or Elle and ask them to do something?"

"Because one, those two never shut up. I can only handle talking to them for an hour or less. And two, I'm not friends with them anymore."

"Then why don't you call Jamie?" Jack teased. "I'm sure he'd be more than happy to spend a few hours . . . or his entire life with you."

Sam gave him an unimpressed looked. "Because I just got rid of him a week ago."

"Call Jade," Jack said. "You always liked Jade."

"I'd rather just lie around and do nothing," she mumbled, absently tracing her finger over the birthmark on her wrist.

"Call Jade," Jack ordered.

Jade was Hayley's daughter. She was just a few months older than Sam, and they always got along really well. There was no reason for Sam not to call her. "Call her and I promise not to be an alarm clock for a week," Jack said, knowing how much Sam hated it when he woke her up by calling her name over and over and over again.

She sighed. "If I agree to hang out with Jade for a few hours you'll leave me alone before noon, not just for the week but from now on."

"A month," Jack offered. "After that you'll be back in school, so you'll be waking up early anyway."

"For the rest of the summer, and any days I'm not in school."

"Deal," Jack said. "Now get up, get dressed, and I'll go call Jade. You have thirty minutes!" He walked out of the room, giving Sam some privacy so she could get dressed.

CHAPTER 23

$\mathcal{S}$am got up out of bed and had a quick shower before brushing her teeth. She pulled on a pair of jeans and a t-shirt, not bothering to look at what she was dressing herself in before she put it on. She rarely ever paid that much attention to what she wore, at least not anymore.

Clothes didn't matter. What was the point in dressing nice when no one was there to notice?

Despite the fact that she had fifteen minutes left before Jack would barge in and drag her outside, she used Magic to dry her hair. Not just because it was easier and less time consuming than using a hairdryer, but because ever since Sam had openly started using her Magic she'd used it for pretty much everything.

Drying her hair, mending clothes if they started to look worn, keeping the house clean, making food taste better. Since she'd turned fifteen Magic had become a part of her daily life.

She never used it to apply make-up though.

Not because she *couldn't* use it for that, but because Magic for make-up was nothing more than a glamour. And people could see through glamours if they cared to look closely enough.

After spending about five minutes making her face look slightly more presentable she placed the amulet that Jack had given her on the counter beside the sink. Then, using a pair of scissors from her desk she cut her finger, allowing a drop of her blood to fall on the crystal.

The blood seeped into the clear teardrop shaped stone. It mixed around inside it for a few seconds, floating within the gem like a red mist. Then the amulet started to glow, before it went clear again.

Cool, Sam thought as she picked the amulet up and held it in her hand. She felt the warm pulse of ancient Magic seeping from it and thrumming against her skin, melding into her flesh and becoming a part of her.

She squeezed the gem tightly in her hand for a moment, allowing herself some time to adjust.

Then she put it around her neck.

Sam gasped as soon as the stone touched the skin on her chest. Her heartbeat momentarily increased. She felt a small stabbing pain go through her heart. Sam turned around and looked at herself in the mirror. A drop of blood ran down from her chest, directly behind the amulet, and behind her t-shirt.

For a few seconds breathing was more difficult than breathing should be. Then, after a few moments, the pain cleared and her breathing returned to normal, as another drop of blood—this time travelling from Sam's heart—seeped through the stone and into the centre. But this time as the blood swirled around inside, it stained the amulet purple.

Sam ran the tap and used the water to wash the blood off her chest. By the time the amulet had relaxed, and grown used to Sam, she noticed that the colour it had turned was the same colour as her eyes.

Sam took a breath, then when she was ready, she put on a pair of shoes and walked downstairs. Jack was in the living room waiting for her. "Ready?" he asked turning to face her as she stepped off the last step.

"I guess," Sam mumbled. She took her jacket off the coat rack in the hallway, then put it on, checking her pocket to make sure her keys were still where they should be. Sam opened the front door, and had taken just one step when she almost fell flat on her face. Jack, still in his corporeal form, reached out and grabbed her, keeping a firm grip on Sam's arm, doing his best to keep her upright. Sam fixed herself, regaining her footing, before she let her gaze travel down to find whatever had tripped her up.

A vase was rolling around on the front porch, eighteen red roses spilled across the ground.

"The fuck?" she mumbled. Sam looked at the vase, then at Jack. He scrutinised the vase in confusion, obviously it hadn't been there when he'd come in. He looked at Sam and shrugged.

Sam bent down, picking the roses up off the ground; she put them back in the vase, counting them as she did. She had been right, there were eighteen, and each one had the thorns removed from their stems. There was a card accompanying the flowers, though it was just a generic piece of white card. It didn't say where the flowers had come from and it didn't say who had sent them. All the card said was 'Happy Birthday'.

Sam stood up with the vase in her hand. "Who are they from?" Jack asked, turning his head sideways to try read the card.

"I don't know," Sam answered, her jaw clenched as she spoke, while the back of her head whispered, *Yes, you do.* "It doesn't say." Sam brought the flowers inside, walking through the hallway quickly; she reached the back door, swung it open with her free hand, then dropped the roses, and the vase they came in into the trash can outside.

She heard Jack let a sigh and knew it meant he'd figured out who they were from. "You didn't need to do that you know? A gift should be appreciated, even if you're mad at the person who sent it."

Without a word in response she walked back to the front door, slamming it shut behind her.

Sam had barely made it up the driveway to Jade's house, when Jade walked out the front door with her jacket on. "Hey Sam," she said. "Ready to go?"

Sam forced a smile and nodded. Jade walked past her, over to the fence where Jack was waiting for them. Before Sam turned to join them she noticed movement at the living room window in Jade's house. She saw Hayley standing there, staring at her boldly, her lips curved in a smirk. Sam felt her teeth clench as she held back her anger.

She wasn't sure what it was about Hayley that pissed her off so much. There was just something about her that seemed . . . *wrong*.

Sam turned to walk away, when she caught sight of a shadow in the corner of her eye. She turned back sharply to try get a better look at what she thought she saw. But when she looked, there was nothing there.

No shadows.

No monsters.

No Hayley.

There was nothing evil . . . at least not that she could see.

CHAPTER 24

$\mathcal{J}$amie walked down a dark and dingy street, the light
that should have been emanating from the streetlamps
was virtually nonexistent. Not that Jamie minded much, with
his heightened senses he could have found his way through the
streets blindfolded.

He turned off the dingy street, into an even dingier alleyway
around the side of the seediest, most rundown hotel he had
ever seen. As he moved forward, he suddenly noticed a
hunched figure on the ground hidden behind the bins. Jamie
jumped slightly when he first noticed him, then for a moment
afterwards just looked at the man curiously.

He hadn't sensed him before he'd seen him, which was odd.

But that was something that seemed to be happening to him
a lot lately. Running into people that his senses told him didn't
exist.

Jamie cast his eyes over the spindly man. He was pale and
dirty, his clothes worn and torn; he looked as though he hadn't

shaved in a month and he smelled as though he hadn't washed since then either.

It didn't take very long for Jamie to determine that the man was dead. He had no audible pulse, his chest was completely still, and no heat radiated from his skin.

Jamie peered over his shoulder at the vacant streets and wondered if he should call someone.

The police?

An ambulance?

After a moment of waiting for someone who he could *persuade* to be the one to make the phone call, he turned, stepped past the man and walked to the door at the end of the alley — the one marked 'Emergency Exit' — after deciding it would be simpler to inform the people within the club he was on his way to.

The door was broken, so it was easily opened. Beyond that door was another one that had been painted black, making it barely visible in the darkness. He stood in the small entryway, the door in front of him swinging open before the one behind had even closed.

Jamie was surprised but he hid it as best he could. *Vampires,* he thought, *they can sense me.*

A girl with vibrant red hair stood on the other side of the door. She looked at him curiously for a moment, then smiled widely as though she were trying to be friendly, but the width of her smile and the amount of teeth she exposed made the action look more threatening than friendly.

Jamie listened carefully, he could hear her heart beating steadily, and her lungs expanding as she breathed in and out. *Human,* he thought, overcome with disappointment, though he tried not to allow his disappointment to show externally. After all, the odds of him finding somewhere that was actually a club for Vampires had never really been very high.

She's dressed quite oddly, Jamie thought as he did a quick evaluation of her attire. She was wearing a pair of thigh-high leather boots over what appeared to be leather trousers, a black long sleeved top, over which she wore a vest that appeared to be made of silver chainmail.

"Hi," she said after a moment.

Jamie smiled nervously, her attire filling him with a slight unease. "Hello."

"My name's Heather," she said, then slowly looked him up and down. "You're new?" she observed, but stated is as though it was both a fact and a question.

Jamie wasn't sure if she meant to the club or life as a Vampire. To the first one he was new, not so much to the second. Given the fact that she was clearly human, Jamie treated her as he would any other human and assumed she had no knowledge of what he was. He nodded to let her know that she was right, he was new to the club. "I'm Jamie," he said.

"Jamie," she repeated. "I like it, you can come in." She stepped aside to let him pass.

He took a step forward, then paused when he remembered the man outside. "I actually need to ask you something first."

Heather paused for a moment, and looked at him, her eyes widened and she looked around nervously as though she expected their interaction to end badly for her in some way. "Oh . . . what do you need to ask me?"

He placed his hand on the door behind him and pushed it open, pointing outside. "What should I do about *him*?"

Heather stepped forward hesitantly and poked her head around the doorframe to see where Jamie was pointing. She visibly paled at the sight of the dead man. "Oh," she breathed and quickly turned away.

"Should I call the police?" Jamie asked. Feeling slightly guilty for exposing her to the sight of a dead body. He would have looked around inside and found someone else, but he was here for a purpose and he'd rather not waste too much time on things that didn't fit into his plans.

Heather shook her head. "No, we can't have police back here," she replied, then turned to the door. "Nick!" she yelled inside. Less than half a second later a tall man showed up at the threshold, dressed in a pair of jeans and a red check shirt. Jamie was relieved to see someone dressed normally; when he'd first seen Heather he had been worried there would be some kind of chainmail dress code.

"What?" he asked, then gave Jamie a curious look. *He has no heartbeat,* Jamie thought excitedly as he smiled a hello. The man . . . the Vampire, Nick, nodded politely.

Heather just pointed to the body, still facing away from it as if she couldn't bear to see.

Nick looked at the body for a moment, before he sighed in annoyance, as if this was something that he dealt with regularly. Then he walked to the dead man and slung the body over his shoulder. "I'll be back in a minute," he said to Heather, before he disappeared.

Jamie watched Nick run away with the fascination of a child who had just witnessed something magical. He could run that fast himself, but to see someone else move at such a speed was an amazing sight to behold.

He'd done it; he had found another Vampire.

He was so happy he could have clicked his heels in excitement.

He didn't . . . but he could have.

Jamie turned to look at Heather who was watching the place where Nick had been, her expression somewhere between amazement and fear. She was human, but obviously she knew about Vampires, which made him wonder how she knew and how — with knowledge of Vampires, which supposedly included knowledge of their dietary preferences—she had wound up working in a place such as this.

Heather turned to Jamie and gave him a queasy smile. "Come in," she said, and led the way inside.

"What's he going to do with the body?" Jamie asked, his curiosity getting the better of him.

"He'll take the body to the park, leave it on a bench then make an anonymous call to the police from the nearest phone booth."

Jamie nodded his head as he looked around. The place was not at all as Sam had described it.

As his thoughts turned to Sam he felt his heart twinge with longing. He promptly washed the feeling away before it had a chance to grow.

Despite the dingy exterior, the inside of the club was quite . . . lush. The walls were painted a deep red and were decorated with black velvet curtains. The room he was standing in was lit entirely by candles, all safely contained in glass jars. Soft music could be heard over unseen speakers.

"The bar is through there," Heather told him and pointed to a doorway framed with black curtains. "If you're looking for a room you talk to me, I'll get you a good one. It's fancier on the inside than it is on the outside."

"Thanks," Jamie said. "Uh, you wouldn't happen to know a Vampire by the name of Aleczander would you?" he asked. Hoping beyond reason that this human girl would have some helpful information.

The only reason Jamie had come to this place was because he was hoping to find the Vampire who had made him this way; a man who he knew nothing about apart from his name.

Heather shrugged. "I've only worked here for like a week," she said. "But I do know that if you're looking to track another Vampire, go into the bar, take a seat and tell Eric . . . the bartender, that you're looking for Claudio."

"Claudio?" Jamie asked.

Heather nodded. "Claudio is one of the oldest dudes around. He knows everyone, he'll find whoever it is you need."

Jamie nodded. "Thanks," he said, and walked towards the bar.

"Remember to come to me if you want a room," Heather called after him.

Jamie laughed a little to himself. "I will."

He walked through the curtained doorway into the bar. Its decor was more or less the same as the reception area only with a countertop to the left of the entrance, lined with stools. There were about a dozen tables, and the walls, instead of being lined with black velvet curtains were lined with black velvet sofas that were partitioned to make little booths around the room.

Jamie sat down on one of the barstools. The bartender was there almost immediately. "What can I get you?" he asked. Jamie could sense no heartbeat from the man. Another Vampire.

"Um, I'm looking for Claudio," he replied. The bartender nodded, this was obviously a familiar routine for him.

He pointed to one of the velvet sofas. "That's him there." Jamie allowed his gaze to follow the bartender's pointed finger and found himself looking at a man who had his mouth on the neck of a brunette in a navy dress. The bartender turned back to Jamie. "He'll be over in a minute. Can I get you a drink while you're waiting?"

Jamie wondered if he was supposed to order blood or not. Was he expected to, or would any beverage suffice? "I'll have a beer, thanks," he said, deciding he'd rather not ask for blood. He didn't know where they got it from, or how fresh it was, or if it was even something they served.

"Any preferences?" he asked. Jamie shrugged. The bartender

opened a bottle and set it down in front of him.

"Thanks," Jamie said.

As soon as he took the first sip, Claudio sat on the seat next to him, fastidiously licking traces of blood from his lips. "You rang?" he asked with a curious glance at Jamie. "I don't believe I know you."

"My name is Jamie, and you don't know me because we've never met."

Claudio smiled at that.

The bartender placed a glass of brown liquid in front of Claudio. Jamie could smell it from where he was sitting, bourbon.

He leaned back on the stool and peered over his shoulder at the woman that Claudio had been feeding from. She was lying on the sofa with her eyes closed and a black jacket draped over her body. "What did you do to her?" Jamie asked and turned his attention back to Claudio.

Claudio glanced towards the woman and smiled. "I told her to sleep, so she sleeps," he explained. "No one will touch her, they all know she is mine," he added, as if assuring Jamie of the woman's safety. "Do you know how to manipulate the mind?" Claudio asked conversationally. Jamie noticed that he spoke with a slight accent. French, maybe.

"Yes," he replied. "I wasn't Turned yesterday. I have learned a few things over the years."

Claudio nodded, sipping his drink while he looked at Jamie as if assessing him. The corner of his lips twitched in a smile as he said, "What has you so shaken?"

Jamie stared straight ahead, choosing to ignore Claudio's question. "I need help finding someone. I was told that you could help me."

He heard Claudio chuckle. "Oh? And who might you be trying to find?"

"The Vampire who Turned me."

"Your Sire?" Claudio sounded baffled. "When was the last time you saw him . . . her?"

"Last I saw *him* was the night before I woke up a Vampire . . . so, late August . . . eighteen-twenty."

"But that was almost two centuries ago!" Jamie turned to look at Claudio's face in an attempt to understand why he sounded and looked so confused. Claudio's expression was a mix of anger, confusion and pity. "What happened?"

Jamie sighed. "I don't really enjoy dwelling on it . . . the basics of the story are that there was a girl who came to my home, butchered my family, kidnapped me . . . took advantage of me—" Jamie turned to glare at Claudio when he heard him stifle a laugh. "It is *not* funny . . . I'm scarred for life."

Claudio covered his mouth, almost choking on his drink. He shook his head. "Sorry," he breathed through his laughter, coughing to help calm himself down. "My apologies. It's just, you rarely hear a man state that a woman took advantage—"

"Well she *did*." Jamie gave Claudio his most unamused expression. "*Anyway*, while I was wherever the girl took me, a man showed up, cut his wrist, forced me to drink his blood, then forced me to sleep . . . like *that*." Jamie pointed to Claudio's sleeping woman. "Then I woke up like *this*, and I haven't seen either of them since."

Claudio furrowed his brow. "That is unusual," he stated. "I've never met anyone who Turned a person for no apparent reason. We tend to only Turn those with whom we've formed an attachment." He tilted his head, watching him with sceptical eyes. "You hadn't met either of them before that night?"

Jamie shook his head. "No."

Claudio stared straight ahead, as if contemplating what that might mean. "Why look for your Sire now? After all this time?"

"I didn't just start looking now," Jamie stated. "I've been

looking for centuries."

Claudio laughed as if he found that amusing. "And after so long you *finally* decided you might be in need of some assistance?"

"I would have welcomed assistance at any time, but tonight is the first time I've managed to find other Vampires."

Jamie could sense the disbelief rolling off Claudio in waves. "You've never met another Vampire?"

Jamie shook his head.

"Not even one?"

Jamie was about to respond with a no, but stopped himself when he remembered that technically he *had* met another Vampire before. "Just the one I Sired," he stated. "Though, as you can guess, I wasn't much help when it came to teaching her as I was just figuring things out for myself."

Claudio nodded. "And where is she now?" He looked around as if trying to spot someone he didn't recognise.

Jamie sipped his drink. "She died." Claudio gave him a sympathetic look. "I'd rather not go into detail."

"Of course," Claudio said. "I understand."

He let a shaky breath before getting back to the reason why he was here. "So, my Sire . . . do you think you could help me find him?"

"That depends, did he at least introduce himself before he Turned you? Do you know what he looks like?"

Jamie nodded. He would never forget the face of the last man he saw with his human eyes. "His name was Aleczander."

"Aleczander!" Claudio spoke the name as if he were shocked. A few of the people — Vampires — sitting nearby as well as the bartender turned their heads to look at him. Jamie looked at each of them in turn. Wondering why they were staring at him. Claudio moved his stool closer to Jamie's so that there was barely a foot of space between them. "Describe him to me!" he ordered.

Jamie moved his chair back slightly, he didn't like it when people came too close to him. It always made him feel uncomfortable. "He was maybe the same height as me, brown eyes, light red hair, he had it long and I believe he was German."

For some reason what he'd said was extremely amusing, because it made Claudio laugh. Loudly. "And the girl?" he asked. "Was she perhaps five foot tall, long brown hair, big green eyes, about fifteen years old?"

"You know them?"

Claudio laughed harder. Which caused Jamie to not only be confused, but extremely annoyed. This man obviously knew who he was talking about, and was laughing hysterically instead of giving Jamie the help he was seeking.

The other man must have seen the expression on Jamie's face, because he stopped laughing and excused himself. "*Pardonnez-moi.* It's just that I know those two quite well, and I would expect such behaviour from Victoria, but Aleczander has always abhorred what he is, and for so long has enforced the laws against Turning humans with no cause. And then you say *he* Turned *you.* A boy he had just met. And not only that, but he abandoned you."

"And my abandonment is funny?" Jamie couldn't help the aggression in his voice. "Do you not realise how difficult it is to wake up disorientated with *no idea* as to what's happened to you, or where you are, or *what* you are? To not understand yourself anymore, and have no one there to help you through it."

Claudio's expression sobered. "I didn't mean it like that," he said, his tone regretful and apologetic. "It wasn't my intention to offend. Turning is difficult for everyone, it takes at least a year to fully adjust, I can only imagine that it would be twice as hard to have to do it alone."

Jamie let a sigh. "Can you help me or not?"

"Not," Claudio stated. "It would be highly irresponsible of me to allow you access to Aleczander when you clearly hold some resentment over him Turning you. For all I know, the reason you want to see him is because you want to exact revenge. And if he were any other Vampire, I would allow it. But with Aleczander I cannot."

"Because he's your friend."

Claudio's smile was almost bitter, he shook his head. "Aleczander is our king."

Jamie raised an eyebrow. "King? . . . There's a king?"

Claudio laughed. "Yes. He is in charge of keeping us in line. He protects us in exchange for our obedience."

"Great." Jamie stood up. He put a fiver on the countertop and slid it in the bartender's direction. "Keep the change."

Then he turned and walked towards the exit, not bothering to say goodbye to Claudio or thank him for his time. He pushed through the black curtained door to the candlelit reception area. Usually he would have made an effort to be polite to other people, but after that conversation his mood had soured so much that he stormed past Heather, completely ignoring her as she spoke to him.

He pushed through both doors, leaving himself back in the seedy alleyway.

Jamie had spent so long wishing for the day he would find others like him, but at this very moment, he wished that he hadn't even bothered. He'd spent almost two centuries alone, what was the point in trying to change that now?

"I can't tell you where he is." Jamie turned to see Claudio emerge from the hotel's doorway. "But I *can* tell him where you are."

"You can?"

Claudio smiled. "I'm not *completely* unhelpful you know." He handed Jamie a phone. "Put your number in there. I'll pass along a message to Aleczander, the odds are he'll call you eventually, whenever he has the time."

Jamie took the phone out of Claudio's hand and typed his number into the contact directory. "It may not be for a while, so you'll have to be patient."

Jamie nodded. "I'm used to being patient. A while longer won't kill me." He gave the phone back to Claudio, who put it into his pocket.

"Speaking of which, you never answered me . . . what is it that has you so shaken?"

Jamie stared at him. Although he was a Vampire like Jamie, he felt no kinship towards the man like he had always thought he would when he found other Vampires. Instead, he felt distrustful of him.

"We take care of each other," Claudio stated. "It's how we survive. If you have a problem it could quickly become everyone's problem, so tell me. Perhaps I can help."

Jamie sighed and shook his head. "It's nothing really."

Claudio smirked as if he didn't buy it.

Jamie shrugged. "It's just a girl."

"Isn't it always?"

Jamie laughed a little. "There's just something *off* about her."

Claudio furrowed his brow. "Off?"

"She's just . . . at first I thought that she was human, but then I felt her inside my head. She was trying to manipulate my thoughts. And she was strong, but . . . After that I thought that perhaps she was a Vampire, but her heart beats, she breathes, she's out in the daylight and sleeps at night."

"What's her name?"

Jamie paused for a moment, unsure as to whether or not he should give Sam's name to a Vampire. What if he tried to hurt her?

Claudio chuckled as if he could read Jamie's thoughts. "I'm not going to steal her away. I'm asking because perhaps I've heard of her."

Jamie nodded. "Her name is Sam . . . uh, Samantha Jacobs."

Claudio immediately reeled back, his expression filled with fear. "Stay *away* from that girl."

"Why?" Jamie asked, confused as to why Claudio seemed so terrified. Sam's abilities were perplexing, but they were nothing worth fearing.

"She is *cursed*." Claudio stepped towards Jamie and placed a hand on his shoulder, gripping him tightly. "*Sorcière*." He shook his head. "If you want to live, you stay away from her, or you will be cursed too."

"Cursed?" Jamie took a step away from the man, he was obviously insane. "What do you mean cursed?"

"Listen to me." Claudio walked towards Jamie, not allowing him to back away. "Understand what I am telling you. Samantha Jacobs is *poison*. Everything around her dies. *Everyone*. If you value your life, you will stay away. Do you understand?"

Jamie nodded his head, his eyes wide as he stared at the Vampire.

Claudio let a sigh of relief. He backed away from Jamie, nodding, mouthing the word 'good' under his breath. "I'll pass your message along to Aleczander. He'll be in contact."

Jamie watched as Claudio turned from him and walked back inside. He stood alone in the alleyway for countless moments, replaying the words Claudio had spoken again and again. Obviously he was paranoid. People couldn't be cursed.

He remembered what Heather had said about Claudio being one of the oldest Vampires around. So he must have been from a time when people believed in such superstitions.

Jamie shook his head as he started walking home. Sam was unusual. She could do things that she shouldn't be able to do. But to believe she was cursed was insane.

Obviously there was another explanation.

There had to be.

CHAPTER 25

*I*t was the last Saturday before school was due to start, which meant that Sam had to spend most of the day dragging herself around the mall, searching for all of the back-to-school necessities.

Like every year before, Jack was supposed to accompany her, to keep her amused and awake while she wandered through the stores. But before she left the house, he'd claimed that there were 'things' he needed to do. And he hadn't stuck around for long enough to tell her what exactly those *things* were.

As a Ghost, she would have assumed that he didn't have anything better to do than to spend all of his time haunting her. It wasn't as though he had any friends to hang out with and it wasn't like he had any physical needs. So as she wandered lifelessly through the mall Sam found herself unable to do anything but wonder what exactly Jack was doing right now.

With a sigh, she blinked hard and gazed around. In her dazed state she had walked right past the book store. Without pretending she was lost—or pausing to put on an act for the people around who were sure to stare at her as if she were an idiot—she turned around sharply, startling the woman who had been walking near her, and walked back the way she came.

She stepped into the book store, and walked straight towards the stationary section, where she picked up some pens, notebooks, pencils and other school stuff such as highlighter pens and Post-Its.

Once she had picked up pretty much all of the items she needed and placed them in her shopping basket, she wandered over to the fiction isles where she spent countless moments staring at the rainbow of book covers.

It wasn't as though she was looking for anything in particular, and she already had more than enough books to read at home, but it just didn't feel right to be inside a book store and not browse through the actual books.

Sam had spent maybe five minutes staring at the books with barely focused eyes, when her vision became suddenly clear and her senses alert as though someone had just come up behind her and given her an injection of caffeine.

The fine hairs on the back of her neck stood on end as her senses registered the presence of another non-human. Without drawing attention to herself—because she had yet to find out if the other presence was here for her, or was just *here*—she walked at a slow pace beside the shelves. Pretending as though she was scanning the covers with little interest, before she sighed and turned towards the register.

It was when the presence behind her didn't dim as she moved that she knew for a fact whoever—*whatever*—it was, was following her. She took a breath, and held her head high as she joined the line and waited for her turn to pay. Knowing that no matter who, or what it was, they wouldn't risk exposure by attacking her in a place as populated as this.

She paid for her things and made her way out of the store, pausing for a moment by the glass door to check the reflection of the room behind her.

When she noticed *him* she sighed in both relief and annoyance.

Stupid Vampires, she thought irritably as she made her way out the door.

Knowing that the only thing following her was a Vampire who couldn't take a hint calmed her down considerably and she decided to continue shopping as she had planned, trying as best she could to pretend that she couldn't see him following her around, hoping that eventually he'd get bored and go home.

And hopefully he'd leave before she did, because one of the things she wanted to get while she was out was some new underwear, and *no way* was she getting those with some pervy guy watching her like a creep.

Although after what she'd originally thought had been stalking her, his presence didn't irritate her all that much. Earlier she'd felt strange being out alone, it had been a long time since she'd left her house without another person being there with her, and to have someone following her who she knew wasn't a threat, was oddly comforting. As long as he didn't try to talk to her, or get himself into any trouble while he was there, she was content to let him stay.

The weather was supposed to be dreadful all day, so there was no chance of him having to stay in a dark corner for long enough for Sam to lose him and buy everything on her list; so when the clock struck five she decided to head home where she could give her legs a well deserved rest.

So she headed to the parking lot, the whole way there thinking of the many things she could do to freak him out for her own amusement.

Sam didn't generally gain enjoyment from other people's suffering, but it would serve him right for stalking her after she specifically told him to stay away in a fake conversation that she planted in his head.

As Sam reached the parking lot she decided to just let it go. Falling back to her original thought that he'd get bored eventually and go away.

The parking lot was virtually vacant; there were only about five cars on the level she was parked on. Sam walked toward hers, which was near the end of the lot. She pushed her shopping bags up onto her arms, freeing her hands so that she could flick through her keys to press the unlock button. The car beeped just before she reached it. She opened the trunk and put her bags inside, inconspicuously looking over her shoulder to see if Jamie was still there.

From what she could see, he wasn't. Which meant he'd either gotten bored and gone home, or he was hiding somewhere she couldn't see.

There was a moment when she thought about using her psychic senses to see if she could find where he was hiding, but decided not to. Thinking it would just be a useless waste of energy.

Just as Sam closed the trunk she was hit with something.

Something that sent her flying back into the wall and slamming to the ground.

Her head smacked into the ground when she fell, but she didn't feel any pain.

At least not until she stood up.

That was when the part of her brain that kept her vision clear decided to start doing back flips in her head. And that brought on a throbbing headache.

She looked up, squinting at the shadows with blurred vision in an attempt to see who had attacked her.

Her eyes cleared a few seconds later, allowing Sam to see her attacker sauntering toward her as if she were easy prey.

He stepped under one of the lights. It wasn't very bright, but it was enough for Sam to make out the blood coloured marks on all of his visible skin.

A feature which she knew identified him as a Hunter.

He was one of Jack's kin. But unlike Jack, this guy was obviously not here to be her friend. Judging by the malice in his eyes, he wasn't even here to take her in alive. He wanted the bounty that was offered for a dead Sam.

He flashed a grin, which was probably meant to scare her. And if Sam were human, or easily frightened, or hadn't been through this process a thousand times before with other Hunters, it probably would have. Without having to put much effort into it, her Magic began to manifest, she could feel the energy dance around her fingertips, ready to show him that easy prey was the very last thing she was.

He was edging nearer, taking his time. A simple scare tactic meant to prolong anxiety or provoke an escape attempt.

Hunters could be very malicious, and dangerously harmful. Especially when in pursuit of their intended victim. So Sam stood still, her chin raised defiantly as she gave him her best 'bring it on bitch' stare, waiting for him to get close enough for her to make her move.

He was closer now, and just as Sam was about to release the Magic lingering on her fingertips, someone tackled the Hunter.

He was bowled over in a flash, which moved so quickly Sam could only make out a blur. The Hunter had been hit with such force he left a giant dent in the concrete wall where he had been thrown.

The Hunter quickly scrambled to his feet and switched his focus from Sam to whoever had run at him. Sam followed his glare to see, to her surprise, that Jamie had been the one who sent him flying.

Jamie glared back at the Hunter with such rage in his expression that it made Sam feel slightly unsettled. She'd spent so much time away from the Vampires that she'd forgotten how aggressive they could get.

The Hunter straightened his stance, and turned back to Sam. Raising his arm, he called his enchanted weapon to his hand. A crossbow appeared, the wood was adorned with runic symbols, and Sam knew without getting too close that the arrow was most likely laced with poison.

He aimed the weapon at her and fired.

Sam didn't flinch. Instead she took a deep breath and concentrated all of her energy on creating a shield that would cause the arrow to rebound if it hit.

But the arrow didn't hit her shield.

Jamie ran in front of her at a speed that only Vampires and some types of Faeries could manage, catching the arrow before it even came close. He stood with his back to her, his stance protective and territorial.

Sam stood there, watching Jamie with slight confusion. She'd always known that he was a terrible Vampire, he made himself too obvious in front of people . . . or perhaps it was just in front of her that he forgot to play pretend, she couldn't be sure. But even so, exposing himself *this* much to someone who he believed to be human . . . Aleczander would have completely freaked if he'd known.

The Hunter made a guttural noise, that sounded somewhere between a growl and an exasperation. He looked at Sam, his expression making it appear as though he were about to attack her again. But then his eyes went to Jamie, and he slowly backed away, before taking off, running in the opposite direction.

Sam frowned, feeling a little insulted that the Hunter found a run of the mill Vampire more intimidating than her.

Jamie stayed standing in front of her, his arm extended to the side slightly as if blocking her from view. His head turned in either direction, checking to make sure there was no one else around.

Sam sighed internally, knowing that she'd have to play the damsel in distress in order to keep Jamie believing that there was nothing unusual about her. She squeezed her eyes tightly shut to make them water, then opened them widely and let a soft whimper, trying to make it sound, and look, as though she was scared.

" . . . Is he gone?"

Jamie turned to face her, his mouth set in a harsh line. His eyes wandered over her, as if he was trying to assess her.

How much she knew, how much she saw, how much she understood.

Before Sam had a moment to say — or do — anything else, he was standing less than an inch away from her. He placed both of his hands on the wall, either side of her as if trying to hold her in place so she couldn't escape.

Sam took a breath, and stayed where she was. Her mind racing through all the possible reasons for why he would be acting like this. If he was going to try kill her, she couldn't keep playing human. If he was trying to figure out what she was, she'd have to erase his memory again. And if he was trying to do anything else, well . . . she wasn't sure what she'd do. She didn't exactly have protocols for what to do if a Vampire had her pressed against a wall.

Jamie didn't speak. He just continued to stare at her intently as if he were trying so hard to figure her out and couldn't quite understand. She let her bottom lip shake a little, trying to make it appear as though she was terrified and about to break down in tears.

His expression softened a little at that. He slowly, hesitantly, reached his hand up to her face and brushed her hair away from her eyes. He let his hand trail along the side of her face, and held it under her chin.

Sam had the strange thought that he might kiss her. *Talk about taking advantage,* she thought, trying not to let that thought show on her face.

He brought his other hand to her face, stroking the other side. He stood up straighter and looked down at her, not breaking eye contact. Then he leaned in and . . .

And then he froze.

His eyes broke contact with hers, and he stared at her forehead. Sam watched him carefully, balling her hand into a fist, ready to fight him if he even tried.

But then, slowly, he backed away from her, leaving about a foot of space between them. Sam took a step to the side, still with her eyes on him. She wasn't stupid enough to turn her back. He was watching her, holding his breath, his hands clenched into fists. Sam saw streaks of blood run down through the cracks between his fingers.

She backed away from him and hurried to her car. Feeling better now that she knew he was making an effort to control himself.

She got in her car quickly and drove herself out of the parking lot. Knowing that Jamie was still standing there watching her.

CHAPTER 26

*J*amie watched as Sam drove away, not moving until her car was out of sight.

Usually he couldn't bear the sight of blood. The smell was something he was able to force himself to ignore, but the sight of it was a completely different matter.

Sam's blood had scared him.

The sight of it caused his pulse to quicken, his muscles to shake, his teeth to ache with a familiar craving. And in that moment he'd known it was only a matter of time before his predatory nature would overtake his composure.

That realisation had caused him to feel dread, an emotion uncommon to him in this situation.

And once the dread had gotten a hold of his consciousness he'd been able to react. Pushing himself away from her, inflicting physical pain on himself in order to keep his mind distracted, hoping that the stinging in his palms would help deter from what his instincts demanded.

But his efforts only worked for a brief moment. The urge quickly became too much and he felt his defences crumble as his instincts obliterated his inhibition. He breathed in the scent of her blood which still lingered in the air surrounding him, hoping as he did that the urge would dissipate before he managed to catch up to her.

He wouldn't kill her, it wasn't as though he hadn't fed in days, but the idea of using Sam to sate his hunger, to cause her that kind of distress, filled him with concern. He planned to see her again, and didn't want to feel guilty every time he laid eyes upon her.

Jamie felt a brief stab of panic . . . before he finally realised the urge was no longer there.

In fact when he'd breathed in her scent it helped to calm him rather than incite him.

Jamie blinked, totally dumbfounded.

When he breathed in, it wasn't the scent of blood, it was simply the scent of Sam. And Sam's general scent didn't fill him with a bloodlust, it filled him with an entirely different kind of lust.

With a sigh, he walked over to the wall where they'd been standing and slowly he let himself sink down, until he was sitting on the cold concrete ground.

He didn't really know this girl, but he'd seen enough for him to learn that she didn't make sense. She worked a human job. Lived in a human house. She had human friends. And today he was pretty sure she'd been shopping for school supplies.

Everything she did screamed human.

But everything else about her . . .

She was attacked by a man with a crossbow! Jamie couldn't remember the last time he'd seen *anyone* use a crossbow. And not only that but he seemed to conjure the weapon from nothing. One minute his hand was empty, the next he had a crossbow.

He couldn't make sense of it.

Everything was just . . . things just weren't right.

Somewhere in his mind he knew that Claudio wasn't just a paranoid, superstitious fool. He knew that he should back off, he should leave Sam alone.

But he couldn't.

He *had* tried.

For a whole week he'd left her alone, not bothered her at all, he tried to forget about all of the things that didn't make sense.

But he couldn't.

The curiosity was keeping him awake every day. And the longing for her, someone he didn't even know, it filled him with the urge to see her. To be near her. Even if she couldn't see him, he needed to know that she was okay.

He'd started going out more and more during the day. He'd always known that he could, not in direct sunlight as his skin burned too easily and it was painful and took *so outrageously long* to heal, but going out while the sky was overcast had always been fine providing he stuck to the shade as much as possible. Even so, it was a dangerous habit to get into. Even with clouds, the sun was still there, waiting to make an appearance at any moment.

And on days when the clouds weren't out he'd sit at home and stare at the clock, hoping that it would make the sun set faster.

And then when the sun *had* set he'd find her, no matter where she was. He'd keep safely to the shadows and be as unnoticeable as possible. If his parents could see him now they would have been ashamed to find him basically stalking a girl. Doing something people usually got arrested for.

He had never been the type to become obsessed over things,

but with Sam . . . there were too many unanswered questions, too many confusing thoughts and sleepless days for him to simply ignore her.

He thought that it should be pathetic that the day he had met her was possibly the best day of his entire existence. Even though she'd made it painfully obvious that she didn't return his affection.

There was just something about her that he felt drawn to. She was like a memory from a dream he'd had long ago, her presence living somewhere in the back of his mind. She was the most familiar thing in the world to him, despite the fact that he'd only met her recently.

I've lost my mind, he thought with a sigh. *Sam was right . . . Claudio was right . . . I need to stay away from her. I mean, I almost attacked her! I just . . . I need to stay away. I've been coming into this town for years and never run into her, it shouldn't be too difficult to avoid her. Maybe she'll go to college and move away . . . I hope I don't have to move away.*

With a resolute sigh he stood, deciding that all thoughts of Sam would now be forbidden. It was for the best.

He pushed himself away from the wall, about to walk out of the car park, when he heard a small piece of metal fall to the ground. He turned and saw a glimmer in the light. Frowning, he walked back to where he had been sitting and bent down.

There was a necklace.

Jamie picked it up and turned it over in his hands. He remembered seeing it before. Sam had one just like it. But the stone in hers was a different colour. This one was clear, where hers had been purple. He brought the necklace closer to his face and inhaled.

It was definitely Sam's, her scent still lingered on it. He looked at the stone again. He *knew* that Sam's was a different colour. *Perhaps it's mood jewellery*, he thought. *That would explain* why the colour changed.

But how did it get here?

He was sure that he hadn't been sitting on it, if he had he would have felt it beneath him. He tried to think back to whether or not Sam had been wearing it when she left, in his mind he could clearly picture it around her neck as she walked away from him.

Again he frowned. Then how did it get here?

He turned slowly, assessing every inch of the car park he was standing in. Attempting to sense another presence.

There was nothing, at least not as far as he could tell.

Unless there was someone that he couldn't sense.

"Is someone here?" he asked, feeling slightly foolish as he spoke to the empty space.

Silence.

He sighed and peered down at the necklace in his hand thinking it was typical that he would now have to return her necklace, right after he had decided to stay away from her. "Am I not supposed to stay away?" he mumbled, wondering if there was a higher power at work. He had never been one to have faith in such things, but he also wasn't completely closed off to the idea that there was something else out there, watching over the world. "If I'm not, I'm afraid I may need a more obvious sign."

He looked up, his eyes scanning the shadows once more. A shape emerged from behind one of the cars. Jamie stared in confusion as a small white cat strolled out into view.

He was sure that the car park had been empty of any kind of presence, both human and animal. Yet there stood the cat, walking towards the far end of the car park. Jamie watched it as it moved, taking a hesitant step towards it. He reached out his senses and probed at the cat's mind, somewhere in the back of his head thinking that perhaps the cat could shield its presence from him as Sam had. But once he realised that the animal was just a cat, he couldn't help but laugh slightly at his own foolishness.

The cat stopped walking and picked something up off the ground, holding the item sideways between its teeth. He looked at it curiously as it turned and began making its way over to where he stood watching it.

When it was less than three feet away, the cat stopped moving and dropped the item on the ground at his feet. Jamie stared down at it, realising that it was the arrow that had been fired by the crazy man with the crossbow.

The cat sat down and gazed at him with its large red eyes and meowed, before nudging at the arrow with its nose. He put the necklace into his pocket, thinking he would find a way to return it to Sam eventually, knelt down and picked the arrow up off the ground, staring at it as he absently stroked the cat's head.

She's in danger, his body froze as he was stuck with that thought. She *was* in danger. The man who attacked her was still out there. He had escaped and he could come back.

What if he hurt Sam?

What if he killed her?

When Jamie looked up he found that the cat was gone and his hand was stroking the air.

He shook his head, and tried not to think on how strange his life had become over the past few weeks. He couldn't focus on that now, not when he had a job to do.

Jamie walked over to where the man had run out, his scent was still in the air. He wasn't going to let anyone hurt Sam. For as long as he was living he'd make sure that she was safe. Even if it meant hunting down the people who wished her harm.

Jamie breathed in deeply, and followed the scent.

CHAPTER 27

$\mathcal{J}$amie followed the trail for miles, all the way out into the forest beyond the town, where even the furthest reaches of the suburbs disappeared behind a blanket of wood and leaves.

It didn't take him long to find the cabin.

For a moment he studied it, wondering why the trail led here, to such an abandoned area.

The cabin's similarities to his own home did not escape him, but he didn't have any time to dwell on it now; his senses picked up movement, and he realised the property wasn't as desolate as it had originally appeared.

There were three of them, sheltering inside the house, all of them male.

"I failed," a voice spoke up. Jamie crept closer, listening intently.

Another replied, "Join the club . . . everyone fails." He spoke with the tone of someone trying to be reassuring, but unable to hide their anger.

"I'll inform Kraven," the third sighed, the sound of his voice followed by the slam of a closing door.

"She had help," the first man said, and Jamie realised it was the one who had carried out the attack. "A Vampire."

With that, Jamie froze, stunned.

The man spoke those words as if Vampires were commonplace. With the air of someone talking about the weather. Why would he speak as though it was nothing unusual?

How could he possibly know?

Who were these men?

"A Vampire?"

"He protected her."

"Aleczander?" the second man asked, the beginnings of fear creeping into his voice.

For a moment there was no reply, but Jamie could hear the rustle of movement from inside the house. After a while, Sam's attacker responded, "No . . . it was probably one of his though. I didn't wanna hurt him in case it started anything with the rest."

The other man sighed. "If they're actively helping the girl then they're already starting something."

There was more sounds of movement from inside. Footsteps, then doors opening. "There was a Vampire," the second man said, his voice quieter as he was now in a room nearer to the back of the house. "We need to know who he is, and who he's aligned with."

Jamie just listed, barely taking in the words that the men were speaking. Deeply shocked and incredibly confused, Jamie clenched his fists tightly. How could they know what he was?

Not to mention, Aleczander?

Was this the same Aleczander Jamie was looking for?

Why would they assume *he'd* be with Sam?

From the way these men were speaking, it was obvious that their attack on Sam was not just a random act. It was a part of some greater conspiracy.

There was a jumble of movement sounding from inside; sensing that his time was running short, Jamie didn't waste another moment asking himself questions with no possible answers.

He darted towards the back door, where he sensed just one man, speaking into a telephone.

Moving swiftly, using his increased speed he barged inside the house and before the man even knew that Jamie was there, his neck was snapped and he was lying dead on the kitchen floor, the phone still in his hand.

After taking the biggest knife he could from the drawers, he silently made his way through the hallway to the door leading to the room where the other two men were talking in hurried tones.

Jamie paid no attention to whatever they were saying, he only listened to their voices to determine where in the room they were. Instinctually he knew their positions within seconds, he could see them clearly in his mind.

Gripping the knife tighter, he kicked at the door to force it open, splintering the wood and knocking what remained off its hinges, charging into the room. Both of the men yelled at each other in a sudden panic. The same man who had attacked Sam made a dive for the crossbow sitting on the floor.

He was the first to die.

Jamie jammed the knife through the man's throat. He fell to his knees, choking on his own blood as red sputtered from the wound.

Before Jamie could do anything else, the other man tackled him to the ground. He quickly pulled a dagger from his belt.

Jamie pushed the man off with ease and sent him flying across the room and through the wall before he had a chance to use the blade.

The man tried to get to his feet, but he was too disorientated from being thrown through four inches of plasterboard.

Jamie reached down and pulled the knife from the throat of the dead man. He threw it through the hole in the wall just as the other one managed to stumble numbly to his feet. The knife sliced through the air and struck the man directly in the heart, sending him falling back to the floor in an instant.

Jamie stood in the middle of the room, breathing heavily as he looked around, barely aware of what he'd just done. He put his hand to his head and tried to calm himself as the scent of blood assailed his nostrils. *Something's not right about that smell,* he thought as he fell to his knees. The scent, instead of making him hungry was making him feel sick.

Jamie brought his red stained hand up to his mouth and licked blood from his knuckles. His stomach churned with the taste of it. He spat onto the floor, trying to rid his mouth of the foul taste.

He took another look at the men he'd just killed. All of them looked normal, but their blood smelled and tasted wrong. *They're not human?* he thought in confusion, wondering how they could look like something they weren't.

He turned and walked out of the house, trying to figure out what was going on.

Out in the fresh air his head cleared, and he looked back at the open door, remembering that the first man he had slain had been on the phone to someone.

A person he was reporting to.

His eyes shifted along the tree line, half expecting to see more people . . . *things,* creeping out of there.

He shook his paranoia away . . . *Sam was safe,* Jamie thought as he ran from the house.

She was safe . . . for now at least.

CHAPTER 28

The voice on the other end of the line went suddenly silent, while the warlock was halfway through giving his report on the latest incident with Sam. Kraven pulled the phone away from his ear and looked at the screen for a moment, checking if the issue was with the device or with the person on the other end of the line.

The little screen was still bright and clearly displayed that the call was still active. With a frown, Kraven placed the phone back to his ear and listened carefully. There were very minimal noises from the other end, just white noise really.

Then a very loud crash.

At the sound of the crash, Kraven hung up the phone, ending the call.

With a sigh he threw the phone to the table. Beside him, Malachi looked to the discarded phone, the turned his curious eyes in his direction. He didn't ask what had happened, he didn't need to as the question was obvious on his face.

Kraven pushed himself to his feet. "We've been attacked," he stated, moving towards the exit.

Malachi stood quickly and followed. "Attacked? By who? Where?"

"The surveillance base, just outside of that town where the Witch girl lives."

Malachi let a heavy sigh. "Was it her?" he asked, though the tone of his voice suggested that even if Kraven had claimed that it had been the girl, Malachi wouldn't have believed him.

Kraven just shrugged, walking through the tunnels to where there were portals that they could use to travel to the surface. "It could have been, we'll have to check the tapes when we get there."

When they came to the portals Kraven placed his hand on the runes that were etched into the stone walls, activating one of them. In his mind he envisioned the location that he wished to travel to. Once the image was clear, he nodded his head towards it, indicating to Malachi that it was now safe to step through.

He did with no hesitation.

Once Malachi had disappeared through the portal, Kraven followed. The opening closing behind him once his feet touched off the wooden floors of their surveillance cabin.

The place was a mess, everything covered in blood. Spatters of it on the walls and ceiling and pools of it on the floor around the dead men.

Kraven stepped over one of the bodies and looked towards the window. Outside he saw a man—well, he was boy really, too young in appearance to be considered anything but.

Though it wasn't the boy's youth that caused his heart to hammer rapidly against his ribs.

No, it was the face.

That face.

The boy ran away swiftly, making his way into the woods and completely disappeared within the trees.

Kraven turned sharply to see if Malachi had seen him, and was deeply grateful to find that Malachi was not even in the room.

He had stepped through the giant gaping hole in the wall and into the kitchen. His back to the window, so surely he hadn't seen.

Trying as hard as possible to hide his panic and fear, he rushed from the room to where Malachi stood. "You need to leave," Kraven stated sharply.

Malachi looked up at him from his place on the floor by the third body, his expression confused. "What . . . why?"

Kraven huffed in annoyance. Malachi was the only member of their society who ever dared to question him, who never just did as he was told. So, knowing an outrageous comment would be the only way to get him out of here, he said, "I'm moving you back to recruitment."

Malachi's expression turned to one of indignation, and he stood gazing at Kraven in disbelief, his lips parted as though he would speak but couldn't think of the words.

"This girl just became too dangerous, so for now, I'm moving you back to recruitment. Get out of here, *now*."

"But you can't do that! This . . . this is *my* job. You promised I could be in charge of this one!"

"Malachi!" Kraven shouted. The other man just stared at him. "What I've said is an order. Now go home."

With a glare, Malachi turned and stormed off, taking the portal home without speaking a word. Only taking time to look in Kraven's direction with the expression of someone who had been betrayed.

Kraven let a sigh of relief when he was gone. Malachi was angry now, but anger over this little disagreement was something that he would get over quite quickly. Within a week they would once again be on speaking terms.

However, if Malachi found out about *him*.

That he was alive, that he was here, and most importantly what Kraven had done to him all those years ago . . . that was one thing he would not be forgiven for.

So he searched the base for the security tapes, and kept hold of them. Knowing that the only other piece of evidence he had left to get rid of was the boy who should have been dead.

*J*ack appeared out of nowhere just as Sam had gotten herself comfortable in bed. "I have news from the Hunters that you may be interested in."

Sam was all ready for school tomorrow, so she really hoped that this news wouldn't affect her ability to play normal for the next few months.

"Have they all decided to leave me alone from now on?" she asked, while knowing that what Jack had to say would be nothing close to that.

But she couldn't help hoping.

"No," Jack said simply. "But someone has put a bounty on your Vampire boyfriend stalker."

Sam didn't smile or laugh. That would only encourage Jack to say more stupid things like that. Which he was doing a lot lately, and he seemed to find it amusing. *Being a Ghost must be super boring.* Sam shook her head, sighing. It had only been a matter of time before they tried to get to Jamie. Especially if he'd been following her around more than just the times she knew of.

"You're not going to ask me why?" Jack sighed dramatically and let himself fall to the floor, sitting cross-legged beside her bed.

"I wasn't going to ask," Sam stated. She didn't care why someone wanted Jamie dead.

She didn't know him.

It didn't concern her.

She didn't want to get involved.

She had her own problems to deal with.

Jack sighed. "Ask me why."

"Uh, okay . . . Why?" Sam asked reluctantly.

"He killed the Hunter who attacked you, along with two higher level Warlocks who were running a secret base just outside of town." Jack did an overly dramatic air grab. "To protect thine honour!"

Sam rolled her eyes. "You're *way* too easily amused." Jack laughed. "If he killed two higher levels and a Hunter, what makes them think that a team of Hunters will be able to kill him?"

"They haven't hired Hunters to kill him."

"But I thought you said —"

"No," Jack interrupted. "They hired a team of *Vampire* Hunters to kill him, don't ever mix up Hunters and *Vampire Hunters* . . . It's insulting. And just in case the Vampire Hunters don't do the job — which less face it, they probably won't because they're shit at everything except being stupid — they also put a message out across the whole magical community offering a reward for whoever kills him."

Shit, Sam thought, *that's bad*.

A community wide bounty was what was put on Sam too. So she knew better than most that it wasn't an easy thing to have to deal with. Especially when a lot of the people who go after those bounties are the type who want to take you back dead rather than alive.

The whole magical community.

And poor stupid Jamie didn't even have much knowledge of Vampires. With knowledge as limited as that, she seriously doubted he knew that other supernatural beings even existed.

Sam couldn't help but feel partly responsible for Jamie's situation. If he had just stayed away from her he never would have felt the need to kill those Demons or that Hunter and he wouldn't be in this mess right now.

Sam sighed, and closed her eyes. She had been starting to believe that she could make it through the year without someone getting killed because of her.

Guess that's another hope gone.

CHAPTER 30

*I*t was another dull and cloudy day, which Jamie thought was perfect. Because it meant he could go outside without the fear of ending up bedridden for two weeks.

He walked towards the old redbrick building that was the high school, thinking as he jumped up the steps about what to say when he found her. Ideally, he'd simply give Sam her necklace and she'd be so happy she'd swoon and fall in love with him and want to be with him forever.

Except that wouldn't happen because Jamie had forgotten to bring Sam's necklace with him.

Alright . . . that was a lie.

He had purposely left her necklace at home. Just in case she wouldn't speak to him today. After all, she *had* told him to stay away from her. Well, technically she had. It still confused him to think about what really happened.

Either way, if she wouldn't speak to him today, he had an excuse to come back and see her tomorrow.

He had chosen to wake up early and go to the school to speak with her. Thinking she would be more comfortable around him if they were both in a public place. And if he went to her house she'd wonder how he knew where she lived, which would most likely lead to an awkward conversation that he didn't want to have and maybe end up with her calling the police on him.

Jamie walked through the doors into the school which was filled with students, all talking and laughing and walking about. There had to have been at least four-hundred people in the building, which made finding Sam very difficult.

A group of students walked through the doors behind Jamie. He only looked at them for a second, before he moved forward and stopped one of them. "Excuse me," he said to a boy with brown hair.

The boy looked at him curiously, and Jamie knew by the expression he wore that he was trying to figure out who he was and what he was doing here. "Hello," the boy said politely. "I'm Scott, are you new?"

Jamie shook his head. "No, actually, I'm just looking for someone. I was wondering if you could help."

Scott gave him a friendly smile, which made Jamie feel that he had picked a good person to ask. "Sure," he said. "Who are you looking for?"

"It's a girl named Samantha Jacobs."

The smile disappeared from the boy's face almost immediately, he eyed Jamie suspiciously. "Why are you looking for *her*?"

The air surrounding Scott suddenly became very heavy and stale; Jamie could sense some very unpleasant emotions emanating from him. He was upset and angry because Jamie was looking for Sam. Which made Jamie think that either Scott hated Sam, or hated the idea that someone was looking for her.

Maybe he hadn't picked the right person after all.

"Uh," Jamie thought quickly. *The necklace.* " . . . I found something of hers and I need to return it."

"You can give it to me," Scott said, holding his hand out, his body language giving the impression that he didn't want Jamie anywhere near Sam. "I'll make sure she gets it."

"That's okay," Jamie said, eyeing him with suspicion. "I'd rather give it to her myself."

Scott gave him a glare, making it obvious that he didn't feel like being friendly anymore. Despite the fact that he was watching Jamie in an unpleasant way he pointed to the end of the hallway. "Go right, her locker's at the end." Then he stormed away before Jamie had a chance to say thank you.

Jamie walked to the end of the hall, then turned right. The hallway was crowded with students, all walking or rummaging through their lockers. He spent a few moments scanning the crowd, standing on his toes so he could see over everyone. He spotted Sam's white-blonde head at a locker near the end of the hall. He moved towards her, pushing his way through the throng of humans. "Sam," he said as he approached her.

She turned to look at him. He could tell by her expression that she wasn't pleased to see him.

"What do *you* want?" she asked, as she closed her locker door.

"I want to talk to you," Jamie said.

"About?" she asked, seeming as though she was making an attempt to keep the conversation to a bare minimum.

Jamie hesitated for a moment. There were so many things he wanted to say to her and so many questions he needed to ask, and yet right there and then, he couldn't think of a single word. Sam looked at him impatiently, her hand on her hip. He just shrugged and said, "Want to go out some time?"

Sam rolled her eyes and turned away from him, hurrying down the hall. Jamie stood there for a moment feeling frustrated by the fact that she was ignoring him, especially since he had saved her life only two days ago. *How could she be so ungrateful?* She could just say no. She didn't have to ignore him.

Sam disappeared into a classroom. Jamie followed her. The teacher looked up at him in confusion, as did all of the students in that class.

"Are you Elliot?" the teacher asked as she looked at him.

Jamie gazed at the woman, then at the twenty seven students in the room. Realising that he should have better shielded himself before walking into a school he had no reason to be inside of.

He hadn't thought this through.

With one last glance at all of the faces in the room, he sent out a wave of Power. *<I am not here>* he said. *<Pay no attention to me>* One by one all of the students, as well as the teacher, looked away. All except for Sam, who kept a steady gaze on him every moment he stood in the doorway.

Jamie sent a current of energy directly into Sam's mind. *<You don't see me>* he said. *<Look away>*

She didn't.

Her gaze didn't falter in the slightest.

Jamie saw a trace of a smile at the corners of her lips. He tried again, this time saying something different. *<At four o'clock call this number>* He put his phone number into her head. *<You want to talk to me>*

Sam looked down at her notebook and started writing. *She must be writing the number down so she won't forget,* Jamie thought triumphantly and turned to leave the room, when Sam held her notebook up for him to see what she had written.

In big black letters across the page, were the words;

Jamie stared open-mouthed at Sam as she placed her notebook back on the desk.

Quickly, he backed out of the classroom and frantically looked around the hallway at the students that were wandering into classrooms. *Had she told people? Did they all know?* Surely if she found out there was a Vampire in town she would have told *someone*. Jamie left the school in a hurry, convinced that there had to be at least one other person in the town who knew his secret.

And wondered if they believed her, knowing that if one person believed it, it was only a matter of time before rumours began to spread, especially in a town so small.

Someone would come for him. It was only a matter of time.

He had to find out who she'd told, and the only way to do that was to confront her. His influencing Power didn't work on her, so what else could he do? Scare the information out of her?

She hadn't seemed very fearful of him as she'd held her accusation for him to see. If anything, she'd seemed amused.

Jamie wandered out of the school in a daze, thinking that he would have to leave town. It was the only way to keep his secret.

CHAPTER 31

There was a knock on the door just a few minutes after Jamie ran out of the school. Sam looked up as it opened and in walked a boy with short, dark hair.

"Elliot?" Ms Mason asked, looking up from her desk. The boy nodded. Ms Mason smiled at him, then she turned to face the class. "Everyone, this is Elliot, he's new so be kind." She turned back to Elliot. "You can take one of the empty seats."

The boy didn't even look around the room at the empty seats. He didn't spend even second assessing the people at the desks around the empty ones to find one that would be most suitable.

Instead he walked forward confidently as if he knew exactly where he wanted to be.

He walked past Sam, smiling at her as he did, then dropped his bag to the floor and took the seat directly behind her. "Hi," he said.

Sam didn't turn around to look at him even though she knew

he was speaking to her. She heard him move and a shadow was cast over her desk. Sam leaned back in her chair, her arms hovering inches from the desk, not wanting the shadow to touch her.

It was too dark. Pure black actually, which it shouldn't have been.

She turned her head to find Elliot leaning forward in his chair, his arms resting on the table. She noticed he had a tattoo on his left wrist, a black star and crescent moon. She looked at it for a moment, the image filling her mind with a vague sense of recollection. Elliot grinned at her in a predatory way, showing all of his teeth. Sam narrowed her eyes at him, and pushed out with her senses. This guy was obviously *something*. She could see it in the way he was watching her.

Elliot's mind was surprisingly easy to get inside of. Which only caused Sam to feel confused. Anything non-human would have mazes and walls and barriers that would make reading their thoughts extremely difficult.

But she was inside Elliot's head with no effort whatsoever, and he didn't even seem to notice she was in there. Because if he knew she was in there she was sure he would have cleaned up his thoughts a little. Because most of them consisted of the various ways in which he believed he would be able to get Sam naked. And then various images of what he thought would happen after.

Sam rolled her eyes and groaned internally. Retracting her psychic net, no longer wanting to see all of the disgustingness inside his mind. The memory of what she'd seen left her feeling like she needed to go home and scrub her brain with bleach.

He wasn't a non-human. He was just a creep. He nodded towards her notebook, and chewing on the lid of his pen said, "You're impervious to Vampires?"

"Yes," Sam replied, her tone serious and unamused. She had

no time for humans or boys who thought of her like *that*. "I'm impervious to Vampires."

Without wasting any more of her time or energy speaking to him, she turned around to face the front of the class where Ms Mason was going on about Shakespeare or something. Sam wasn't really paying attention, because all she could see was that the shadow on her desk had vanished.

And all she could do was wonder what it was and where it had gone.

CHAPTER 32

 t was lashing rain and the sky was a dark shade of grey.

Jamie stood outside the school building, the rain wetting his hair and dripping into his eyes, making them blur as he stared at the doors, too scared to go inside in case Sam had told people his secret. As he thought back to yesterday, again he wondered how she knew. *Am I really that obvious?*

The school bell rang, indicating the end of whatever class had been in session. Students from the outside buildings ran towards the main one, holding either umbrellas or coats above their heads. Jamie stepped aside to let them pass.

Sam was with the crowd.

She scrutinised Jamie passively as she walked through the doors. He held her gaze as she watched over her shoulder, and followed her into the building. Once inside she looked away and continued through the halls.

She knew he was following.

She didn't care.

Jamie walked through the halls with a crowd of students. A red-haired girl bumped into him, her books fell to the floor.

"Sorry," she mumbled, as she went to pick them up. Jamie bent down and helped her.

"It's okay," he said reassuringly as he stacked the books into a small pile and handed them to her.

She looked at him curiously. "Are you new?"

Jamie thought for a moment. "Sort of," he said and relaxed a little. This girl didn't know him at all. In fact, as he looked around he noticed that not only was there not a single person who looked at him as if they knew him, but none of them were looking at him at all.

Which they surely would be doing if Sam had told everyone about him.

The girl stood, as did Jamie. She smiled at him. "I'm Madison," she said, clutching her books to her chest with one arm as she extended the other.

Jamie took her hand and shook it momentarily. "Jamie," he replied.

"Is it your lunch period now?" she asked. "Because it's mine, so I'm going to the cafeteria if you need to get there."

"I'm actually just waiting to talk to someone," he said. "Thanks anyway."

"Oh." She looked disappointed. "Is it the principal? Because she usually doesn't see people during lunch."

"No, actually, it's a girl." Jamie assessed Madison, allowing his psychic senses to seep into her mind, not to read her thoughts exactly, but to get a grasp on what type of personality she had. He smiled to himself when he found confirmation of what he'd been thinking. "You seem like the sort of person who knows everything about everyone," he stated.

She smiled proudly, taking his observation as a compliment. "If you're looking for gossip, you came to the right girl."

"Her name is Samantha Jacobs," he said. Jamie saw a look of recognition sweep across Madison's face. "What's her deal?"

Madison smiled. "That's a story that could take a while." She directed him down the hall. "Walk with me." Madison started walking towards the lockers. Jamie moved alongside her. She stopped at one of the lockers, opened it, put her damp books inside, then closed it and started walking again.

"She moved here when she was thirteen," Madison began, linking her arm through Jamie's. "She didn't start in school until she was fourteen, though. She was homeschooled until then, so she didn't really have any people skills, I guess. She and her brother moved in with their grandparents after their parents were murdered."

"Murdered?"

Madison nodded. Then paused for a moment as if to think. "I suppose it was twice as bad for Sam, because her birth parents were murdered when she was a baby, then her adoptive parents were murdered when she was thirteen."

"Damn," Jamie mumbled to himself. "No wonder she seems so closed off."

Madison nodded. "She wasn't always like that," she said. "She was fine until her grandmother was killed. A week after that happened, she came into school, broke up with her boyfriend, told all of her friends, me included, that she never wanted to see them again. She just stopped talking to *everyone*. I mean, not like, *totally* stopped talking. Like, she'll talk to you for a few minutes about whatever it is you want to say to her. And after that she'll just walk away. She never hangs out with anyone."

Jamie sighed. He couldn't imagine what Sam's life must be like, to lose that many people in such a short amount of time . . . it was tragic.

"Things got worse three years ago," Madison continued.

"When her brother left for the army, then a year after that her grandfather died." They walked through the cafeteria doors. "You wanna sit with me and my friends?" Madison asked, and pointed to a crowded table which Scott was sitting at. Jamie remembered how he'd behaved yesterday at the mention of Sam's name. *Her ex perhaps?*

Jamie tilted his head, turning his attention to the other side of the cafeteria where he could see Sam sitting by herself, eating lunch and doing homework.

"No," he replied. "But thank you for the offer, and for the information."

Madison smiled. "Remember who to call when you need dirt on your neighbours."

Jamie smiled as Madison walked away, before he began making his way towards Sam.

Feeling slightly morose now that he knew her story.

Losing people was something he could relate to, they were feelings he could share. Not that they were good feelings to have.

A long, *long* time ago Jamie had lost his brother. No one ever found out what happened to him. He was just gone one day, vanished into thin air. Then a couple of years later both of his parents were killed. When Jamie had been Turned he had to leave behind everything that was familiar to him. Which wasn't an easy thing to do, but he'd had a lot longer to adjust to his situation than Sam had to hers.

And then there was Bethany, who had been taken from him.

He knew what it felt like to be alone.

Not to have a single person left in the world.

Jamie sat down on a seat across the table from her. Sam looked at him and sighed. "What do you want *now*?"

"We need to talk," Jamie stated.

Sam chewed her lower lip as she stared at the notebook in front of her. Almost as if she was thinking about speaking to him. She closed her eyes for a moment. "No, we don't." She stood and gathered her things.

"You can't run from me Sam," Jamie said.

"I'm not running," she stated. "I'm calmly collecting my things so I can casually walk away."

Jamie reached into his pocket and took her necklace out. He held it up for her to see, holding it by the chain, the gem swinging back and forth. Sam looked at it for a moment, then she reached out to snatch it from his hand, but Jamie moved it out of her reach. "If you want it back you have to talk to me."

Sam glared at him. "Give it back right now, or I'll scream Vampire as loud as I can. I swear to the Gods, I will out you right here." She threatened him despite the fact that she kept her voice low and was looking around as if to make sure that no one was listening. It gave Jamie the impression that 'outing' him was something that she didn't want or plan to do.

Jamie put the necklace back into his pocket and stood. He blanketed every mind in the cafeteria with his Powers, influencing them to forget that he or Sam were ever there. Then he persuaded them not to see what happened next.

Jamie moved across the table, using his heightened speed to his advantage he seized Sam around the waist, slung her over his shoulder, and grabbed her bag before running out of the school with her struggling to get free.

They were through the woods and inside his house in less than two minutes.

He slammed the door behind him and set Sam down on her feet, dropping her bag by the door.

She shoved him away from her, then took a step back and looked around. "Where am I?" she asked, striking him on his left side with her hand. "Where did you take me?"

"My house," Jamie replied simply, keeping his back pressed against the door so she couldn't leave.

Sam tried to push past him but he kept himself planted firmly in front of the door, not allowing himself to be swayed. She wasn't leaving until he got the answers that he wanted.

"Move!" she demanded.

"Not until you talk to me," Jamie said, staying calm.

"Fine," Sam exasperated. "What do you want to talk about?"

"How did you know?"

"Know what?" she asked. Giving him a look of pure innocence, one which she had shown him more than once during their last few encounters. It made him wonder how long she had been playing him for.

"How did you know that I'm not human?"

She laughed humourlessly. "You're stupider than you look if you haven't figured out the answer to that one by now," she snapped. "The answer is simple. Three guesses."

Jamie took a step towards her. "I'm not playing games Sam. Now tell me, how did you know that I'm not human?"

"Easy!" she yelled. "Because I'm not human either!"

Jamie took a step back in shock. He could feel his eyes grow wide. Even after all he had witnessed, and after everything that Claudio had said, hearing Sam say it out loud shocked him. "What?"

She wiped stray strands of blonde hair away from her eyes. "I'm not human," she repeated quieter and calmer than she had the first time, fidgeting nervously with her hands as she spoke, almost as though speaking those words aloud made her feel extremely uncomfortable.

"But you're not . . . I mean, are you . . . " Jamie took a breath. "Vampire?"

Sam laughed a little and shook her head. "No."

"Then what?" Jamie demanded. "What are you?"

Sam looked away. She sighed, then shrugged. "I don't know."

She's lying.

"How could you not be human, and *not* know what you are?" he asked rhetorically. "You're *lying*, now tell me how you really knew."

"I just did!" she yelled. "I knew you were a Vampire the first time we spoke. I could see it in your soul."

She's crazy. Jamie gave her a look that reflected his thoughts. "I don't believe you," he said.

"Fine," Sam snarled. "You believe whatever the fuck you want to believe. I don't care. Just give me back my amulet."

"Not until you answer me!" he replied, speaking to her in the same manner and volume she had used when she spoke to him.

Her mouth formed a tight line, the corners of her lips twitching in anger as her expression filled with fury.

"Give me back my amulet," she repeated through gritted teeth. Jamie's mouth opened, as he attempted to say no, but the word stuck in his throat as he saw what appeared to be fire . . .

A ball of purple fire, which had begun to form in the palm of Sam's hand.

"Now!" she screamed as she released the fire-ball.

Jamie flinched instinctively, his arms coming up to shield his face from the impending impact. Only realising once he heard the smashing of wood that she had aimed it at the bookshelf, destroying it and all of its contents, rather than throwing it in his direction and causing what could have been potentially fatal injuries.

When he turned his head away from the wall where the paint was now scorched and looked in Sam's direction, he could see her fingers twitching as if preparing for another fiery release. He got the feeling that if he didn't give her what she wanted, he would end up like the bookshelf and be in pieces all over the floor.

But no matter how his brain attempted to coax him into movement, he couldn't bring himself to reach into his pocket to pull out the necklace. His body frozen by the overwhelming shock of what he'd just seen. "You're really not human," he whispered. Sam shook her head in reply. "What are you?" Jamie asked in astonishment.

Sam sighed. "I already told you. I don't know."

"But how can—"

"*Because!*" she yelled, she took a breath to calm herself before she continued to speak. "I'm not a Vampire, I'm not a Ghost, I'm not a Lycanthrope, I'm not a Witch, I'm not a Demon, I'm not a Faerie . . . I wasn't human and Turned into something else. I was just born with all of this Power, and . . . " She closed her eyes and put her hand to her head as if talking about this was giving her a headache. "I just don't know. I don't know where I came from. I don't know who I am. So how could I possibly know *what* I am?"

"Sam, I'm—"

"Save the sympathy," she said and held out her hand. "I don't want it. Just give me back my amulet."

Jamie reached into his pocket and took the necklace out. He held it out to Sam, she took it from him and put it around her neck. The clear crystal stone turned purple at the touch of her skin. Jamie watched at it curiously. "How does it do that?" he asked.

Sam looked down at the stone. "Magic," she mumbled.

"Magic?" Jamie asked. "Like . . . *real* Magic?"

"Yeah." Sam waved her hand in the direction of the wall where the bookshelf had been. The pieces of wood and paper that were strewn around the floor picked themselves up and reassembled into a bookshelf and the books that had been inhabiting it.

Jamie leaned his back against the door for support. *How can this possibly be real?* He was feeling conflicted, his emotions a mix of a child who was filled with excitement at the prospect of Magic, and an adult who was filled with an immense fear of the unknown. *Magic is real.*

Jamie looked at Sam's expression. She didn't look happy, or excited. She just looked sad. Jamie stood up straight and walked over to her. "What's wrong?" he asked.

Sam looked at him with cheerless eyes. "You should have stayed away from me," she said.

At those words Jamie got the same nauseating feeling he'd gotten when Claudio told him it would be best for him to stay away from Sam. In the back of his head he knew he should listen. But in his heart and soul he felt like he couldn't.

"Why?" Jamie asked.

She closed her eyes and turned her head away. "Because now you're going to die."

Jamie looked at her, his eyes widened as a thought struck him. *Is that why she stays away from people? Because she thinks that if she doesn't they'll die.* Jamie smiled and put a hand on her face. "I'm fine," he said reassuringly. "I won't die."

Sam placed her hand on his and moved it away from her. "You will," she muttered. "I know for a fact that you will. It's just a matter of how. And wh—"

The rest of Sam's sentence was cut off by the sound of the window next to Jamie smashing. Before he could turn around to see what had happened an arrow pierced through his chest, paralysing him instantly. His body fell to the floor with a hard thud. His eyes started to blur.

Sam was kneeling beside him, shaking him, telling him to stay awake.

But he couldn't stay awake for her.

Her voice was drifting further and further away.

Until he couldn't hear her at all.

And then Jamie lost his hold on reality and everything went dark.

CHAPTER 33

"Jack!" Sam yelled out to the empty room, keeping her hands firmly pressed over Jamie's chest where the arrow protruded in an attempt to stop the bleeding.

Barely a second later Jack was by her side, looking around in complete confusion.

"What—"

Sam cut him off by speaking over him, there was no time for questions. "Corporealise!" she ordered. "You have to hold down on the wound." Jack did as he was told and knelt beside Jamie. Taking her place beside him, keeping his hands around the arrow that was sticking out of Jamie's chest, and putting pressure on the bleeding.

Placing his hands over hers, as she moved away. Her hands now covered in warm blood, so much that it dripped from her fingers, leaving a trail along the floor as she stood and walked to the door.

Throwing it open and looking out, glaring at the Vampire

Hunters that she knew were hiding among the trees. She concentrated her energy and sent it out in a blast at the three Vampire Hunters that were currently running forward, making their way towards Jamie's house. The blast of energy threw all three of them backwards. One of them hit into one of the trees, and was skewered on a low-hanging branch, which fortunately for him meant instant death.

The other two scurried to their feet and pointed their weapons in Sam's direction. Without hesitation, she sent out another wave of Power, this time ensuring it was lethal. The Vampire Hunters shrieked in agony as they were consumed by flames that burned so hot their bodies were reduced to nothing more than piles of ash within seconds.

Sam used her Magic to clear the scene of any evidence of a fight. The body and the ash and the destruction vanished in an instant, leaving nothing behind so that it was as though nothing had ever happened.

Sam closed the door, and put a temporary barrier spell around the house. Moving as quickly as was possible as she was fully conscious of the Vampire currently dying on the floor; his body still as it was probably wondering if it should heal the open wound and seal within itself the poison it had been injected with, or continue to excise the poison and instead die from blood loss.

With the blood that still stained her hands, Sam drew some runes on the wall of Jamie's home, drawing the outline of a portal on the living room wall while simultaneously reciting the incantation to activate the runes. Sam bent down and picked up a piece of broken glass from the floor, stabbing the sharp edge into the palm of her hand, she winced at the pain as she dug the glass in deep enough to draw a sufficient amount of her own blood to give it a kick of Magic that was necessary to open the portal.

She then slapped her bleeding hand against the wall, the runes she had drawn began to glow as the Magic was pulled from her blood and absorbed into the wall. Into the runes she projected a thought of her home, opening a doorway between here and there.

"Can you carry him through?" Sam asked, as she pulled her palm away from the wall, cradling the hand against her chest as she allowed the wound to heal.

"Is he even still alive?" Jack asked unsurely, as he looked from Sam to the deathly still Vampire on the floor.

"He should be okay for a few more minutes . . . maybe," Sam said. "After that he'll be dead from blood loss."

Jack picked Jamie up, carrying him over his shoulder as if he weighed nothing at all. Sam ran to the door, picked up her backpack and followed Jack through the portal, making sure to close it behind her so nothing could follow them through.

Sam ran to the kitchen and found her magical first-aid kit.

When she ran back in she saw that Jack had taken Jamie's jacket off and was about to lie him down on the couch. "Keep him sitting up," she said to Jack, who did as he was told and held Jamie in an upright position.

Sam snapped the head off the arrow, then pulled the remnants of it out of Jamie's chest. She used the scissors to cut his torn and blood stained shirt off, pealing the fabric away from the blood that kept it plastered to his skin. She took out one of the creams she had made up for whenever she got hit with Hunter weapons. The bottle contained enough herbal ingredients and enough Magic that it could pull any foreign toxins out of his body and heal up the wounds.

At least that was what the cream did when she was injured. She could only hope that it would work the same for Jamie.

She didn't know much about Vampire biology, but she could only assume that a cream made to extract poison for a non-human creature like Sam could fulfil the same purpose on another type of non-human.

Sam applied a large amount of the cream onto the wound on Jamie's chest and the corresponding tear on his back. Afterwards she put a bandage on either side.

Jack lay Jamie down on the couch, and they both left him there to rest.

Hopefully he would heal . . . because if not, he would die.

CHAPTER 34

$\mathcal{B}$efore Jamie had even opened his eyes he knew he wasn't at home.

Sam, was his first thought; and as he opened his eyes he knew immediately that he was in her house, even though he had never before seen the inside of it. Her scent was everywhere, so he knew it was hers.

Jamie sat up and looked around slowly, pushing back the navy blanket that had been draped over his body. He tried to clear his thoughts and remember what had happened.

He'd awoken on the sofa in Sam's living room, which was strange because he didn't recall coming to Sam's house, let alone being invited inside. Jamie looked down at himself and noticed that his shirt was missing and that there was a bandage on his chest.

Slowly he peeled the bandage away, and as he moved he could feel that there was another on his back; he removed that one too, curious as to why he'd needed bandaging in the first place. But it seemed that the harder he fought to collect his memories, the further they hid away in his subconscious.

He gazed at the bandages thoughtfully, both of them were stained with blood and what appeared to be a blue dye. There was no blue mark on his chest, so he assumed there wasn't one on his back either, and there was also no scar. But then there wouldn't be a scar. As a Vampire his wounds healed themselves just moments after they occurred. Which made the fact that he had needed nursing all the more confusing.

Slowly, he got to his feet and studied the space in which he stood.

The living room in Sam's home was larger than his own; brighter in its furnishings and colouration, yet just as sparse when it came to decoration. It lacked the family photographs, trophies, and other childhood memorabilia that would usually be found within the homes of all normal humans.

All of the curtains were closed—from what he could tell at least—and luckily the fabric they were made from was heavy enough to keep him safe from the sun. Jamie could tell by the outline of light around the curtains that not only was it daytime but the sun was shining.

Strange, he thought. Last he remembered it was lashing rain.

Jamie turned back to the sofa and noticed that his shoes were on the floor beside it. He sat down and slid them on. When he looked up from his laces he saw that one of his t-shirts was folded on the table.

He picked up the t-shirt and examined it closely. It wasn't the one he'd been wearing. At least it wasn't the last one he *remembered* wearing. But he knew by the scent of it that it was his. He pulled it on over his head, the whole time wondering how one of *his* t-shirts managed to find its way to *Sam's* house.

Jamie stood again, looking towards the hallway as he wondered where Sam was, and whether it would be alright for him to wander her house until he found her.

With a deep breath, he stretched his senses outwards. He could hear Sam upstairs talking to someone.

"I need you to go back to whatever sources you have and find me all of the information you can on Vampire Hunters." Jamie paused at her words, flashes of memories coming back to him like bursts of lightning in his mind. He remembered going to Sam's school, taking her to his home, speaking to her, arguing with her.

She's not human either, he remembered, his mind suddenly buzzing with apprehension. Slowly, he walked out of the living room, through the hall and up the stairs, all the way wondering who she was talking to.

"What?" she asked, as if someone had said something to her. Jamie couldn't hear anyone else and couldn't sense another person in the house. He paused on the staircase for a moment. *Is she talking to herself?*

"No," she said. "It's alright then. Wait 'til later." Jamie came to the top of the stairs, but her voice still seemed far away. He turned the corner and noticed another staircase at the end of the hallway ... leading to an attic perhaps? He continued moving forward. "Don't," she said. "Don't you dare leave me here alone!" Jamie came to the door. He hesitated before opening it. "Don—"

Jamie opened the door just as Sam dropped her head to her hands. "I hate you!" she screamed.

He cast a quick glance around the room; there was no one else there.

"What did *I* do?" Jamie asked as he stepped inside, wondering if her hatred was aimed at him, and what exactly he had done to deserve it.

Sam turned her head and looked in his direction, she sighed. "I wasn't talking to *you*." She was sitting at a table on the far end of the attic. Books littered the top of the desk, some of them open, others closed and in piles that were placed precariously on the edge of the table. Sam put her foot up on the chair across from her and pushed it out from the table; she looked at Jamie and nodded towards the chair, inviting him to take a seat.

Jamie took a step towards her then stopped, unsure as to whether or not he *wanted* to sit with her. After all, she might be completely insane. She had been talking to no one and Claudio had said she was cursed . . . whatever that meant. "Who were you talking to?" he asked, inconspicuously looking around once more, just to be certain there was no one else present.

Sam sighed tiredly and rubbed her eyes. "Jack."

Jamie looked at Sam . . . there was *still* no one else in the room. "Is *Jack* here right now?" Jamie asked carefully.

Sam gave him a sideways look. "Do you *see* anyone else?"

"No," Jamie said. "But I also didn't hear anyone else while you seemed to be having a full conversation with . . . " he paused for a moment, then said, " . . . yourself."

Sam looked at him. Then she started to laugh as if she found his statement amusing. "Don't be stupid," she said. "Jack is a Ghost. Your silly little Vampire brain can't register him when he's invisible. He doesn't bother with the whole making-himself-seen thing when it's just me."

Jamie cringed when she said the word 'Vampire'. It felt strange, hearing someone attribute that word to him after so many years. He looked at Sam in disbelief. "A *Ghost*? . . . Ghosts aren't real."

"By that logic, neither are you," she said.

She has a point, Jamie thought as he finally walked towards Sam and took the seat she had pushed out for him. "So, can I meet Jack?"

"When he gets back," she said.

"Well, where did he go?"

"To find all of the information he can on Vampire Hunters," she stated, looking him directly in the eye. "To prevent you from getting shot again."

Shot, he thought as the remainder of his memories flooded back to him. *That's what happened.* He put his hand on his chest, the pain of his body being pierced coming back with the memory. "The arrow?"

Sam looked at his chest where he had been injured, then used her thumb to point over her shoulder to a small table in the corner of the room. "It's over there if you want to keep it."

Jamie looked at the broken arrow, then back at Sam. "You saved my life?" he said in astonishment. From what he could remember, the arrow had hit him less than an inch from his heart. *I almost died.*

Sam shrugged. "You saved mine. I saved yours . . . though technically I was never in danger 'cause I could have saved myself, but whatever."

"Did you say there were Vampire Hunters?"

Sam nodded. "Three of them. They're dead now, but there's probably a lot more where they came from, so . . . " She took a book from the pile on the table and dropped it in front of him; it hit the table with a thud. "Start reading. Find out all you can about their methods, that way you'll know what to look out for."

Jamie opened the book, then he looked at Sam. "Thank you," he said. "For not letting me die."

"Don't mention it," she said. "You'd do the same for me . . . you did do the same for me . . . technically . . . well, kind of." Jamie laughed a little. *She couldn't just say thank you,* he thought as he shook his head. Then he opened the book and started to read.

"Did Claudio help you find your Sire?" Sam asked a few moments later, while flipping through pages in the book she was studying.

Jamie looked at her in bewilderment. "What?" he asked, not seeing how she could possibly know why he wanted to find another Vampire, and how she knew the name of the one he had talked to. From what he'd gathered from Claudio's reaction at Sam's name, he wouldn't come anywhere near her. And how would she know him?

"Did Claudio help you find your Sire?" she repeated.

"How did you know I talked to someone named Claudio?" Jamie asked.

"Because I gave you the address of where he hangs out, so that he could help you. Because apparently he's the guy to talk to when you wanna find someone."

"And how do *you* know Claudio?" He tried to keep his tone indifferent, but failed.

Sam smiled as if she found his question amusing. She didn't answer, instead she asked one of her own. "What did he tell you about me?"

Jamie paused for a moment, not sure if it would be proper to repeat the things that Claudio had said about Sam, and speak them to her face. He let a sigh. "He said that if I wanted to live I should stay far away from you."

She nodded her head as if that was something she expected people to say about her. "He said that you were a Witch." Jamie paused and looked at Sam, trying to find a reaction in her expression. But she just stared back impatiently, wanting him to finish what he was saying. "He said that you were cursed and that everything around you . . . *dies.*"

Sam smiled bitterly. "Well that's not *entirely* true, I managed to keep those plants alive." She pointed out the small attic window. Jamie couldn't look out to see because the curtains were drawn and from what he could tell it looked bright outside.

"Why did you ignore what he told you?" she asked, her eyes looking down at her arm where there was a red mark on her wrist. Jamie leaned in to get a better look as she traced over it with her finger. It was an odd mark, the design a series of swirls and loops that came together to make quite an intricate pattern which covered half of her lower arm, from her wrist halfway up to her elbow.

"I didn't fully believe him," Jamie replied.

"And do you believe him now?"

"No."

Sam looked up, her eyes staring directly into his. "*How* can you *not*?" she asked, sounding both confused and outraged. "What he told you was true, except for when he called me a Witch, but the rest of it . . . I *am* cursed. People die—"

"I'm not people," Jamie said, cutting her off.

She shook her head. "Neither were my parents," she said quietly. "Neither was my adoptive mother, or my grandmother. Yet where are they now?" She looked at Jamie as if waiting for him to answer. Which he didn't, because he knew where all of those people were now, and he knew what she was trying to say.

"Maybe I can *help* you," Jamie said.

"I don't need help," Sam snapped. "What I *need* is to be left alone. I can deal with my problems, but I can't keep everyone safe, unless I keep them away."

"I can keep myself safe." Sam snorted and rolled her eyes. Jamie felt himself scowl. "You think I can't? I've lived longer than you, I've survived this long alone."

"That was before you had things after you. You don't know what's out there. You don't know how to deal with it. And if I'm attacked by something you can't help me fight, I won't have time to give you a lesson on how to deal, I'll be too busy fighting and keeping *you* from being killed."

Jamie leaned back in his chair and tapped his fingers on the book that was open in front of him. "If I'm such a burden then why not just leave me to die?"

Sam sighed tiredly and rubbed her eyes. "Because now we're even. And the only reason you were attacked in the first place was because you got messed up with me. So, I'm gonna help you get the bounty off your head and then I'm no longer responsible for you."

Jamie could feel his eyes grow wide. "A *bounty*?"

Sam looked at him in confusion. "Did I not tell you that already?" Slowly, Jamie shook his head. Sam sighed and looked at him empathetically. "Sorry," she said. "The men you killed, the one who attacked me and the other two at the base, one of them was a Hunter and the other two were Demons. Well, not *actual* Demons, that's just what they call themselves, they were Warlocks or something. Anyway, when you killed them you made it look like you were on my side, which pissed a lot of guys off, so now there's a bounty out on you. Wanted dead."

"Damn," Jamie whispered. "Not even 'or alive'?"

Sam shook her head. "Sorry," she mumbled. "That's why it would have been better if you had just stayed away from me."

"Why?" Jamie asked. "Why would ... Demons want me dead because they think I'm on your side? Your side of what? Why are they after you at all? Did you do something do them?"

"I exist," she said quietly, looking at the mark on her wrist again. Jamie wondered if it meant something. Was it a tattoo? A birthmark? Or perhaps some kind of magical mark? "I don't think I'm supposed to exist." She shook her head. "I don't *fit*. I don't fit anywhere. I'm not *anything*, and yet I'm *something*. And on top of that I have Power. A *lot* of Power. Like, they come at me with a two-hundred man army and I'm the only one who walks away kind of Power. And they want that for themselves, they're at war and they need to tip the odds in their favour, so they need me. But not *me*. So they try to kill me, because they think it will free my Powers from this body and send it out into the world for anyone to absorb."

"Is that possible? Wouldn't your Magic die with you? And *can* you even die?"

She turned her face upwards and stared at the ceiling. "Theoretically it is possible for me to *give* my Powers, but I'm not sure if they can be taken against my will, except . . . " She let the sentence trail off as she stared up.

"Except what?" Jamie urged her to continue, curious to find out more about this. Although everything she was saying was completely outlandish and fantastical, and hearing her speak of these things filled him with a sense of fear because it couldn't possibly be *real*, he found himself wanting to know about it. His curiosity getting the best of him.

Sam chewed her lip and looked at Jamie. "Except you."

"*Me?*" Jamie pointed to himself, his expression confused.

She smiled a little. "Not you specifically, but a Vampire, or Vampires. They might be able to steal my Powers if they tried."

"Uh . . . Vampires aren't all that magical," Jamie stated. "It's more like a medical condition with no cure."

Sam laughed genuinely, a sound he had never heard before; it made him smile. It was good to hear her laugh. "My Magic is in my blood. If a Vampire consumed all of my blood they would consume my Magic."

"And you know this because . . . ?"

She shook her head. "I don't, like I said, it's theoretical. But, well a Vampire wouldn't attack me, because Aleczander wouldn't allow it. And my blood wouldn't taste very nice either . . . not the right kind of nutrients."

"How do *you* know Aleczander?" he asked, and wondered if she knew that Aleczander was his Sire.

Sam looked at him. He wondered if he had succeeded in hiding the jealousy he felt. By the look on Sam's face, he hadn't been all that successful. She smiled coyly. "He's my Vampire husband."

He almost choked when she said that. "What?"

Sam smiled. "Yeah. I'm Mrs Vampire."

Jamie raised an eyebrow. "Are you messing with me?"

He could tell that Sam was trying not to laugh. "We met in Rio, where we danced upon the sand."

Jamie gave her an unimpressed look as she burst into a fit of laughter. "You're messing with me."

She spoke through her giggles. "You should've seen your face, it was hilarious!"

Jamie shook his head without smiling. "That wasn't funny."

"Why not?" Sam asked.

"It just wasn't," he snapped. "And you didn't answer me, *seriously*. I mean, Vampires are *dangerous*, and if one is following you around—"

"One *is* following me around," Sam stated with a meaningful glance at Jamie. "*You*. And why does everyone think that Vampires are so dangerous all of a sudden? Was there a memo that I didn't get?"

"Vampires *are* dangerous," Jamie stated.

"No . . . they're not. At least not to me they're not."

"Bu—"

"After my parents were killed, Aleczander and his wife Evangeline took me in."

"Wife?"

Sam laughed. "Yeah, they're both my friends. I lived with them, and about two-thousand other Vampires up 'til I was four."

"Oh," Jamie said, for lack of anything better. He ran his hand through his hair. Sam sat there in silence examining her book closely. "Aleczander is my Sire," he mumbled in a feeble attempt to keep the conversation going.

"That makes you his first fledgling. Congrats." She gave him a thumbs up. "You're next in line for the Vampire throne."

"His first what?" Jamie asked in confusion.

"His first fledgling," Sam repeated. "The first human he Turned into a Vampire."

"Oh," he thought for a second. "Are there others?"

"Just Evangeline, but you're *way* older than she is. Like way way . . . *WAY* older. Like—"

"I get it," Jamie said, cutting her off before she could say more about how old he was.

She smiled a little. "You're ancient. Like, *pre-historic*."

"I am *not* pre-historic. I'm . . . *historic*."

Sam laughed. "From ye olde ancient times." Jamie scowled and shook his head, turning his attention away from her and to the book he had in front of him.

"You wanna know something funny?" Sam asked after a moment.

"Sure."

"Evangeline was the one who gave me the address to the Blood-Bar for you."

"She was?"

Sam nodded. "I was looking for Aleczander, but he wasn't home."

"So the friend that you were talking about who goes to the Blood-Bars all the time, was my Sire?" Sam laughed again while nodding. "You could have just given me his phone number."

He couldn't help feeling slightly betrayed. Sam had known how to get in contact with his Sire all along and instead of allowing him direct contact she sent him running around to questionable places.

Sam shrugged. "If I had you would have wondered how I knew two Vampires. And it would have been better if you knew nothing about me. But you just couldn't walk away when you had the chance . . . and now there's a million dollar bounty on your head."

Jamie remembered what Claudio had said about staying away from Sam. And Sam telling him that he was going to die because he hadn't. They both meant what they said. And because he refused to listen he was sitting here right now with Sam, having enjoyable conversation inside her home.

He knew that with the situation he was currently in — with Vampire Hunters and who knew what else suddenly taking an interest in him and wanting him dead — that he should have been wishing he'd followed their advice. But he was with Sam, which was exactly where he wanted to be, so in all honesty, he had absolutely no regrets about the choices he'd made and if given the option would do the exact same things all over again.

She smiled sadly. "You should have stayed away from me when I told you to."

"I've survived two centuries so far," Jamie said confidently. "There are Demons after you and Vampire Hunters after me, I'm on your side so can I assume that you're on mine?"

Sam hesitated for a moment, but then she nodded. "I'm on your side."

"Well then, I'll watch your back and you watch mine."

"I suppose we could give it a try, it's not like I can abandon you *now*."

The doorbell rang and Jamie jumped slightly with fright, not expecting the sudden noise. He looked towards the attic door, then glanced at Sam. "Who's that?" he asked curiously.

Sam stood. "Dinner."

CHAPTER 35

I found 1 of ur fledglings.

Sam sent the text to Aleczander as she walked down the stairs. She opened the door, there was a guy there with a pizza box in his hand. "Sixteen-fifty," he recited, his tone sounding about as bored as he looked.

Sam handed him a twenty, then took the box out of his hand. "Keep the change." She closed the door before the pizza guy had a chance to say anything else.

She heard her phone buzz on the table beside the door where she had set it down. Sam held the pizza box in one hand and picked the phone up with the other. There was a message from Aleczander.

It read, Claudio told me. I can't see him for a month or so. I have dealings to do with the Lycanthropes and whatnot, best to keep him out of sight, I'll call you when I'm done with that and you can bring him to see me.

Sam replied with, Whatev, tel Eva I said hi.

After shoving her phone into her bra for safekeeping, she

went into the kitchen, hunkering down at the fridge where she got herself the bottle of Pepsi.

As she straightened, a wave of dizziness overtook her, causing her vision to blur momentarily. She turned swiftly, pushing her back against the countertop for stability as she squeezed her eyes shut, giving her head some time to clear.

There was a moment before she felt her body calm, when her instincts caused her lips to part, a spell almost escaping her.

Snapping her jaw shut and clenching her teeth together, she ignored the voice in the back of her mind that told her she should call Jack for help and with a determination, bordering on stubbornness, wrote it off as nothing more than a moment of vertigo before she made her way back to the attic.

When she opened the door, Jamie was standing by one of the shelves that lined the walls, leaning against it, flipping through the pages of one of the books. He looked up when she entered and smiled. "You didn't tell me you wrote poetry."

Sam looked at him in confusion. "What?" she asked. "I don't write poetry . . . I don't even *read* poetry."

Jamie smiled then looked down at the book in his hand. "I will not shed a tear for life, for death I will not—" Sam rushed forward and slammed the book he was reading closed.

He smiled at her again. "They're not bad you know," he said. "Some of them even rhyme."

Sam rolled her eyes and set the pizza box and the Pepsi bottle down on her chair, discretely placing her phone on the table before he had time to notice where she'd stashed it. She picked up the book Jamie had been reading from, then slapped him across the head with it, putting as much of her physical strength into it as possible.

Jamie looked more surprised than angry or hurt. He put his hand to his head, though Sam knew that it would take more than being slapped with a book to cause him pain. "What was that for?" he asked.

"For being an idiot," Sam replied, then placed the book back on the shelf. She cleared a space on the table for the pizza box and left the Pepsi on the floor. "That's not a book of poetry, it's a book of spells. I didn't write them, they were already written. And you don't read a spell out loud unless you want to put it into effect."

"Oh," Jamie said and ran his hand through his hair. He smiled awkwardly. "Sorry . . . So what was that one?" Sam opened the pizza box while glaring at him.

"That one was a belated birthday present from Jack . . . it's a spell for immortality," she said. "Want some?" She pointed to the pizza.

Jamie looked at the pizza as if it were diseased. "No . . . Thank you."

Sam bent down and searched under the table for her bag. Inside it was the plastic flask she had taken from Jamie's house when she'd gone there to get him a blood-free t-shirt. "Here," she said. Jamie looked at the flask curiously, clearly recognising it as his, then at Sam. "When was the last time you ate?" she asked waving it in front of him.

"Uh," Jamie shifted uncomfortably. "Two days ago, maybe."

"You're probably hungry," she said. Then placed the flask directly in front of him.

Jamie shook his head while staring at the flask. "I'm fine," he told her and forced a smile. "I'm not *that* hungry."

Sam smiled to herself as she bit into the first slice of pizza. "Liar, liar pants on fire," she mumbled.

"I can wait 'til later," he said.

Sam rolled her eyes. "Just drink it," she snapped with impatience. "It's not like I care, I've seen Vampires drink blood before, sometimes even from living flasks."

Jamie tried not to laugh. "You don't refer to humans as living flasks!" he scolded.

Sam sighed internally, he'd drink it if she just left it there. She turned her face upwards to stare at the ceiling for a moment while she considered the weirdness of Vampires. The bare light bulb on the ceiling glared into her eyes, causing her to have to close them to block out the light. "I have something for you," she said to Jamie as she thought of how she didn't necessarily *have* to have the light on.

She threw the pizza crust into the box, then made her way across the room to a small wooden jewellery box on one of the many shelves. She opened the box and took out a ring. Then she walked back to the table and held it out to Jamie.

He took the ring out of her hand as she sat down, and looked at it. "Are you proposing to me?" he asked with a smile.

"Not even in your dreams," she scoffed. "It's a protection amulet."

Jamie tilted his head to the side slightly, looking at her curiously. "Protection from what?"

"The sun," Sam stated. "The best way to protect from the sun is to take a piece of jewellery, a ring, necklace, earrings, bracelet, whatever. Preferably one with a stone that already has protective properties. Then you charge the stone and put an enchantment on it." Sam leaned forward. "You see the way the stone has three different colours in it?"

Jamie looked at the ring. "Yeah."

"The light blue is for the morning sky. The normal blue is for the evening sky. And the navy-blue swirls around them both, bringing the night to every time of day. Which means that whoever wears it carries with them a piece of the night and can't be harmed by the sun."

"What type of stone is that?" Jamie asked curiously.

"Well, it's not any specific type of stone anymore." Sam took the ring out of Jamie's hand and moved it around, trying to see it from different angles in different lights. "I *think* this used to be garnet. It's a type of reddish, orangey-brown colour. It's really good for protection." Sam held the ring on its side and pointed to the stone. "You can still see little reddish sparkles in it."

Jamie looked at the ring, then took it out of Sam's hand. "Are you sure this will work on me?"

"Yes. It will."

There was no question about it, Sam *knew* it would work. She had enchanted it herself so she was one hundred percent sure.

"How can you be so sure?" Jamie asked.

"Put it on," Sam ordered. He hesitated, then slipped the ring onto his finger. She waved her hands at the window, sending out a gentle current of energy to throw the curtains open.

Jamie made a dive for the floor as soon as he saw the first beam of sunlight. Sam tried to suppress her laughter. He peered up at her from practically under the table and gave her an unimpressed glare. Sam smiled. "Hey look . . . it worked."

Jamie picked himself up off the floor, then sat back down while dusting off his clothes. "I could have *died!*"

Sam rolled her eyes. "Don't be such a drama queen. You're fine."

"Don't call *me* a drama queen," Jamie mumbled to himself. He opened the flask, took a sip of the blood inside, then looked towards the window. "How am I not on fire right now?" he asked himself.

Sam answered him anyway. "Because I'm amazing," she said proudly.

Jamie smiled at her fondly.

"How long will it work for?"

"Forever," Sam said through a mouthful of pizza. "As long as you wear it you're safe from the sun. Oh, and I texted

Aleczander, he said he's busy for the next few weeks, but he'll call me when he has all of his duties sorted out and I can bring you to see him."

"You texted him just a minute ago?" Sam nodded. "Are you *allowed* to talk to him?" he asked. "I thought he was King of the Vampires or something."

"He is," Sam said.

"I thought you'd have to talk to his guards before you get to talk to him."

"He doesn't have any guards," she said, laughing at Jamie's ignorance. "And even if he did, he's one of my Guardians, so I could talk to him directly whenever I feel like it."

"He's one of your what?"

"My Guardians," Sam said. "One of the people who were assigned to protect me."

Jamie raised an eyebrow in confusion. "Assigned by *who?*"

"The Moirai," Sam sighed, thinking he was asking *way* too many questions. She saw the look of confusion on his face at the word Moirai and decided to explain before he could ask yet *another* question. "Clotho, Lachesis and Atropos. They're called the Moirai but are better known as the Fates."

"The Fates?" Jamie asked. "Like the mythological hags who spin the threads of life."

Sam nodded. "Don't call them hags," she said. "They can hear you. They're like most immortals, and look a *lot* younger than they are. Clotho spins the thread of life, Lachesis determines the extent of the thread, and Atropos cuts the thread when time is up."

"So if you have the Fates, or the Moirai on your side, why are there Demons after you?"

"Because fate is on no one's side," Sam explained. "All the Moirai do is tell the story, everyone has control over their own actions. But every time you make a decision it puts a chain of events into motion. So every time you go left instead of right, the Moirai know everything in your life that will be influenced by that decision. They don't control what happens, they only know about it."

"Oh," Jamie said thoughtfully. "Do they at least give you fair warning?"

Sam shook her head. "If they did that it would alter any decisions I would have made and inevitably change my life in ways it wasn't supposed to be."

"So basically . . . they do nothing."

Sam nodded. "Basically."

"Have you ever met them?"

Sam shook her head. "No, but—"

"I have." Sam tried not to laugh when Jamie jumped as Jack materialised beside her. "They're three of the most useless, annoying bitches you will ever meet in your entire life. I despise all three of them. And I say this knowing full fucking well that they can hear every single word I'm saying. They may not be able to influence peoples destiny, but they make up for that by making up a load of bullshit rules that certain defenceless Ghosts have no choice but to go by, because they were threatened with spending an eternity in the godforsaken shithole known as Limbo."

Sam gave Jack an amused look. "Feel better now?" she asked simply.

Jack smiled in satisfaction. "A little." He turned to Jamie who was staring at him in confusion. "I'm Jack," he said, pointing to himself. "I'm sure Sam's told you *so much* about me, because, well let's face it, who *wouldn't* want to talk about me? I'm amazing."

Jamie laughed a little. "Jamie," he replied.

Sam rolled her eyes. "What did you find out?"

Jack sat on the windowsill, his feet on the edge of the table.

"You were right," he said to Sam. "Like us awesome Hunters, they poison their weapons—such copy-cats, I mean can't they get an original idea? They use wolfsbane, which is poisonous to Vampires," he added to Jamie. "And dead man's blood, not poisonous, but does make Vampires weak. They also treat some of their weapons using UV radiation. That's the same thing that's in the sun, so it can burn a Vampire from the inside out.

"They hunt in groups, usually the men do the killing. They sometimes try to lure Vampires into drinking drugged bait blood, which is usually hosted in the veins of an attractive female, or male, depending on the preferences of the Vampire they're hunting."

"So how do we notice one if they're undercover?" Sam asked.

"Easy," said Jack. "They'll smell irresistibly sweet."

"What?" Jamie asked in confusion.

Jack sighed. "He *is* the worst Vampire ever," he mumbled to Sam, then turned to Jamie. "Vampires are attracted to humans because of their warmth, their life-force and their energy. But the first thing a Vampire picks up on is a scent, how a person smells . . . do I *really* need to tell *you* something you should have learned a bazillion years ago, you dumb fucker?" Jack didn't wait for a response, though Jamie frowned slightly and opened his mouth as if he was about to speak. Jack continued, "Vampire Hunters drink a special potion. In that potion there's wolfsbane, the wolfsbane is absorbed into their blood while the rest of the potion protects them from being poisoned themselves. The potion also gives off a 'come get me' smell. So you'll try to get close to them, and you'll try to drink from them. But Vampire plus wolfsbane equals bad . . . If a Vampire drinks from a Vampire Hunter they'll be paralysed after one taste. Then the Vampire Hunter will kill the Vampire."

"So . . . I should be on the lookout for people who smell good?" Jamie asked as if that was the most ridiculous thing he'd ever heard.

Jack smiled and nodded. "Exactly."

CHAPTER 36

$\mathcal{T}$he room filled with an awkward silence after Sam left. Jamie sat on his chair and stared down at the book he was supposed to be reading, but he barely paid any attention to the words. He could feel Jack watching him, even without looking up.

What can you talk to a Ghost about? he thought to himself, feeling as though he should be the one to break the silence, since it seemed as though Jack wasn't going to do it.

"So . . . um . . . is there really a heaven?"

Jack simply stared at him like he was asking the strangest thing that he could have possibly thought of. "How the fuck would I know? I'm not there, am I?"

"I suppose not."

"I know there's a Limbo. I've been there. Technically still am."

"Okay, so what's Limbo like?" Jamie asked.

"Boring," Jack said vaguely, as he stared out the window,

chin resting on his fist.

"That's it? It's just boring?"

Jack nodded. "Speaking of which, I have stuff to do. So when Sam comes back, just tell her I had to go."

"O—" Before Jamie had time to finish saying 'Okay' Jack vanished into thin air.

Jamie sat alone in the attic for countless moments, before Sam finally came back up the stairs.

Sam looked at the empty place where Jack had been when she'd left, then at Jamie. "Where did Jack go?" she asked.

"Oh, he said he had some things he needed to do. He just left about a minute ago."

Sam sighed. "Okay." Jamie watched her as she walked over to him. She leaned over his shoulder to peer at the page he had been staring at. His stomach flipped, his breath momentarily stuck in his throat as her hair brushed against his cheek. "Find anything useful?" she asked coolly, as if his proximity didn't affect her at all.

"Not sure," he said, taking a deep breath to calm himself. "All the words started to blur together about an hour ago."

Sam nodded her head as she stepped away from him. "We'll just work with what we know so far, and maybe we'll figure out some more stuff later."

The book made a thud as Jamie closed it. "Alright . . . what are we doing now?" he asked, while hoping she wouldn't tell him it was time for him to leave.

Sam walked over to one of the shelving units on the far side of the attic and rummaged through it. She took some jars and what looked like stones and plants off the shelf. "We're going to your house to make it safer for you to be there."

Jamie stood and walked over to Sam. "Why does it need to be made safer?"

Sam looked at him as if he was asking a question to which

the answer was extremely obvious. "Um ... because a whole load of Vampire Hunters know where you live and will probably come back for you when you least expect it."

"Oh ... " Now he felt stupid for asking. " ... right."

She opened the lids of all the jars and started to pull apart the plants, putting even amounts of each into all of the jars, then she placed a stone in each one before she twisted the lids back on and carefully placed them into a bag.

"How many times in your life have you used a weapon?" Sam asked, as she walked over to some wooden chests in the corner of the room.

"Not many ... " Jamie said slowly, not sure why she was asking about weapons. "Not at all really, I've never needed a weapon. I mean, I've been in a few fights, but I just use what I've got, and anything that's lying around. Why, how many times have *you* used a weapon?"

"I don't really need weapons. I carry a dagger around with me, but that's just because Jack insisted. I've never had to use it before. I've got enough strength to get by without having to."

"Okay, now *why* are you asking about weapons?"

"Just wondering if you knew how to use them if you needed to or if I needed to teach you how to sword fight or anything."

Jamie's head was immediately filled with the image of Sam, a girl who couldn't have weighed more than one hundred pounds soaking wet, wielding a sword to fight off monsters. He laughed. "*You* know how to sword fight?"

"Yes," Sam said defensively. "Jack taught me. He taught me how to use all kinds of weapons. Not that I need to, but it's a 'just in case' sort of thing."

"Um ... okay. Should I be afraid?" Jamie asked with a smile.

"You mean of me killing you? ... No. But not because I *can't*, because I don't feel like it. If I wanted you dead, you'd be dead before you could blink."

"Wow . . . thanks," Jamie said sarcastically.

Sam laughed. "I said I *wasn't* gonna kill you . . . Chillax."

Jamie stared at her for a moment. It was difficult to picture her using a weapon to fight someone off without laughing . . . it was difficult to picture Sam fighting at all. When he looked at her he didn't see someone with enough Power to burn him alive without so much as blinking, he simply saw a human girl. Even though he knew she wasn't human, it was difficult for him to think of her as anything but.

He sighed to himself. "So what are we going to do once we get to my house?"

Sam kneeled down on the floor, opened the wooden chest and pulled out three daggers. She placed two of them in the bag with the jars she had taken from the shelves, and held the third one out to Jamie. "You keep this one on you, leave one in your bedroom, under your pillow or somewhere you have easy access to it, and keep the other in whatever room you spend most of your time. Again, leave it somewhere you'll be able to get to quickly if you need to."

Jamie stared uneasily at the dagger she was holding out to him. "I told you I don't need weapons."

She stood and walked over to Jamie, then she took his hand in hers and placed the hilt of the dagger in the palm of his hand. "Just in case you do."

She walked away from him, leaving him holding the blade. *At least it's sheathed,* he thought as he tucked it into his belt. *Now I just have to be careful not to stab myself.*

"I've got some spell jars we can bury around your house," Sam said as she picked her bag up off the floor and pulled the strap up to her shoulder. "They'll keep people away. And I can place some barrier runes around your house so that once people get to a certain place they can't get any closer without an invitation from you."

"And this Magic stuff, it will *actually* work?"

Sam gave Jamie a sideways glance. "You're walking around in the sunlight, and you're unburned, and you're *still* questioning my Magic?"

Jamie smiled guiltily. "Sorry. I just want to make sure."

"Well *be* sure," Sam said, holding her head high, her eyes burning bright with Power and confidence. "My Magic *never* fails."

CHAPTER 37

$\mathcal{I}$t took well over two hours to make the trek to Jamie's house. Before they left Sam suggested using a portal to travel. Because *apparently* she has the power to open up a hole in the universe, and step through it and land somewhere else in the universe.

And she suggested they travel through a hole in the universe, as though he'd be alright with that.

It was an interesting concept, the ability to move from one place to another without taking more than one step. But Jamie was more scared by the thought of doing it than he was fascinated, so they ended up walking the whole way there.

"Okay, we can dig the first hole here." Sam pointed to a spot on the ground twenty feet from the front door.

Jamie looked at Sam and arched an eyebrow, the corner of his mouth twitched in an amused smile. "*We?*" he asked rhetorically. "Are you going to be digging too?"

Sam stared at him as if he were insane. "You're a Vampire!"

she yelled, too loudly and casually for him to feel comfortable with her saying it aloud. "You don't need help with manual labour. It's not like it's a strain for you or anything."

Jamie laughed a little, partly from a nervous feeling that someone had heard her, but mostly from amusement. He took his jacket off, and threw it on the grass beside him. It was September, so the weather was at that awkward stage where mostly it was damp and colder as the days got darker, yet every few days there were a couple of hours where during the daylight it was too warm to be comfortable in winter clothing, yet if you wore clothes designed for warmer weather, by the time the night came you would wish your coat was heavier.

Jamie had heard—or rather read and seen on TV—that Vampires didn't feel the effects of the weather. That was one of those things that he had managed to figure out for himself was untrue. His experience was that he was generally unbothered by the cold, unless the temperature dropped below freezing point, and the heat made him feel uncomfortable, as though his body was suffocating despite the fact that oxygen was, for the most part, optional.

He gazed up towards the sky, knowing by the position of the sun that he wouldn't have to suffer through the heat for much longer. The sun would set in an hour or two, and the night would bring cooler weather. With a sigh, he started digging, using the shovel that he had carried here all the way from Sam's house. "How deep am I digging this thing?"

"Not too deep. About a foot maybe. The jars aren't huge or anything."

"And what will you do whilst I dig?" he asked with a smile. "Watch and hope I get warm enough to take some clothes off?"

Sam rolled her eyes and sighed while shaking her head. "Don't flatter yourself. I'll be putting some protection runes on those trees." She placed the bag containing the jars on the ground beside Jamie. He watched as she took her jacket off, leaving her in a set of lightweight clothes; a light grey t-shirt—which seemed well fitted around the top and became looser near the end, flowing past her hips—a pair of patterned leggings covered her legs, and on her feet she wore a pair of black hiking boots. It was the first time he'd noticed that she changed her clothes. When he'd first found her in the attic she had been wearing a dress. He briefly wondered when exactly she'd changed, and why.

Sam cleared her throat, Jamie glanced at her face to find her glaring at him. "You can stop perving on me now." She dropped her jacket on top of his. "That's *all* the clothes I'm taking off."

Jamie laughed a little, out of embarrassment more than amusement, as she walked over to the tree behind him.

He looked over his shoulder just in time to see Sam climbing it with ease. He watched her curiously. "What are you doing?" he asked. When she told him she would be carving things into the trees he didn't think she meant she would be climbing them first.

She took the knife out from between her teeth where she had kept it while she climbed.

"What's it look like?" she asked rhetorically as she started carving things into the bark as near to the top as she could climb. Although the trees appeared strong, the branches near the top were old and weathered. And she was standing on them, perfectly balanced without a hint of nervousness, as if she didn't feel them bowing beneath her.

"Please don't fall," Jamie mumbled to himself as he whispered a silent prayer to whatever God was out there, then he started digging. Keeping his ears on alert for the sound of a falling Sam.

The hole didn't take all that long to dig. A little less than five minutes. Jamie dropped the shovel next to the little hole he had dug in the ground and turned to Sam, who was now standing on the tree a few over from the one she had started on. He gazed at her curiously, wondering how she had moved between them without him hearing a sound.

"What now?" he asked, thinking she should have explained what he was supposed to do in more detail. It wasn't as though he was incompetent and needed to be given instructions one step at a time, but he didn't say anything about that. He just assumed it was how Sam liked to work.

Never giving away more information than was necessary at the time.

Sam looked at him over her shoulder. "You need to dig another one to your left."

Jamie sighed. "Okay . . . how far to the left?"

Sam continued carving her symbols into the tree she was perched in. "Give me a minute!" she shouted down to him. She took a few more seconds to finish her carvings, then she jumped out of the tree, knife still in hand.

Jamie leapt forward a little in an attempt to catch her, though he hesitated for long enough to not get there in time. She had already landed, feet first, on the ground. Sam fixed her clothes, wiping away flecks of dirt and broken leaves, then looked up to see Jamie staring at her.

"What?" she asked and put her free hand to her cheek as if to wipe something away. "Is there something on my face?"

Jamie shook his head. "You just jumped out of a thirty foot tree."

Sam shrugged. "So? I landed on my feet."

"Is that how you've been getting down from all the trees?"

"No," Sam laughed. "I jumped from one to the other."

Jamie stared at her in shock. "Are you *joking*?"

She shook her head. "No. Why waste time climbing up and down when I can jump?"

"What if you had fallen and hurt yourself?"

Sam shrugged in a half 'whatever' half 'I don't know' kind of way, then walked past him to the hole in the ground. She moved about twenty feet to the left of it and pointed down. "About here should be good."

She's completely insane, Jamie thought to himself as he walked over. "Okay. Can you tell me how many of these holes I need to dig and where they need to go so that I can *not* get my hopes up and think I'm done, then find out that I'm not?"

Sam half smiled. "Sure."

She went back to the first hole where she had left her bag. She picked it up and took out a jar, placing it by the hole. After which she took out another and handed it to him, pointing down to indicate where it would go.

"There needs to be five," she said. "They'll make the five points of the star. And your house will be in the middle." She continued moving to the left, about another twenty feet and placed a jar on the ground. "When you're finished digging the holes the jars get buried." She walked another twenty feet, then left a jar to mark the spot. "But before they get buried you need to cut your hand or something and put a drop of blood into each jar."

"I have to put my blood into those?"

Sam continued in the same direction, then placed the final jar on the ground. "Well yeah. To make them protect you, you put your blood in them. Otherwise they won't work."

"Does it *have* to be blood?"

Sam rolled her eyes and mumbled, "Vampires." Jamie didn't know whether he should be insulted or not. "No, it doesn't *have* to be blood. Blood is just the least disgusting bodily fluid you can use. So do you think you can man up and control yourself around *your own* blood or would you rather pee in the jars?"

Jamie looked down, creasing his brow thoughtfully. He ran his hand through his hair and sighed. "I think I'll pee in the jars."

Sam scrunched her nose up in disgust. "Eww."

Jamie laughed at her expression, then, sighing dramatically, he threw his hands up in defeat. "*Fine*, I suppose I can use some blood."

Sam shook her head and walked back to the trees to continue carving into the bark, leaving Jamie with his shovel to dig four more holes in the earth.

About twenty minutes later, Jamie heard a thud indicating that Sam had just jumped out of a tree. He looked behind him to see where she was.

"Over here," she called.

Jamie jumped a little, then swiftly faced forward to find Sam standing there. "It's been a really long while since someone's been able to sneak up on me."

Sam shrugged as if it was no big deal. "I must be a ninja." Jamie laughed at her nonchalance. "You almost done?" she asked.

"Yeah, just finished."

Sam handed Jamie the knife she had been using to carve symbols into the trees. "You can use this to cut your hand or finger or whatever. You only need one drop in each jar."

Jamie nodded. He stared at the blade nervously, he could tell that it was sharp enough to slice through skin quite easily, which was good . . . the easier it cut the less it would hurt. Not that he had to stab himself to get some blood out. Sam said he just needed to shed a little, he could probably squeeze five drops from a cut as small as one he'd get from paper.

He dragged the knife across the palm of his hand just hard enough to break the skin. Cuts didn't hurt Jamie all that much, the most difficult part of getting a wound like this was concentrating on not letting it heal too fast so that he had enough time to get some blood out.

Sam unscrewed the lid from one of the jars and held it under his hand. Jamie squeezed it tightly in a fist and let the blood drip into the jar. She placed it on the ground and ran to get another one. They did this a total of five times, until all of the jars had drops of his blood in them.

Sam took the knife from Jamie. He stared at the hand he had cut and watched the skin stitch itself back together until there wasn't even a scar left.

"Do you have people over frequently?"

Jamie looked at her curiously. *Well, that's a random question to ask.* He shook his head. "I don't really know any people . . . except you."

"Okay," Sam said. "That saves us a lot of time."

Before Jamie had a chance to question her, Sam slid the blade across her palm and let her blood spill into the jars. He watched the crimson liquid drip from her hand in rapt fascination as it fell into the jar and mixed with his blood. Jamie swallowed hard. "What are you doing?"

Sam handed the dagger to Jamie, then showed him her hand. "All gone," she said with a smile. She had been able to heal the wound almost as quickly as Jamie had been able to heal his.

"How come you had to put your blood in there too? And why did you need to know if I had people over?"

"Because," she said as she started twisting the lids back onto the jars. "If you have people over on a regular basis, it would be smart for you to put their blood in here too. With these jars, no one can get into your house without an invitation from you . . . well except me. The reason you need to put other people's blood in there is so that they don't need an invitation. That way if they ever send Shape-shifters—"

"Shape-shifters?" Jamie asked incredulously.

"If they ever send Shape-shifters after you, disguised as people you know, they can't get in without an invitation, and you'll know they're not really the person they're disguised as."

Jamie stared at her, unable to believe what she'd just said. " . . . Shape-shifters?"

Sam rolled her eyes. "Assume everything is real, that way we won't have to have these conversations on a regular basis." Sam picked up two jars and handed them to Jamie. "Now let's bury these things so we can call it a day . . . I have school tomorrow and tons of homework to do, so I don't wanna be doing this all year."

CHAPTER 38

An entire month had passed by without a single strange occurrence. Life went on as it would have if Sam had been a completely average eighteen year old high school student.

Which was why she felt on edge.

The attacks on her had been happening on and off for her entire life. Over the past couple of years, they had stuck to a bi-weekly schedule. But the attack on Jamie was the last run in she'd had with any form of Hunter.

She knew that her Magic was strong enough to shield Jamie from Vampire Hunters, which explained why there had been no more attacks against him. But all the bad guys knew where she lived, and even though they couldn't step foot inside her house, they had in the past—on more than one occasion—caught her outside of it. So she knew they *could* get to her, and was confused by the fact that they hadn't tried.

Jack was keeping a look out for any activity from them

during the day, while Jamie slept and Sam was at school. Not that she'd been able to pay all that much attention in her classes, due to the overwhelming dread that knotted at her stomach when she thought of what was surely coming.

The locker next to hers slammed shut loudly, causing her to jump slightly and shake herself out of her own thoughts. She peered around the locker door, looking towards Elliot who was now on his way to class.

His silhouette grew darker the further away from her he moved, and as she watched him go, his shadow growing darker than was possible with each step he took, her mind was transported back to her time at the library, where she had encountered those strange shadows. She shook her head, willing those thoughts away as she turned back to her locker.

Something about Elliot always brought her mind to dark places. It was one of the reasons why she always went out of her way to ignore him whenever he was around.

With a sigh, she threw her math book into her locker, exchanging it for the ones she needed for English.

"Sam!"

Sam turned sharply to find Scott standing behind her, watching her with *that* expression again. *This can't be going anywhere good*, she thought warily. Scott looked down at his shoes, his hands nervously fidgeting with the end of his hoodie. "Um, I was just wondering if you're going to the dance with anyone?"

Sam sighed tiredly. *I knew this wasn't going anywhere good.* "I'm not going to the dance," she said firmly, hoping that Scott could just leave the conversation at that.

He didn't.

"Would you go with me?" he asked.

Sam sighed again, this time more impatiently. She hated when he did this. Why couldn't he just hate her and go be with someone else? "Scott," she said. He gazed at her hopefully. "We broke up almost *two* years ago."

"Yeah," he said. "I know. But I was still kinda hoping that maybe we could un-breakup."

Sam looked at him sadly. Of course she still had all of *those* feelings for him. Which was exactly why she couldn't be with him. She shook her head. "You could do so much better than me."

"But there is *no one* better than you."

Sam instantly looked away, deciding she'd rather stare at the footprint smudges on the linoleum rather than at Scott's sad expression. *Why does he always do this?*

She heard him sigh dejectedly. "Does this have anything to do with that guy?"

Sam looked at him in confusion. "What guy?"

Scott scowled. Which was honestly the angriest expression she'd ever seen him wear. "Sam, I *know* about the guy." Sam gave him the same confused expression. He elaborated, "The guy that you've been hanging around with . . . He meets you outside of school every day."

"Oh," Sam said and quirked an amused smile when she realised he was talking about Jamie. Sam didn't really consider him to be a *guy*. He was just . . . *Jamie*.

"*That* guy." Sam shook her head. " . . . No, it has nothing to do with him."

"So he's not your boyfriend?"

Sam laughed despite the fact that she was vexed by the idea that anyone could think she was *with* Jamie. "No."

"Well, then who is he?"

"He's just a guy." Sam shrugged. "That's it."

Scott gave Sam a scrupulous look. "That's it?" he asked, as if he found that hard to believe. "You're not, like, best-friends? You haven't been on a date . . . nothing?" Sam shook her head.

"Well, then why do you spend so much time together? Madison told me that he's at your house almost every day."

"You have Madison spying on me?" Sam asked in angry disbelief.

Scott looked taken aback. As if he hadn't realised that he'd said that last part. "No." He shook his head. "It's not like that. You know the way Madison is. She feels the need to know everything, and tell everyone about it."

Sam sighed. "We're not friends. We've never been on a date. We've never kissed. We've never even hugged. I don't even know why I'm telling you this." She gave him a sombre look. "We're not together anymore, Scott. I don't have to explain myself to you."

Scott turned his face away. "I know," he said sadly.

Sam sighed, thinking that she should say something just to make him feel better. "I'm just helping him with some stuff. That's it."

Scott looked at Sam curiously. "What kind of stuff?"

"You know . . . just . . . *stuff*."

His eyes were wide with disappointment and sadness.

Sam let a sigh of exasperation. She *really* hated when he did *this*.

"I don't like him like *that*, so can we just drop it?"

Scott paused thoughtfully for a moment, then sighed as he decided to drop the conversation. "Are you going to Madison's on Halloween?"

Sam shrugged. "I don't know."

Scott nodded. "Okay, well maybe I'll see you there?"

She forced a smile and nodded slightly. He was still trying to push her, but asking if she was going to a party was better than the countless times he'd asked her out directly. "Maybe," Sam answered as she closed her locker door. "I'm late for English."

"See ya 'round," Scott said with his ever hopeful smile, as

Sam walked away.

CHAPTER 39

The lunch bell finally rang.

Scott felt like he'd been in that class all day and it was only one o'clock. He made his way out of the room, through the halls to his locker. As always, he took the long route, which led him straight past Sam's locker. He couldn't help feeling disappointed when he found she wasn't there.

He walked to his locker, put his math book inside, then took out his lunch and made his way to the cafeteria. As soon as he'd pushed through the doors, Madison waved him over to her table.

Scott inconspicuously scanned the cafeteria crowd for Sam's blonde head.

Another wave of disappointment ran through his chest when, yet again, she was nowhere to be found.

He took a seat next to Madison, which was where he usually sat for lunch. "Hey Scott," she said as he sat down.

"Hi," he replied, trying not to show how upset he was.

Scott had known Madison for his whole life, they lived directly across the street from each other and had been best friends up until junior high, when they went their separate ways. She was popular. Scott wasn't necessarily. People liked him, but it wasn't like he was captain of the football team or anything.

He started hanging out with Madison again when they entered high school. But that was because Madison and Sam were friends, and Sam and Scott were dating. But still, they'd been friends for so long that he felt comfortable enough talking to her about pretty much anything. He looked around the table to make sure that no one was paying attention to him. Elle was flirting with that new kid, Elliot.

Everyone thought that Elliot was cool, but Scott got this eerie feeling around him.

The guy was creepy.

But he wasn't paying attention to anyone other than Elle right now. Aaron had his back to Scott and was in the middle of a heated discussion on something to do with sports with Mike and Chelsea. And Chelsea was flittering in and out of the sports talk, and talking to Madison.

When Chelsea tuned back into the discussion, Madison turned to Scott. She took one look at him, rolled her eyes and asked, "What's up?"

Scott took a breath. *Is it wrong to still be obsessing over Sam after all this time?* Everyone else seemed to think it was. But Scott couldn't help how he felt about her. It was like a sickness that lived inside him and only grew stronger with each passing moment.

Filling up his brain with constant thoughts of her.

And no matter how hard he tried, it was impossible for him to let her go. It had been two years, it should have gotten easier to not have her around, but it had only gotten more difficult.

"You know that guy Sam's been hangin' out with?"

Madison sighed. "I only talked to him for like ten minutes that *one* time, so all I can tell you is his name is Jamie and that he's, like, foreign or something. And that he has a major crush on Sam."

Scott bit into his sandwich. He *knew* there was something going on between them. With all the time they've been spending together how could there not be? "Do you think she likes him like that?"

"In my female opinion?" Scott nodded. "Sam is very hard to read, so I'd say if she does like him she doesn't realise it. Do you want another opinion?" she asked. Again, Scott nodded. "Get over her," Madison said bluntly.

"I tried," he replied quickly. "But I can't." He shook his head and looked away. "You just don't get it."

Madison sighed. "I *do* get it," she insisted. "You have feelings for somebody who doesn't feel the same about you. Lots of people go through that same situation. They deal with it by finding someone they *can* have so then eventually those other feelings go away."

"But I *love* her," Scott said lamely.

"Well she doesn't love you!" Madison said loudly. The sting of her words bit into his heart like a needle made of ice. A few people turned to look out of curiosity. Scott quietly gathered his things and made his way out of the cafeteria.

Out in the halls he started to walk faster, wanting to get as far away from Madison's words as possible.

"Scott, wait!" Madison called after him. Scott kept on walking, barely resisting the urge to break into a run.

Madison grabbed onto his arm. He turned to look at her, not bothering to mask his pain. "I'm sorry," she said. "I didn't mean to be so harsh. It just came out."

Scott looked at her. A lump formed in his throat. "You're

right," he said, shaking his head. "She doesn't love me. I just —
" Scott covered his face with his hands. He would *not* cry in the
middle of the hallways. "I don't know how to not love her."

Madison wrapped her arms around him. "You know I'm
here if you need me," she whispered. Scott nodded, Madison
was a good friend. He knew she hadn't intentionally tried to
hurt him.

He let a breath and took his hands away from his face when
he was sure no tears would come. Then he wrapped his arms
around Madison and returned her hug. "Thanks," he
mumbled, as he let her go.

"Do you want to skip out early?" she asked. "We could go
hang out somewhere."

Scott shook his head. "No, I'm fine." He smiled as
convincingly as he could. "Thanks anyway."

"You sure?" Scott nodded. Madison thought for a moment,
chewing her lip. "Are you going to the dance?" she asked. Scott
was grateful for the subject change; he knew she was trying to
take his mind away from Sam.

He shrugged. "I don't know, I don't really have anyone to go
with."

"You could go with me," she suggested.

"Aren't you going with Aaron?"

Madison waved her hand dismissively. "We broke up, like,
two whole days ago."

"Oh," Scott said, wondering why she hadn't mentioned it
before now. "*Sorry?*"

Madison shrugged. "We only went out, like, four times. It's
not like I planned to marry him."

Scott smiled, a little happier. "Sure, we can make a night of
it." He figured having a day out with a friend would keep his
mind busy enough to forget about Sam.

"Cool," Madison smiled. "You better be coming to my

party."

Scott grinned and rolled his eyes. "Wouldn't miss it for the world."

"Good," she said.

They both started walking back to the cafeteria, but before they made it to the doors the bell rang. Scott sighed. "So much for lunch time," he muttered, voicing the thoughts of his stomach.

He and Madison said their goodbyes, then Scott went to his locker and took out his chemistry book. When he was ready, he made his way to the chem labs.

One by one, the seats in the lab filled up with students.

And once again, Sam wasn't there.

CHAPTER 40

After talking with Scott, Sam decided to leave school early. As she always did whenever he tried to talk to her about how they should get back together. She hated dealing with that conversation again and again.

And again, and again, and again.

. . . and *again.*

Scott would make it worse by always walking past her and looking at her dejectedly. It just made her feel guilty, even though all she was doing was keeping him safe.

Sam walked out the school doors as soon as the lunch bell rang, only to walk right into Jamie.

Actually, no, scratch that, she didn't walk into him . . . *he* ran into *her.* Sam felt a huge jolt as his body crashed into hers, but he caught hold of her so she wouldn't fall. "Sorry," he said quickly. "I should have slowed down sooner."

Sam gave him a little push so he would let her go. "It's fine," she grumbled, straightening out her jacket as she fixed the strap of her bag onto her shoulder.

Jamie looked around. "Is school over?" he asked, obviously confused by the lack of other people.

"No," Sam said, running her hand through her hair to fix it in case he'd messed it up. "I just wanted to leave early."

She paused as she was struck by a sudden thought, *Wait . . . I left early . . . the fuck is he doing here?*

Turning to Jamie suspiciously, she asked, "Do you just stand around here all day and wait for me to finish?"

Jamie shook his head. "No," he said defensively. "I was keeping tabs on you, and I sensed that you were upset so I came to see if you were okay."

Sam blinked, surprised not only by the fact that he was spying on her, but that he'd just openly admitted to it as if it wasn't a big deal. She sighed and closed her eyes. "Jamie . . . "

He looked at her and smiled excitedly, as if he were anticipating some words of kindness. "Yes?"

She shook her head. "You are such a *stalker*." Jamie's smile faded. "Stop keeping tabs on me, I'm not okay with that. If I need you I can just call you." Sam walked towards the school gates.

He walked along behind her. "Would you?"

"Would I what?"

"Call me if you weren't okay?"

Sam shrugged. "Maybe," she said. "Not that I'd need to considering the fact that you *never . . . go . . . away*."

Jamie looked up at one of the posters on the notice boards by the school gates. He pointed to it. "Are you going to that?" he asked.

Sam looked to where he was indicating. She saw the poster for the Halloween dance and sighed, turning away. "No."

"Would you like to go with me?" he asked.

Sam gritted her teeth. "No!" she said again, this time firmly.

What was with people and wanting her to go places with them?

"Oh," Jamie said, looking deflated.

"I was already asked, and I said no because I don't want to go," she explained in an attempt to make him feel better. "And why would you ask?" Sam wondered out loud. "You don't even go to school."

Jamie shrugged. "I've never been to a dance before."

"What? They didn't have dances back in ye olde ancient times?"

Jamie smiled. "They did," he said. "I just didn't go." His gaze shifted around the street in confusion, brow furrowed as he looked behind him. "Uh, Sam?"

"What?" she asked, her voice sounding more irritated than she actually was.

"Isn't your house that way?" he asked, pointing in the other direction.

"Yes," Sam stated. "I'm not going home yet."

"Then where are we going?"

Sam noticed that he said '*we*' as if she had invited him on her journey. Then, after she spent a moment thinking about it, she realised that he would assume he had been invited because she hadn't told him to go away yet.

He could come along, Sam decided, as long as he didn't talk anymore about dances or dates. "Tír na nÓg," she answered as if she had said something normal like post-office or laundromat.

Jamie laughed as if he thought she was joking. "Good one," he said. "Now where are we really going?"

Sam looked at him. "Tír na nÓg," she repeated with a serious tone to match her serious expression.

He looked confused. "Tír na nÓg? . . . As in the *mythological* world of Faeries?"

Sam nodded. For someone who had two centuries to learn all sorts of things, he could be pretty stupid sometimes. "Yeah," she said.

"But Faeries aren't *real*," he said, stressing the word 'real' as if he were trying to convince her of that fact.

Sam grinned widely. "Do you realise that by that logic you're not real either? And neither am I, or Jack, or —"

"Okay!" Jamie held his hands up to stop her from speaking. "But *I* am real, and *you* are real, and Jack *is* real, but Faeries are *not real*."

"Yes they are," Sam stated.

"No they're not," Jamie said adamantly.

Sam laughed. "Why not?"

"Show me the evidence that Faeries are real!" Jamie demanded.

"Show me evidence that they're not."

Jamie looked around him and directed at all of the trees. "Do you see any Faeries?" he asked.

Sam laughed and shook her head. "Not right now I don't."

"Well then," he said with a satisfactory grin. "How can you say they're real when you can't even see them?"

"Do you believe in God?" she asked.

Jamie got a half confused, half surprised look on his face. She had caught him off guard with the question. "Yes . . . maybe . . . I'm not sure. I used to, but . . . anyway, that's different. That's a matter of belief."

Sam smirked at his naivety. "Everything is a matter of belief, Jamie. You fall asleep every night without fear because you *believe* you'll wake up the next morning. You drive when the traffic lights go green because you *believe* that means it's safe. You lock all of the doors every time you leave the house because you *believe* if you don't you'll get burglarised. But just because you believe all of that, does it mean that you will wake up every morning? Or that you won't crash your car? Or your house won't get broken into?"

"Well, no, but—"

Sam interrupted, "So does that mean that Faeries aren't real, just because you believe they're not?"

"Yes," Jamie said in an 'I know everything' matter-of-fact tone.

Sam laughed and shook her head. "Well Faeries are real. And I don't *believe* that, I *know* that. And I'll prove it . . . when we get to Tír na nÓg."

CHAPTER 41

They made their way through the woods until Sam found the fallen tree she was looking for.

Sam stood on the fallen log, she stretched out with her arms so that each was resting on the bark of the trees on either side. Jamie watched her curiously. "Uh, Sam . . . "

"What?" she asked without turning back to look at him.

"What are you doing?"

Sam rolled her eyes.

The fact that Jamie was a Vampire, yet knew nothing about the supernatural could be very frustrating. Especially when he questioned *everything* she did or said. "Opening the portal," she informed him as if the answer had been obvious. Which it would have been, if he knew *anything*.

Sam reached up, keeping her hands on the trees until she felt the pinprick on each of her index fingers. A drop of blood from each hand was pulled from her wounds and sucked into the bark of the ancient trees.

She jumped backwards off the log, a pile of dead leaves crunched beneath her feet; she watched the air between the trees shimmer slightly, a cool breeze flowing through it. She took a few steps backwards so she was standing next to Jamie, who was rooted to the spot, watching the space where she had been intently. "I don't see anything," he said after a moment.

"That's because you have to go through it."

Jamie pointed ahead. "Through there?"

She nodded her head. "I used my blood to open it, so it will close when I go through. *You* have to go first."

Jamie looked at her as if she were crazy. Then he hesitantly walked towards the trees, stepped onto the fallen log and disappeared before he reached the other side.

Sam followed quickly, knowing that if she waited too long Jamie would get so scared he'd probably cry like a small girl. Which was what she assumed he did when she wasn't around, and what he had probably spent the last two centuries doing.

As Sam stepped onto the green grass, she felt the portal shut behind her. Her energy feeling more drained than it should have been by the time she got to the other side. She let out her breath slowly, closing her eyes as she attempted to regain some of her lost strength.

"Where are we?" Jamie asked. When she opened her eyes to look at him she saw that his expression was filled with bewilderment, amazement and wonder, with the slightest tinge of fear.

Sam brushed past him, walking forward confidently despite the fact that her legs felt weak. "We're in Tír na nÓg, stupid."

CHAPTER 42

*J*amie stood on the greenest grass he'd ever seen and gazed out at what Sam had referred to as *'Tír na nÓg'*. It seemed like a suitable name, considering that it looked like some place out of a children's fairytale.

Green fields that appeared to stretch for miles were filled with a rainbow of plants that Jamie had never seen before. Large, ancient trees stretched out into the forest behind him. The sky was a twilight blue, with streaks of green and pink and even a vanilla colour.

Jamie felt something nudge at the back of his knees, his stomach filled with an overwhelming feeling of apprehension. He turned and looked down . . . behind him there was what looked like a black panther sniffing at his legs. "Sam," he whispered in panic. "What do I do?" he asked, his body rigid, too scared to move in case it lead to the panther trying to maul him or Sam.

She laughed a little. "Relax," she said calmly. "It's just a Cat

Sídh. It's making sure you're not human, or a threat."

Jamie looked down at the thing Sam had called a cat in disbelief. *That* was definitely not a cat. Cats were small, and that . . . *thing* wasn't. Another one padded through the trees behind Jamie and over to Sam. He let a hiss to try scare it off but all that accomplished was a smile of amusement from Sam. The 'cat' sat down beside her, nudging its head against her hand. Sam scratched its ears, and the cat let out a purr.

The other cat was still sniffing around Jamie's feet. After a few seconds it finally moved away and Jamie heard a deep, melodic voice say, "*Vaimpír.*"

Jamie felt his eyes grow wide and he turned around to stare at the animal. "Did that cat just talk?"

Sam laughed. "Come on." She grabbed Jamie by the sleeve of his jacket and pulled him away from the trees and the talking cats. He looked over his shoulder to see both of the animals retreating back into the woods.

They were talking to each other.

As if that was a regular thing for giant cats to do.

Jamie looked to Sam. "It talked."

She rolled her eyes and let go of his sleeve. "It's a Cat Sídh," she repeated, as if that explained everything.

"Cats don't talk."

Sam shook her head. "No," she said. "It's a Cat *Sídh*. A Faerie cat. They guard the entrance to Tír na nÓg, they're Faeries."

Jamie checked behind him again. The cats were gone. "They look like panthers," he said. "I thought Faeries had wings, and were three inches tall."

Sam gave him a smirk. "I thought you said Faeries weren't real."

Jamie pretended he didn't hear her.

They walked through an open patch of green field that was growing too many flowers for this time of autumn. Strange looking human shaped creatures and animals wandered around in the distance.

"Maybe I was wrong," he said reluctantly. It was difficult to argue the non-existence of creatures that were walking around right in front of him. "Sam?"

"What?" she asked without looking at him.

"What did that cat say?"

"Vaimpír," she said with a laugh. "It was identifying your species."

"Oh." They walked through the grass, which Jamie thought was slightly longer than it should have been. But who was he to dictate how the Faeries should maintain their fields? They were supposedly nature spirits after all.

"So, why are we in Tír na nÓg?" he asked, as they came near to what he could only describe as an ancient rural village.

Or at least, it looked like what he would imagine an ancient rural village to look like.

"I come here every month to restock my shelves," Sam answered.

"Restock your shelves of what?" Jamie asked.

She gave him a look, suggesting that he should know the answer to that. When Jamie didn't respond she rolled her eyes and said, "Herbs and plants and candles and gems and potions . . . you know, stuff that *usually* goes on shelves."

Jamie couldn't help laughing at that. "Who's shelves?" he asked, wondering if she actually believed that she had listed the kind of stuff that regular humans kept in their homes.

"Mine," Sam said with a coy smile.

Jamie watched with childlike fascination as what he could only describe as a Tinker Bell type Faerie flew past. It was like a three inch tall strangely shaped firefly. Jamie reached out to touch it, but Sam grabbed his arm before he could.

"Insects," she said. "Their bites are poison."

Jamie let his arm fall back down to his side, and just watched the Faerie insect as it flew by. That was when he noticed they were being followed.

CHAPTER 43

$\mathcal{S}$am . . ."

"What?" she asked without looking in his direction.

"There are two girls following us," he whispered staring straight ahead, acting as if he hadn't said a thing. "And one of them looks just like you."

Sam stopped walking; her heart skipped a beat. She took a breath and looked over her shoulder, already knowing what she would see.

A thin girl with silver hair, deathly pale skin and large dark eyes.

A Ban Sídh.

And beside her was a ghost, shedding silent tears as she looked at Sam with a face that was identical to her own.

A Feit.

Shit, Sam thought with an internal sigh, suddenly aware of how weak she felt as her eyes set upon the melancholic faces of the death fey.

"How long?" Sam asked. The Ban Sídh shook her head, refusing to answer as Sam knew she would. With a sigh, she nodded and turned back to Jamie, who was watching her intently. "It's okay, they won't hurt either of us."

"But—" Jamie tried to protest.

"It's *fine*."

Jamie looked at her, uncertainty written clearly on his face, then he sighed and nodded resignedly. They moved out of the grass and onto the cobblestoned streets of the marketplace.

"That's where we're going." Sam pointed to the store at the end of the road, where a boy with violet hair and green eyes sat holding a mandolin in his lap. He had the appearance of a sixteen year old, but Sam knew that he was actually more like a hundred.

Cayden smiled as Sam approached. He started strumming his mandolin, momentarily glancing at Jamie beside her. "Do I need to make changes to my ballad?" he asked Sam. "Do I need to make it more upbeat since the last time I saw you?"

She suppressed a grin and rolled her eyes. "Not now Cayden." Sam pushed the store door open and walked inside with Jamie close behind her.

"Who's that?" he asked, peering out the window at Cayden, who was still strumming his mandolin.

"That's Cayden."

Sam turned swiftly to look at whoever had spoken.

"He sits there all the time and makes songs about the people he sees," said the small girl as she looked from Jamie to Sam and back again.

Sam eyed the girl warily; she had been coming to this store once a month for the past three years and had *never* seen her before.

Not even once.

Which was weird because most of the people who came here

did so on a regular basis.

Unless of course they were a new recruit to the world of Faerie.

The girl held an empty glass jar, turning it around in her hands as she stared inside it. Her skin was white as snow, she was paler than anyone Sam had ever seen in her life, including Jamie, and much like snow her skin appeared to have an unearthly shimmer. Almost as though whatever Power the girl possessed lived within every cell of her being. Her hair was pale pink, though Sam doubted it was her natural colour. Judging by the tone of her skin and the luminous reddish-purple shade of her eyes, Sam guessed that the girl's natural hair was probably the same shade as her skin.

The girl's eyes creased around the corners in a smile as she watched Sam assess her.

Sam didn't smile back.

There was something *wrong* about this girl. By the look of her it was obvious that she wasn't human. Sam could practically see the Magic leaking from her. But her senses picked up no traces of it.

Meaning that this girl had the ability to shield herself from Sam.

Which *no one* should have the Power to do.

Sam looked over the girl's body. Assessing the threat level. She was pretty small, barely five feet. And she was young. Perhaps thirteen, maybe fourteen. Her species of origin wasn't obvious by her appearance, though she did have some form of markings on her face. One across her forehead, just around the area of her third eye and two identical markings under each eye. Sam had never seen marks like those before, but she was sure they probably meant something important.

Her left hand was wrapped up in a bandage that looked like it hadn't been changed in years. It was torn and had both red and black stains on it.

"Poison," the girl said when she noticed Sam looking at it. Sam looked the girl in the eyes. She was smiling in a friendly manner, which just made Sam feel uneasy. *Something is seriously off.* "My blood is poisoned," continued the girl, "it makes it turn black."

"Will it kill you?" Jamie asked. Sam jumped slightly at the sound of his voice. In all the time she'd spent looking at the girl she had forgotten there was anyone else in the room.

"Eventually," the girl said conversationally, turning her head to the side to look at Jamie. Assessing him the same way Sam had been assessing her.

Sam stepped in front of her gaze, taking her attention away from him. If this girl was a Faerie, Sam didn't want her to pay that much attention to Jamie. He wouldn't last here. And if she wasn't a Faerie, she still didn't want her to pay *that* much attention to him. He probably wouldn't last anywhere on his own.

The girl gazed at Sam and smiled as if she knew something that Sam didn't. She placed the jar down on the countertop. "But everyone dies eventually."

"My blood can heal," Jamie said and held his arm out to the girl. "You can take some if it will help."

The girl smiled. "Thank you Jamie," she said. Sam looked at her in surprise. *He never introduced himself.* "But I'm afraid I'm immune to Vampire blood. It won't help."

"How did you know my name?" Jamie asked, allowing his arm to fall back to his side.

"'Cause I know everything," the girl said as if it were obvious. She walked past Sam and tugged on Jamie's arm to make him lean forward. Sam turned and watched as the girl stood on the tips of her toes and whispered something to him. She couldn't hear what was being said, but halfway through whatever it was Jamie looked up at Sam. And spent the rest of the time the girl was whispering staring at her.

The girl finished speaking and slipped something into Jamie's hand before she stepped away. She smiled at Sam, as Jamie put whatever she had slipped him into his pocket. "Bridget's back," she said. "You can get your things now."

"What did you say to him?" Sam asked accusingly, taking a step towards her.

The girl just smiled and walked to the door.

"Effie?"

Sam turned at the sound of the voice to see Bridget behind the counter. "Did you find what you were looking for?"

"Yes," she said quietly, with a barely noticeable glance towards Jamie. "I did."

Sam watched as the girl walked out of the store. Then she turned to Bridget.

"Who's that?" she asked as if Bridget was in on some kind of conspiracy with that girl. Though couldn't help being paranoid; that girl was creepy and Bridget knew her.

"That was Effie," Bridget said, as if that was all the explaining that needed to be done.

"And *who* is Effie?" Sam asked. "*What* is she?"

Bridget took a moment to think, then frowned. "You know . . . I'm not sure. I never really thought to ask."

Sam sighed and closed her eyes, wondering what that girl had said to Jamie.

She turned her head to look in his direction. He was staring at Bridget unabashedly, his eyes wide. *He must be having a system overload with all the things he's seen today.*

Jamie always seemed to have a hard time coming to terms with anything that didn't appear normal. He'd either deny the existence of anything that was inhuman, or, when he had been proven to be wrong in his denial, stand there and stare open-mouthed in a state of shock.

She could understand why Jamie appeared freaked out by Bridget. She still looked more humanesque than most other Faeries, but her skin had taken on a pale green glow as had her once chestnut coloured hair. Which gave her an aura of pure undiluted unearthliness. She would be a shock to anyone's system if they weren't used to seeing things like that.

"The usual," she said, turning her attention back to Bridget.

Bridget smiled and started gathering Sam's usual items.

Jamie looked away from Bridget and turned to gaze at Cayden through the window. "Um . . . so, why was he asking you about his ballad?"

Sam sighed. "He writes songs about everyone, and there's one about me too."

"Oh."

"Here you are," Bridget said, and placed a paper bag on the countertop.

"Thanks." Sam took the bag and squished it into her backpack.

Bridget removed a glass jar from the shelf behind her, twisted the lid off and placed it on the table. Sam positioned her hand over the jar and projected some energy waves into it. She took her hand away when the energy inside turned a shade of lightning blue. Bridget put the lid back on, trapping the Magic inside, and replaced it on the shelf.

"See you next month," she said with a smile.

"Bye." Sam roughly pushed Jamie out the door in front of her and walked out behind him.

"What was that?" Jamie asked. "Don't you have to pay?"

Sam smiled. "I did," she replied. "They have no use for money here, things are paid for with Magic or bodily fluids or favours. I choose to pay with Magic."

Jamie didn't say anything in response. He was too busy

watching Cayden.

Cayden smiled at Jamie before he turned his attention back to his mandolin and started singing.

"Her heart was filled with sadness – "

Sam grabbed onto Jamie's arm and pulled him back towards the woods, where the portal was. She could still hear Cayden singing as she walked, with Jamie trailing along beside her. His melodic voice sounded through the streets.

"Yet tears would never flow
Her eyes that shone like sapphires
Were filled with wisdom's glow
Childish thoughts of laughter
With time hath fade to dust
Come gather 'round me passers-by
For listen now you must
The worlds lay on her shoulders
Such a burden for one to bear
Come listen to the ballad
Of the girl with golden hair – "

CHAPTER 44

I wanted to hear the rest of the song," Jamie whined as they reached the other side of the portal. "What does it go like?" he asked with a smile.

Sam sighed irritably. "I don't know."

That was a lie, she knew what the rest of it went like.

The whole of Tír na nÓg knew what the rest of that fucking song went like.

But that doesn't mean he *has to know,* she thought to herself.

"How could you not know?" Jamie asked doubtfully. "Surely he would have told you . . . did he not have to ask you questions about yourself to write a ballad about you? Or was it just an observational song?"

Sam hadn't really told Cayden anything. She met him on her first trip to the Faerie markets—well, not so much met as she did look at him.

But that was all it took, one look into her eyes and he knew everything about her. Of course Sam hadn't realised that until a minute later when he started strumming his mandolin and singing that ballad.

That was when she found out that Cayden had the unique ability to view a person's past. One look into their eyes and he could see everything that had ever happened in their life. If Sam had known that she never would have made eye contact. She hated that he could know so much about her without her saying a word, and the fact that he wrote a song about her only made it worse.

"I didn't tell him anything." Jamie looked as though he was about to say something else. "Have you ever been to the cliffs?" Sam asked, quickly changing the subject before he could ask anything else about Cayden's song.

Jamie looked away for a moment as he thought. " . . . I don't think so."

Sam pointed ahead, and walked in that direction. "They're right down here," she stated. "I usually walk along them on the way back from the market."

"That sounds awfully dangerous," Jamie said nervously.

"It would be kinda funny," Sam laughed as she spoke, "if I died from falling off a cliff." Jamie's head snapped around in her direction. He looked at her seriously, his expression one-hundred percent unamused. *I'd find it funny,* Sam thought with an internal sigh. "Just because of all the attacks and stuff," she clarified. Jamie's serious expression softened slightly. "It would be funny if I ended up dying a human death."

"Can't you just make yourself immortal?" he asked. "I saw the spell, so you could if you wanted, right? And that way you wouldn't have to die at all."

"I could," Sam said, as she looked towards the parting in the trees ahead, " . . . but I don't think I'd like living for an eternity."

Jamie stepped into the clearing first and Sam came in behind him. This was one of her favourite places. Just standing there made her feel at peace.

The grass was overgrown and wild plants grew haphazardly around the field, some of which dangled over the cliff's edge. In front of her stretched a beautifully endless ocean. "Every time I stand here I feel like I'm at the edge of the world," Sam said quietly, so as not to disturb the peace.

"I can see why," Jamie said as he looked around. "This place is nice."

Sam smiled. "Not dangerous then?"

"Well, yes, it is. But only if you step too close to the edge . . . or get bitten by a rat."

Sam looked at him sharply. "There are no rats here!"

She saw him trying to suppress his smile. "There's a couple right over there," he said, pointing at the long grass to the right of Sam. "I can hear them."

Sam looked to where Jamie was indicating. "I didn't need to know that!" she said and Jamie laughed. *He ruins everything I like,* she thought with a sulk.

"Sam?" Jamie spoke when his laughter had died down. She turned towards him; he had been eyeing her nervously, averting his gaze when she made eye contact. "You know a lot about all things supernatural, right?" he asked, chewing his lower lip.

Sam nodded. "That I do."

"So, then, you know a lot about Vampires too?"

She smiled, pretty sure she knew where he was going with this. "Yes."

Jamie ran his hand through his hair and gazed at her expectantly. "I know that you said I could go see Aleczander sometime soon and he'd tell me all the stuff I need to know, but, well, that's just gonna be a while because he's so busy with all of his kingly duties . . . so, I was wondering, could you do it?"

Sam raised an eyebrow. "You want *me* to give you a lesson on Vampires?" Jamie nodded. She laughed a little. "Sure, I suppose I could do that."

Jamie beamed. "Great."

Sam stared straight ahead and chewed her lip. She cast a glance in Jamie's direction and saw that he was looking over the edge at the ocean. Sam let a sigh. "So . . . what did that creepy girl say to you?"

Jamie looked at Sam, the corner of his mouth twitched up in a smile. "Why do you ask?"

"'Cause I'm curious," she said with her most uncaring expression. Which only seemed to add to Jamie's amusement.

"Are you *sure* that's why?" he asked, taking a step towards her. "Are you sure you're not jealous that a pretty girl was talking to me?"

Sam rolled her eyes. "Get over yourself!" she snapped and folded her arms across her chest. *She wasn't that pretty.* "I was just curious to know what was so secret that I wasn't allowed to hear it. *And* I know she said something about me 'cause you looked at me when she was talking."

Jamie just smiled more. "I'm not gonna tell you what she said."

"Well, what did she give you?" she asked with a glance towards his pocket.

He shook his head. "That's also private."

Sam scoffed and turned around, marching towards her house with Jamie following behind her, giggling to himself like an idiot.

CHAPTER 45

$\mathcal{S}$am got up off the couch at the sound of the bell and walked to the front door, expecting to find Jamie on the other side. She felt her expression turn to a frown when instead she found a relatively tall girl with dark skin, shiny black hair and green eyes smiling at her.

Jade raised an eyebrow. "Expecting someone else?" she asked with a knowing smile.

"Maybe." Sam looked Jade up and down, from the gold gladiator sandals on her feet to the gold jewels in her hair. "Or maybe I just wasn't expecting to open the door to Cleopatra."

Jade laughed and stepped inside, shutting the door behind her. "Where's your costume?" she asked as she looked at Sam's outfit disapprovingly.

"I'm dressed as a human," Sam said with a smile as she looked down at her jeans, then back at Jade. "Can't you tell?"

Jade rolled her eyes. "Very funny." She grabbed onto Sam's wrist and marched through the hall, pulling her upstairs. "I *knew* you'd try to get out of it."

"Get out of what?" Sam asked innocently.

"You know wh—" Jade was cut off by the chiming of the doorbell. She frowned as she looked at the door. "Whoever it is won't get you out of this."

Sam stayed on the landing at the top of the staircase while Jade went downstairs and flung the door open.

"Nice try Sam!" Jade called when she saw Jamie standing on the threshold. She threw the plastic bag she had brought with her up to Sam, who leaned forward and caught it with one hand. "Go put that on!"

"What?" Sam opened the bag and looked inside to find a black dress and a Witch's hat. "You brought me a costume?" She gave Jade her most unimpressed look.

Jade just smiled. "I already told you. There's *nothing* that will get you out of going. Now go and dress up."

"Get her out of going to what?" Jamie asked Jade, then looked at Sam. "I thought we had plans."

"We do," Sam stated. "I promised—"

"I don't care!" Jade interrupted, then turned to Jamie and said, "We're going to a Halloween party ... You're coming with us."

"I am?" Jamie sounded surprised. He looked towards Sam. "You mean I'm actually *invited* to be seen in public with you?"

Sam frowned, knowing that, at this point, there was nothing she could do or say that would get her out of having to go out tonight. She stormed off to her room with the bag swinging in her hand.

"That means yes," she heard Jade say as the front door closed.

CHAPTER 46

I'm Jade," Cleopatra informed Jamie as he followed her up the stairs. "You must be Jamie."

"You know my name?" he asked in surprise. Jade laughed. "It's just, um . . . does that mean that Sam talked about me?"

Jade nodded in reply and knocked on one of the bedroom doors. "We're coming in, so you better have clothes on!"

"I'm in the bathroom!" Sam yelled just as Jade opened the door to the room. Jamie took a hesitant step inside. *This is Sam's actual bedroom,* he thought as he looked around, memorising every detail, from the cream carpet to the purple walls. *I'm in her bedroom!*

Jamie carefully seated himself on the edge of Sam's bed. "So what're you dressing up as?" Jade asked.

"What? I have to dress up for this party?"

"Yeah." Jade nodded. "It *is* a costume party. Do you think I dress like this every day?" Jamie laughed and shook his head. "I'm sure I can find you a costume somewhere."

The door to Sam's bathroom opened and she walked out. Jamie could do nothing but stare. She held her arms out to the side and slowly twirled around, the end of her dress moving with her. Jamie studied her outfit; she was wearing tights with silver spider webs on them, a black long sleeved dress that stopped about eight inches above her knees and a Witch's hat to pull the outfit together.

She stopped twirling and glared at Jade. "Happy now?"

Jade smiled widely. "*Ecstatic.*" Sam pressed her lips together tightly, looking as though she was trying to repress a smile and shook her head. "What about Dracula?" Jamie hadn't realised that Jade was speaking to him until Sam looked at him expectantly.

"What?" Jamie asked and looked at Jade.

"Dracula," she stated. "What about him?"

"I can't be Dracula," he said with an amused smile. "I don't have any Vampire fangs."

"Hmmmmm . . . " Jade pursed her lips and looked at Jamie thoughtfully. "Smile for me." He did as commanded and grinned, flashing all of his teeth. His canines were longer than the average human's, but in their current state they weren't long enough to pass as Vampire fangs.

He was safe.

Jade moved towards him, and before he had any time to make sense of what she was doing or react, she pressed down on his gums with her thumb.

Forcing his canines to extend to their true size.

He heard Sam snort as she tried to suppress her laugher.

Jamie's eyes grew wide. He slapped Jade's hand away and covered his mouth with his hand. "What the hell?" he asked in a muffled voice.

"What?" Jade asked innocently, blinking her eyes as if she hadn't done anything wrong. "You said you needed Vampire fangs and now you have some."

Jamie looked to Sam for an explanation. "Did you *tell* her?" It wasn't as though he had confessed his secrets to Sam, but she knew, so he had expected her to keep his secrets exactly that.

Secret.

Especially from humans.

Sam rolled her eyes. "I didn't need to," she explained. "Her mother leads the local Witches coven. They knew about you before I did."

Jamie felt himself relax slightly at that. "Oh," he said simply, not overreacting to the word Witches; after a few months of listening to Sam talk about a variety of magical and mythical beings, he found it easier to accept things like 'Witch' being thrown into everyday conversation. Even so, it still freaked him out slightly that *they* knew of him before he knew of *them*. It hardly seemed fair that they should be aware of his existence, yet leave him thinking he was alone amongst humans.

Jade scoffed. "More like leader of the local bitches coven." She giggled at her own joke. Sam rolled her eyes and shook her head. Jade turned her attention back to Jamie. "So, are you going as Dracula or not?"

Jamie gave her a look implying that the answer was obvious. " . . . *Not.*"

He wouldn't have minded dressing as Dracula, but after Jade forced his fangs out he felt slightly violated, and was no longer in the mood to play dress up for her amusement.

Jade sighed impatiently. "Then what are you going as? And don't say 'Human' because Sam already tried that one and it didn't fly."

"Do I *have* to dress up?" he asked, his voice coming out more whiney than he'd intended.

"*YES!*" she replied aggressively. "It's a *costume* party. That means you *have* to dress up. What is *with* the two of you? First

Sam didn't want to dress up, and now you! Do neither of you enjoy having fun?"

Jamie tried not to laugh. "I enjoy having fun," he said. "I just don't enjoy looking ridiculous while doing it."

Jade raised an eyebrow. "*Ridiculous?*" She placed her hands on her hips. "Are you saying *I* look ridiculous?"

He shook his head quickly. "No, I—"

"Are you saying *Sam* looks ridiculous?" Jade interrupted.

"Sam feels ridiculous," Sam interjected.

"Shhhhhhhh!" Jade ordered.

Jamie took a breath. "That's not what I'm saying," he stated calmly. "You look great," he said to Jade, then looked at Sam. "And Sam looks . . . um . . . she looks . . . " He glanced at Jade questioningly when he heard her repress a laugh.

Jade turned to Sam and sang, "I think someone *likes* you."

Jamie looked at Sam to see what her reaction was. She was watching the door like it was the most interesting thing she had ever seen. The light rose-coloured flush of her cheeks was the only visible response to that statement. "Danny might have some Halloween stuff in his closet," she mumbled as she walked out of the room.

"Who's Danny?" Jamie asked curiously.

Jade looked at him as if he should know the answer to that. "Sam's brother," she said. "Duh."

Jamie had forgotten that Sam had a brother. Which wasn't surprising considering that she never said a word about him. "He's in the army, right?" Jade nodded. "How come Sam never talks about him?"

"Because Sam doesn't like to," Sam said as she walked into her room carrying some clothes hangers with costumes on them.

"Oh, I'm sor—"

"Just drop it." She placed the costumes out on her bed for

Jamie to sift through. "You can wear one of those. Change in the bathroom, and then we can all get this over with."

CHAPTER 47

*J*ade knocked on the door. "Smile," she hissed at Sam.

Sam grinned widely, showing all of her teeth. "How's this?" she asked through them. Jade elbowed her in the ribs. Sam laughed.

Jamie sighed beside her and looked down at the torn and fake blood stained clothes he wore . . . after spending forever searching through some of Danny's costume choices he'd decided to dress as a zombie. "I feel ridiculous."

"Stop complaining!" Jade ordered, just as the door swung open, allowing the music that was blaring inside to spill out into the streets.

"Hi guys." Madison, dressed as Little Red Riding Hood, smiled and stepped aside to let them pass. "Come on in." Jade walked in first, followed by Jamie. Sam hesitated before stepping inside.

The air within the house felt cold and heavy. Like a dark mist was infecting the building.

Something was wrong.

"I'm glad you could make it." Madison placed her arm around Sam to lead her inside.

She shied away from her touch. "Me too," she lied, forcing a smile to make it convincing.

Jade gave her a questioning look. Sam's hands started shaking. *Something is* very *wrong here,* she thought and tried her best to project that thought to Jade with her eyes.

Jade smiled and shook her head. "You're fine," she said dismissively. "Go get a drink and calm down."

Sam looked at Jamie, who was watching her intently. *His senses are more fine-tuned than Jade's, maybe he feels it too.*

<*Can you hear me?*> Sam projected to him. Jamie nodded, his eyes never breaking contact with hers. <*Jamie, there's something evil in this house*>

Jamie's eyes widened as he looked around the room. His hands clenched into fists at his sides. <*Do you know where?*> he asked.

<*No*> Sam replied as she smiled at Madison and pretended to be listening to whatever she was babbling on about. <*But I can sense Power in this house, and not the good kind*>

Sam steadied her shaking hands. She knew there was a threat, there was no need for her hands to still be shaking. She had dealt with threats before. She always survived. *It's everyone else who dies.*

Sam looked around the open space. There were people everywhere. Standing around in groups or sitting on the couches that Madison had moved to the room on one side of the staircase to clear out space for dancing on the other. *Would they really attack with this many people around?*

She concentrated on the people in the rooms that she could see, attempting to separate their auras so she was no longer surrounded by one massive pulse of human energy. If she could separate them, then maybe she could single out the source of her discomfort.

Sam took a breath to calm herself. "I think I need a drink."

"I'll get you one," Jamie volunteered. "Anything specific?"

She shook her head. "I don't mind. Surprise me."

He gestured to the others. "Anyone else want a drink?"

Madison held her cup up for Jamie to see, indicating that she already had one. "I'll go with you," Jade said with a smile. "I know where she hides the good stuff."

Madison laughed. "Stay away from my parents' liquor. They know what's there and I am not getting in trouble because of you."

Jade laughed before walking away with Jamie, who glanced over his shoulder at Sam. *<You'll be alright?>*

<I'll be fine> she assured him, even though she didn't feel so sure. He looked away and continued making his way towards the kitchen.

"Come meet my date!" Madison grabbed onto Sam's arm and pulled her through the crowd of people to the corner of the room, where a tall man with broad shoulders and dark hair stood on his own, looking at the people around him as if their presence made him uneasy. Madison latched onto his arm, he looked down at her and smiled in amusement. "This is my friend Sam," Madison said and directed to her. The man turned his head to study her.

She froze when she saw his face but tried to keep a mask of indifference covering her expression. *Where have I seen him before?* she thought as she frantically searched through her memories to try place his face. "Sam, this is Malachi. *He* thinks it's funny to come to a costume party in normal clothes and claim he's dressed as a human."

"Hello Sam." He looked her directly in the eyes, his

expression making it appear as though he was placing a dare before her.

Sam simply looked at him for a moment. "Have we met before?" she asked.

He smiled widely. *So the answer is yes then.* "I don't know . . . have we?"

Sam took a step away from him as her brain went back to her childhood. More specifically, when she was twelve. "I know you," she snarled. "You tried to kill me!"

Malachi's brows pinched together, he looked genuinely confused. "*Sam!*" Madison looked shocked. Sam took another step away, not wanting to get too close to him in case he tried anything.

She concentrated on his energy. It wasn't human. *He* wasn't human, he was a Warlock. And from the amount of Power that rolled off him, she could tell that he was quite a powerful one. But . . . no matter how hard she pressed at his energy, or how hard she tried to make it fit, he wasn't the source of her discomfort. He wasn't the entity that tainted the house.

But it had to be him, who else *could* it be?

Malachi slipped his arm out of Madison's grasp. "Perhaps it would be best for me to leave."

"No, don't go." Madison shot Sam an angry glare. "Sam *apologise!*"

"No," Sam said simply, without taking her eyes away from Malachi. "I also think it would be best for him to leave."

Malachi smiled. "Thanks for the invite," he said to Madison. "Be seeing you." Sam watched as he pushed his way through the crowd towards the front door. He stood in the doorway for a moment, and glanced at Sam before stepping outside.

He left the door open.

Leaving her a clear invitation to join him.

"What's your deal!"

Sam ignored Madison, instead she pushed her way through the crowd of partygoers, moving towards the front door. *<I'm going out for air>* She sent the message to Jamie so that he and Jade wouldn't come looking for her. *<I'll be back inside soon>*

"Oh, Sam!" She stopped moving for just a moment to see Scott coming up behind her.

"Sorry Scott." She started walking backwards to the door, in her peripheral vision seeing Elliot at the top of the staircase, sitting on the landing with a drink in his hand, smiling at the people below as if he were watching a mildly entertaining show. "I *really* have to go," she said to Scott, turning away from him and everyone inside.

"No, but . . . wait!"

Sam blocked him out as she walked outside, slamming the door behind her. She hurried down the driveway to the street. Malachi was a few feet away from her, his hands in his jean pockets.

"Why can't any of you just leave me alone!" Sam threw a blast of energy at Malachi that flung him several feet before he crashed heavily to the ground.

She stayed where she was and watched as he slowly pushed himself to his feet, laughing as if she hadn't just attacked him.

"Come on Sam," he said, wiping blood from his lip. "I know you can hit harder than that. And so can I, but if I had come here to hurt you don't you think I would have already?"

Sam shook her head. "I *know* you're one of *them*."

"You know me then?" Sam nodded. He smiled and shook his head. "I don't think you do."

"Yes I do!" Sam screamed as she clenched her unsteady hands into fists.

Why won't they stop shaking?

"Would you like to know a secret?" he asked, taking a few steps towards her and leaned in to fill the rest of the space between them. Sam didn't flinch, instead she stood her ground. *One wrong move*, she thought, *one wrong move and he's dead.* "If it wasn't for me," he whispered, "you'd be dead by now."

Liar! her head screamed.

Sam hit him with all the energy she could manage, which only threw him about ten feet away from her. Her hands started shaking harder.

I should have been able to kill him.

Malachi stood up and looked at her curiously. "You're getting weaker?" Sam opened her mouth to deny it, but Malachi shook his head. "*I* don't want to fight you, especially not like this . . . but others will." He turned his back to her and walked away.

Sam stood there helplessly, not knowing what else she could do.

My Magic never fails.

The streets filled with loud music. Sam turned her attention to the door to Madison's house, where she saw Jamie rushing towards her with Jade following close behind. "What happened?" Jade asked. "Jamie got a distress call."

Sam looked at Jamie, who was staring at her in bewilderment. "I never sent you any call."

"You did," Jamie insisted, as he looked around the street, his eyes frantic as they strained to find a threat. "I felt it. You sent out a distress call."

Sam looked around her, but Malachi was nowhere to be seen; the use of a portal would be the only way he could have disappeared so quickly, but she hadn't sensed one opening, which only added to her distress.

"Sam," Jade said, as she placed her hand above her lip. "Your nose."

Sam wiped under her nose with the back of her hand, then stared at the blood which now stained her skin. "Remember on your birthday when Jack gave you a spell to say?" Sam nodded as she looked at Jade without actually seeing her. She couldn't make her eyes stay focused. "You didn't say it, did you?"

Sam shook her head. "I can't stop shaking." She looked at her hands . . . then at Jade . . . before her eyes finally met with Jamie's. "What's wrong with me?"

CHAPTER 48

$\mathcal{T}$hey left the party pretty quickly after arriving. After her encounter with Malachi, Sam didn't feel in much of a party mood.

Her Magic had been getting steadily weaker over the past few weeks, that was something she wasn't in denial about.

She knew that it was happening.

She knew how to stop it.

And yet, in spite of that knowledge she did nothing.

Jamie walked them to Sam's house and offered to stay. But Sam sent him home. He was the last person she wanted to be around right now, because she knew what he'd say to her when he discovered what the problem was. So she managed to convince him that she was tired and just needed to rest.

In the end, he only left when Jade assured him that she'd stay with Sam and ensure that she was well taken care of.

The only issue then, was that Jade refused to leave.

Sam threw herself down on her bed, face first, and groaned

silently into her pillows.

Jade stepped into the room and shut the door behind her, taking a seat on Sam's bed.

"What the fuck is wrong with me?" Sam asked, her voice muffled by the pillows.

Jade let a sigh. "Where do you want me to start?"

Sam turned herself around so that she could see Jade's face. Jade just watched her, one perfectly shaped eyebrow raised, her lips forming a half smile as she watched Sam, all knowing and disapproving.

With a sigh Sam pushed herself upright.

"Okay," Jade said, moving further onto the bed so that she could get herself in a more comfortable position. "Let's play what the fuck is wrong with Sam . . .

"I think a good place to start is that your life is pretty shitty, what with all those crazy people wanting you dead."

Sam nodded her head. "Always a good place to start."

"So those crazy people do bad things to you and the people around you, and instead of blaming them you blame yourself. And because you blame yourself, you think that you need to be punished. So you punish yourself, by making your own life more difficult than it has to be. You have the Power to fight, so do it. Simple as."

Somewhere inside her Sam knew that Jade's words made sense. But there were other voices within her mind that spoke louder than Jade's reason. Sam rubbed her eyes, smudging her make-up all over her face. "I just want it to be over."

"Sam, listen, I'm your friend and I care about you. But if you don't cut the crap I *will* hit you."

Sam rolled her eyes.

"Seriously," Jade placed her hand on Sam's, "everyone goes through dark times. Ending yourself is never the best way to make the bad things end. You have to fight through all of the crap, because the only way to win against the inside monsters is to get through to the other side. Don't let them win, you're better than that."

There was a long moment after Jade had stopped speaking in which there was nothing but silence. Sam just thought back to when Jack had given her an immortality spell and told her that if she didn't say it before the end of the year that she'd lose her Powers.

That was all he'd said to her, because he didn't need to tell Sam what would happen to her if she lost her Powers completely. As Sam was born with Magic, her body wasn't one that could survive being human.

Jade let a sigh. "I'm not going to tell you to say the spell, but I do think you're being stupid by refusing to . . . I mean, if you die, I'll have to make new friends. And Jamie, he'll have to find a whole new girl to stalk . . . "

Sam laughed a little. Jade smiled. "I think I might be the only other girl he knows in town. So I need you to stay alive, because if you die, I think I might be next. Just saying . . . he *did* say I look great."

Jade kicked off her sandals and lay down on one of Sam's pillows. "I hope you're being nice to him, because I think he *likes* you."

Sam rolled her eyes and lay down next to Jade. "Well obviously he likes me, I'm not stupid."

"So have you kissed him yet?"

Sam stared in Jade's direction and laughed as though that was the most ridiculous thing she had ever heard. "I said I knew he liked me, who said I liked him?"

Jade smiled widely, and rolled her eyes. "Oh, *please* . . . he's like the *only* person—apart from me and Jack—who you've willingly hung out with in the past, like, *two* years . . . why would you hang out with him if you didn't *like* him?"

Sam scoffed a little. "I hang out with him because he's ridiculous and I think that if he's left alone he'll probably die. So I'm doing a good deed by keeping him alive."

Jade laughed so hard she almost fell off the bed. "Yeah right, like I'm falling for that one. You totally like him, and I'll be right here to say I told you so when you're finally ready to admit that."

"Whatever, shut up and go to sleep."

CHAPTER 49

 $\mathcal{J}$ amie leaned forward, his eyes still on Sam. She let an irritated sigh; he had been watching her like that for at least four hours.

"So, how come I have no heartbeat then?"

"*Of course* you have a heartbeat you idiot. If you didn't your body wouldn't have the ability to pump all that blood you drink," she stated. Jamie raised a sceptical eyebrow, then placed two fingers from his right hand onto his left wrist. Sam rolled her eyes. "You won't be able to check your pulse the way a human would. A Vampire's heart, on average, only beats once every two minutes, making it virtually undetectable. You could probably hear it if you listened through a stethoscope or something, but you'd have to have the patience to sit there and wait for it to beat."

"Hmmm . . . " Jamie moved his wrist to his ear. "If I stayed like this for five minutes would I hear it?"

She shrugged. "Maybe."

Jamie smiled and let his arm fall to his side. "I'll check it later."

"Any more questions?" Sam asked with a sideways glance towards the window. Outside the sky was completely black. There were no streetlamps anywhere near Jamie's house, which meant that it was *so* dark outside, she couldn't even see how dark it was. When she looked out the window all she could see was a void, a black space of nothing. Meaning it was very late and she should probably go home soon.

"Yeah."

She turned her attention back to Jamie. He was staring at his knee. *First time he's looked at something else since I got here.* Sam smiled internally.

"Are you okay?" he asked, fixing his gaze on her. "I mean, you were in a really bad way the other night and I didn't hear from you at all yesterday and . . . I was really worried. So, are you okay?"

Sam sighed and closed her eyes. She wasn't in the mood for giving explanations. Especially to him, since all she had to do was say a spell to make it better. Jamie would think it was a simple solution, but it was more complicated than he would be able to comprehend.

She opened her eyes and smiled as convincingly as she knew how. "I spent yesterday in bed sleeping, I'm fine now though."

He studied her carefully. She flashed another smile, hoping it would keep him from noticing that she was wearing a glamour to make her look healthy. He sighed in defeat and closed his eyes. "Okay," he said, nodding his head. "But, you know you *can* tell me if there's something wrong?"

A bubble of guilt rose up through her stomach. *Why did he have to say that?* She suppressed the feeling and rolled her eyes.

"I'm *fine*. It was just a bug or something."

"A bug?" Jamie asked in disbelief.

"Yeah, I was sick, I slept it off, and now I'm fine."

"I didn't realise you *could* get sick."

"Of course I can, so can you for that matter." Jamie looked at her curiously, Sam continued, "We may not be human, but that doesn't mean that we can't be afflicted by illnesses. Most of them are the types that can't be caught by humans, so they're illnesses specific to . . . um . . . " Sam searched for the right word, " . . . *supernatural* beings. Most of those illnesses aren't majorly serious or fatal. Some are, but most aren't. And because of our supernatural resilience, we can get over sickness quicker than humans can. But we can still get sick."

Jamie thought for a moment. " . . . I don't think I've ever been sick . . . at least not as a Vampire. Perhaps as a child, though it's so long ago I can't remember."

"Lucky you," Sam said with a smile. "Being sick is not all that fun."

Jamie placed his hand on hers. Sam froze and she stared at it nervously. Her heart skipped a beat. *Shit, he probably heard that.* Sam glanced at his face, expecting him to be wearing a stupid grin, but he didn't seem to have noticed. *Good,* she thought as she looked back at his hand on hers.

He had never held her hand before.

"You're alright *now*, aren't you?" he asked

She looked at him in confusion, he seemed genuinely concerned for her wellbeing. *Why should he care?* she thought as she nodded her head slowly. "Yeah, I'm alright now."

"Good," he said with a smile.

Sam looked towards the window again, then checked her watch. *Twenty-five to ten.* She could see Jamie in the corner of her eye, he was staring at her . . . again. "Anything else?"

He looked at his hand, which was still holding onto hers and chewed his lower lip. Taking his time to think of an answer.

Jamie stayed like that for what felt like forever, occasionally looking at Sam as if he were about to say something, then looking away after deciding against it.

Sam slid her hand out from under his. "I should probably go home now," she said, not wanting to sit around in silence for the whole night. She stood up and stretched her legs, which were numb from sitting cross-legged for so long.

"Oh," Jamie said, seeming disappointed. "Are you sure?" He stood up and looked at her hopefully. "You could stay for a while longer . . . we could watch a film or something?"

Sam stared at Jamie, who was eyeing her with anticipation. "Why?" she asked.

He paused for a moment, confused by her question. "I don't know," he said, running his hand through his hair, messing it up completely. "I just like having you around."

Sam thought about giving him the 'You'd be better off if you kept me away from you' speech, but decided not to. He didn't listen to her warnings when he should have and now that there was a hit out on him it was probably better if he *did* stay near her. *Safety in numbers.*

"Maybe some other time."

She picked her coat up off the back of the couch, and folded it over her arm. She wasn't sure why she had even bothered to bring it. She'd used a portal to get here and was planning to get home the same way. It would be pointless to wear it since she'd only be outside for a minute, two at most. All it was doing was making it so that she had to stay in the awkwardness of having Jamie look at her in silence for longer than she'd like to.

Note to self: when travelling by portal leave the coat at home. "Bye," she said after a moment, turning and moving towards the door.

Barely four steps later; "Sam!" Jamie called her as if he had forgotten something that was urgent.

Before Sam had a chance to speak, or even fully turn around to face him, Jamie had moved towards her faster than she could see, only stopping when he had her back against the front door and his lips pressed to hers.

She could feel Jamie's surprise, which mimicked her own, as without thinking about it she started to kiss him back.

Automatic reaction, she heard the logical part of her brain whisper, *when somebody kisses you, you have a split second to decide whether or not to go with it or push away. You didn't have enough time to think about it, so you just went with it.*

It's okay, the whisper said, *you've had the time to think about it, you can push him off you now.*

Sam felt her hand clench into a fist, ready to punch him in the chest to make him stop. But then he placed a hand on her head, running his fingers through her hair and wrapped his other arm around her waist, pulling her closer and—

—she froze.

Suddenly unwilling to push him away.

Her head was teeming with activity, as she started arguing with herself in her head.

Stop it.

Images flashed in her memories.

Demons.

Warlocks.

He's not safe.

Shifters.

Hunters.

He saved you.

Always following her. Coming after her. Trying to kill her. Hurting her. Hurting those she cared about.

He won't hurt you.

Jade

Push him away.

Madison.

Elle.

Scott.

He's not like them.

She had tried so hard to push each one away because they're fragile.

He'll die like everyone else.

Because they're weak.

Stop it.

Because they're human.

. . . he's not.

Sam felt her hand relax as her mind came to that realisation.

He's not human.

He's stronger. He's faster. He doesn't act like them. He doesn't think like them. If Sam were to let Scott kiss her like this he'd think it meant that she loved him. He wouldn't understand that she just needed to have someone to feel close to.

Just for a moment.

But Jamie, he wasn't human. He wouldn't think like that.

Think about this, warned the logical whisper in the back of her head as she slid her hand down Jamie's side to the end of his shirt and started moving it upwards.

"Sam," Jamie breathed, his tone infuriatingly similar to the whisper's, his voice wavering slightly.

"Don't!" she hissed and pulled him to her. She didn't want to think about this anymore; with the possibility of attacks every minute of her life, she had to think about everything she did, ten times over, then another twenty just in case, always wondering what would happen after.

Right now, with Jamie, she felt . . . wonderful.

She felt safe.

For once in her life Sam didn't want to think about it, she just wanted to act. She was sick of worrying about what might happen tomorrow.

"Just shut up," she ordered and kissed him again. She knew that right now he wanted her, and she had already decided to give him what he wanted.

I'm not thinking about it, she commanded herself, *I just want something physical, exciting, amazing.*

Don't do it, said a tiny voice in one half of her brain. While the other half whispered . . .

. . . fuck it.

CHAPTER 50

*J*amie couldn't believe he had kissed her so fast, and so sudden. But he had, and it had resulted in her accepting his touch. She wanted him, just like he wanted her.

He pulled her closer, strands of blonde hair falling in front of her face. He wiped them away and kissed her again. This time longer than before. He kissed her until she was left breathless. Her heart pounding so hard that he could feel its beat in his own chest.

He touched his hand to her cheek. Her skin feeling as soft as flower petals, and getting warmer as her body temperature rose. Her indigo eyes met his and she smiled, giving him *that* look. The one that made him feel like she could see into his soul.

Jamie returned her smile and picked her up, wrapped her legs around his waist and ran, carrying her upstairs, both of them laughing as they went. He opened the door to his bedroom and dropped Sam on the bed, she laughed as she landed on the mattress, he smiled and climbed onto the bed in front of her. Pulling her towards him and kissing her, making it deep and meaningful, trying his best to ensure she knew how he felt.

Then, with none of the hesitation he had felt before he first kissed her, he grabbed the end of her t-shirt and pulled it over her head. He got to his knees to take his shirt off and she unfastened his belt, ripping it off aggressively.

Jamie unbuttoned her jeans and they fell back to the mattress, tumbling over and laughing.

He spun her onto his lap and unhooked her bra, throwing it to the floor.

Pressing their bare chests together, he kissed her again, entangling his hands in her hair. She wrapped her arms around him and pulled him as close as she could.

Almost as if she was scared he might try to let her go.

But he never would.

He loved her.

And it was clear in this moment that she loved him too.

CHAPTER 51

*J*amie watched Sam as she lay on her side, with her back facing him. A smile grew on his lips as he watched her body move slightly with each breath she took.

He felt complete.

It wasn't until he had Sam lying next to him that he even realised anything had been missing.

My whole life, he thought, *she's what I've been waiting my whole life for.*

He just hadn't realised it until now.

Not even Bethany, whom he had loved and held so dearly ever made him feel as whole as Sam did right now.

Jamie wrapped his arm around her and lay closer to her. She jerked at his touch and then went very still. He loosened his grip, thinking he may have held her too tightly. He pushed himself up, leaning on his other arm so that he could see her face.

She said nothing. She just lay there silently and in complete stillness with her hair hiding her face from his view.

Jamie smiled at her even though she couldn't see.

He leaned down and placed a gentle kiss on her shoulder where her skin was exposed. "I love you Sam," he whispered, not thinking she would hear.

She jerked again. This time when he spoke. She curled herself up tighter, moving further away. Jamie sat up, now realising that she wasn't asleep. He brushed her hair away so that he could see her face. She moved, trying to bury her face in the pillow. He slid his hand under her head to try turn her towards him. His hand became wet when it touched her skin.

Jamie took his hand away and looked at the wet on his fingers. He knew before he looked at Sam's face that she was crying. "What's wrong?" he asked.

Sam didn't answer.

"Did I do something wrong?"

Sam breathed heavily, obviously trying to stop her tears. Jamie placed his hand on her shoulder, trying to comfort her. She pulled away quickly, causing his hand to fall to the sheets. Sam got out of the bed and frantically started searching for her clothes.

"Sam." Jamie sat up to watch her. She didn't answer; she kept her back to him as she pulled her clothes on. "Sam." Jamie reached his hand out to her.

She pulled away before his hand had even made contact. "What did I do?" he asked as he sat on the bed, feeling helpless, not knowing what to do, or what was wrong. "*What did I do?*" he asked again. A lump formed in his throat, making it feel tighter as he started to panic.

Sam ignored him. She picked up her shoes and started to put them on. Jamie jumped out of the bed and stood in front of her, blocking her before she had a chance to get away. He grabbed onto her arms and tried to make her look at him.

"What did I do?" he asked yet again, his desperation for an answer evident in his voice.

Sam pushed hard against his chest, he let go of her arms and stumbled back. Without putting her shoes on, she ran out of the room. Jamie hurried to throw his trousers on, and followed her out. "What did I do?" he called.

Still, she didn't answer.

"Sam!" She kept her back to him as she opened the door. Jamie thought about following her outside. But all he could do was stand in the doorway, staring out into the night, watching as Sam ran away from him.

All the while thinking to himself, *What the hell did I do?*

CHAPTER 52

With his back to the wall and his eyes checking all directions for as much as a moving shadow, Malachi descended the stone staircase as quietly as possible. He could tell from his last encounter with Sam that her Powers were getting weaker. Which was strange because she was getting older, so her Powers should have been getting stronger.

There was absolutely *no* reason that she should be growing weaker and her Powers diminishing.

It had always been Malachi's job to find a way to get Sam's Powers from her. *He* was the one who made the plans. *He* was the one who told people what parts they played in *his* plans.

And in the past few months he had made no plans.

Because for some inexplicable reason he had been demoted from plan maker . . .

The only thing Malachi could think of to explain why she would be weakening would be if someone *else* was making plans and executing them behind his back.

Even though Sam was *his* job.

Ever since a few months ago things had been strange. He'd notice that people would suddenly stop talking when he walked into the room. Kraven had been avoiding him, refusing to answer his questions about why he was no longer in charge of Sam. And refusing to say who he'd placed in charge instead.

He kept saying that there was no one else. That they were just avoiding Sam for now.

But clearly that was a lie.

Because clearly there was something going on with her.

So *clearly* someone was doing something and they were doing it behind his back.

For a while he had managed to convince himself that he was just being paranoid about his thoughts. But his encounter with Sam proved to him that he wasn't.

Someone was making plans that *he* was supposed to be making. And what was worse was that he wasn't being told about it.

Malachi stepped off the stairs and into the hallway. To avoid making any unnecessary sounds he had taken his shoes off in his room. He needed to get to The Oracle without anyone knowing.

Usually if Malachi was bothered by something, or needed answers, he would talk to Kraven about it.

But in this instance he got the feeling that *he* was the one making the plans behind his back.

So that meant that the only way to get answers would be to ask The Oracle, which was kept in a locked room that everyone thought only Kraven had a key to. But as second in command, Malachi had a master key that allowed him access to any and all rooms on the property.

Malachi came to the door leading to the room where The Oracle was kept. He knew he would find the answers to all of his questions in there. Pushing aside the guilt he felt about going behind Kraven's back, he tried not to dwell on the fact that he was also about to touch one of the man's most treasured possessions.

Respect is a two way street, he thought, *if he can't respect me enough to keep me in the loop, then why should I show him a courtesy he's refused me?*

For eighteen years Malachi had been in charge of dealing with Sam. It was his job to find a way to get her Powers from her. No one else really cared whether she lived or died.

But Malachi did.

He'd prefer not to have a young girl's blood on his hands, so he had been trying to come up with a way to get her Powers without killing her — at times he'd gone completely out of his way to ensure that she stayed living. And there was no way he was going to let someone ruin all of his plans before he even had a chance to execute them.

Malachi unlocked the door and stepped inside, closing it carefully behind him.

The room was dark.

He reached into his pocket and pulled out a short, thin candle. He lit it with a match and used it to illuminate the room slightly. He didn't dare use Magic in this room. Kraven would have been able to sense the residue when he was next in here.

Malachi walked forward slowly, shuffling his feet along the floor to avoid tripping over anything.

Not that he really would; the room was empty of all furniture apart from a small wooden table in the centre. *Still,* he thought, *better safe than sorry.*

He approached the table, carefully placing his hand on the wooden box that rested on top of it.

The Oracle.

He slowly lifted the lid and peered inside.

The box was lined with red velvet, and on top of the lining was a big lump of iolite. Malachi placed his hands on the stone. It lit up so bright it momentarily blinded him. He blew out his candle and put it back into his pocket, no longer needing its illumination.

He stood there for a moment with his hands on the stone, unsure of what he was supposed to do next. He had never called upon The Oracle before. *I probably should have learned how to do this first.*

He took a breath.

"Oh great and powerful Oracle . . . um . . . I seek answers from your . . . wise self." Malachi waited a moment. Nothing happened. "Um . . . I seek answers . . . *please?*"

He sighed again when, once more, nothing happened. He slid his hands off the rock, accidentally cutting himself on the jagged edges.

He jumped back a little and put his finger in his mouth to stop the bleeding. Malachi peered up as he heard a low rumble.

The gemstone shook, then slowly the light inside it shot out as it cracked open.

Oh shit, I broke it! he thought in panic as he looked behind him at the door, wondering how far he could run before Kraven found out what happened. He took one last look at the stone, and gasped.

Floating above it was the ghostly image of a woman. She opened her pupil-less eyes and stared directly at Malachi. "You are not my Master," she stated, her ghostly voice ringing out in an echo. Malachi winced, briefly peering over his shoulder at the door. *I hope this room is soundproofed.* "You have no right to call upon me."

"Hi," he said lamely. "Yeah, I know. But I need answers and I didn't know who to ask. So I thought . . . you know, who better to answer a question than an Oracle?" He smiled hopefully.

The Oracle didn't seem pleased. "I answer questions only for my Master. That is the agreement to which I am bound."

"I know. But Kraven is your master. And my question is about him . . . kind of." Malachi sighed. "I don't know who else to ask."

The Oracle regarded him for a moment. "I should not allow this, but since my current Master will leave me to you when he dies, I suppose I can allow for this one exception."

"Thank you!" Malachi smiled. "Okay, so—"

"You may ask me *one* question," The Oracle interrupted. "And that is all. I will answer you as best I can."

"Okay . . . " Malachi thought hard about the question he would ask. *She probably already knows everything that's been happening and everything I'm thinking of asking.* Malachi looked at The Oracle, hoping she'd have an expression that would confirm his thoughts.

She didn't.

Her expression was neutral.

She probably doesn't have any other expressions. He sighed. "What should I do?"

The Oracle appeared to give him a half smile. If she did though, it was gone before Malachi fully noticed it. "What should you do about the past? What should you do about the present? Or what should you do about the future?"

Malachi opened his mouth to answer 'the present', but stopped himself, shrugging instead to indicate that he wasn't sure which one he meant. *Why get one answer when I can get three?*

The Oracle was silent for a moment, then she said, "Do not trust your past. Presently you should do as you believe to be right."

Malachi waited a moment for her to continue. "And the future?" he asked, hoping since he was simply prompting an answer for the question he'd already asked, that she didn't treat what he said as a separate query.

"Follow the path of jade, to find the truth of your soul."

"What?" Malachi asked in confusion. "What does that mean? Where is this jade path . . . is this a *real* path or a metaphorical one?"

The Oracle looked down at him. "I said I would give you one answer. I allowed you to have three. I will speak with you no more."

"Wait a minute."

The Oracle disappeared in a swirl of light, which seeped back through the cracks in the gemstone.

"That last one doesn't really count," he said to the empty room. "If I don't understand it it's not a real answer!"

Malachi waited a moment for a reply he didn't get. He sighed, then closed the lid of the box and walked out of the dark room.

"Malachi!" He jumped at the sound of Kraven loudly calling his name. "Get in here!"

Lucky timing. Malachi quickly locked the door and hurried down the hall to where he'd heard Kraven call from.

He caught a glimpse of a tall cloaked figure as he . . . or she walked out of the room Malachi was about to walk into. The cloaked figure appeared to be oozing shadows. Malachi shivered, turning his face away as he approached Kraven.

He didn't ask who that had been as he got the distinct feeling that he would rather not know.

"What is it?" he asked.

Kraven opened his mouth to speak, but he paused, furrowed his brow and studied him curiously. "Why are you not wearing shoes?"

"Oh." He looked down at his feet, then back at Kraven. He shrugged. " . . . Because I'm not going outside today?"

Kraven stared at Malachi for a moment, before laughing. "You can be *so* strange sometimes."

Malachi grinned and rolled his eyes. "Why did you call me?"

Kraven pointed to the floor, where there was a locked wooden chest. He eyed the chest in confusion, then lifted his gaze back to Kraven.

"Were you not the one who was complaining about being left out of the plans?" he asked with more sarcasm than was necessary.

"I wasn't complaining," Malachi said defensively. *How the hell did he know that? I never said a thing out loud.* "I didn't even —"

"This box is how we're going to get her," Kraven interrupted. "It's filled with Shadows and about as much Dark Magic as we could manage to cram into it. My friend, who just left, told me that she needs to have a sad heart when she opens it, to make her more susceptible to what's inside.

"So we're going to upset her, then give her the chest. When she opens it, the Shadows will possess her, then her Magic will be drained and sucked into the chest. Then all we have to do is go and get the chest and make everything look normal for when the human police arrive at her house."

"Why would the police be at her house?" Malachi asked curiously, doing his best to hide his concern.

Kraven bent down and picked the chest up. "Most likely to investigate her death. Isn't that what police do?" he asked sincerely, the innocent gleam in his eyes making it obvious that he saw nothing wrong with what he'd said. He held the chest out for Malachi to take.

He reached out slowly, taking the chest in his arms. Malachi could feel strong Power throbbing inside; it wasn't the good kind and being so close to that amount of evil made him feel queasy. He tried his best not to let it show on his face. "Keep it in your room until tomorrow," Kraven said. "I'll send the Shifters to get it from you then."

"Why do *I* have to keep it?" Malachi knew that, in this situation, the right thing to do was to hand the chest back to Kraven and admit that he wanted nothing to do with this plan. Not if it involved killing an innocent girl. And the way Kraven had described it, it sounded like quite a painful way to die.

Kraven smiled slowly. "Because I wouldn't trust anyone else with it," he said as he left the room.

Malachi stood there alone for countless moments, a thousand thoughts rapidly running through his brain.

He sighed dejectedly, then made his way back to his room.

The chest would be in his possession all night.

Which meant that between now and tomorrow when the Shifters came to get it, no one else would see it.

No one else would touch it.

So no one else would know what he had done to it.

CHAPTER 53

$\mathcal{S}$am had always considered herself to be nobody's victim, but as she lay in bed crying she realised how wrong she had been. The dictionary definition of a victim was somebody who experienced misfortune and felt helpless to remedy it. That was Sam; she wasn't nobody's victim, she was *everybody's* victim.

People who didn't know her hated her guts and wanted her dead for no reason other than the fact that they were greedy for the Magic she possessed. There was nothing she could do to stop them, every time she killed one of them another took their place.

She buried her face in her pillow, taking in shallow breaths as she tried to calm herself down. *What the fuck is wrong with me?* She turned over so she was staring at the ceiling. Keeping her arms straight at her sides. Her hands balled into fists, gripping the sheets tighter and tighter as she tried to regain control of herself.

Loves me? Why does he have to be so damn stupid!

Her throat ached. It felt like it was filling up with something. Blocked, so that each breath she took through her nose was followed by the feeling of something trying to force its way out of her mouth. Sam pressed her lips shut, forcing her teeth together so tightly they hurt. She closed her eyes again to try calm herself.

It wouldn't work though.

When she closed her eyes all she could see was the look of hurt on Jamie's face as she had run away from him. Her heart felt like someone had it in their hand and was squeezing it horribly tight.

He doesn't understand, she told herself, *he can't understand.*

Sam felt something inside her break as she recognised the lie in her thoughts. The truth was that he could understand if she would give him a chance to. It was just another lie she had been feeding herself to make the pain of the truth stop hurting.

Her lips parted as she sighed, and with the sigh came the sound of a whimper. She squeezed her eyes closed again and let the tears fall.

Silently at first.

Then with loud sobs.

She turned on her side and buried her face in her pillow again, this time trying to muffle the sounds of her crying.

He wasn't supposed to love me.

"Sa—"

"Don't!" Sam snapped, interrupting Jack before he had a chance to do his impersonation of an alarm clock. She moved the duvet down, so that Jack could see her face. "I'm in a bad mood and I'm *not* getting up."

Jack looked at her, she could see concern in his eyes. "What's wrong?" he asked.

Sam groaned and closed her eyes tightly, trying to make the stinging go away. "I'm just tired."

"Tired?" Jack looked into Sam's eyes. She didn't look away. She knew that her eyes were probably red and puffy from all the crying, but that could also make them look tired. If she looked away he'd know something was wrong.

Jack sat down on the edge of her bed. The covers didn't crease beneath him, which meant he wasn't corporeal. Sam always wondered how he was able to sit down in a noncorporeal form. She never asked though, and right then she really couldn't have cared less.

"Did something happen?" he asked, sounding as concerned as he looked.

Sam shook her head.

"You know you can tell me if you're not okay?" Sam nodded. "'Cause that's why I'm here. To make sure that you're okay."

"I know," Sam said, feeling slightly guilty for not talking, but not enough to make her speak.

Jack nodded. "Okay. I'll leave . . . call me if you need me though, okay?"

"Okay."

"For anything, right? Nothing is too trivial. You can call me if you only need a tissue or something."

Sam forced herself to smile a little. "Okay . . . thanks."

Jack smiled at her kindly, then disappeared, leaving her alone to bury her face in her pillow once again and cry some more.

CHAPTER 54

$\mathcal{J}$ack knew that there was something wrong with Sam. He could always tell when things weren't right with her. It was like a sixth sense he had developed through living with her since she was a child and learning to see through her bullshit.

She used to be good at pretending that she was okay, but he was never stupid enough to fall for it. Although he did, on more than a few occasions, allow her to think that he believed she was completely fine.

Sam wasn't really the type of person who enjoyed sharing feelings. And the older she got, the less she showed them.

To anyone.

But just because she didn't openly show them didn't mean that Jack couldn't see.

It has to have something to do with Jamie. And if it doesn't, well, he follows her around enough for him to have some idea as to what's happened.

Jack corporealised inside Jamie's house. He knew Sam had buried spell jars around the perimeter and carved some protective sigils somewhere. Her spells would keep anyone and everyone out of this place. Unfortunately for Jamie, anyone and everyone only included those with physical bodies.

He gazed around the living room where he had corporealised. Jamie wasn't there. He wandered in and out of all the downstairs rooms trying to find him. When he couldn't locate Jamie, he checked upstairs.

Up the stairs there was just a bedroom and a bathroom. And the stupid Vampire wasn't there either.

Jack walked back downstairs and sighed.

Where the fuck else would he be?

As far as Jack knew the only person Jamie talked to around here was Sam. And since Jack was pretty sure that Jamie wasn't with Sam right now, he should be here.

. . . If I were a Vampire, where would I be?

Jack sighed and sat down on the sofa in the living room. *All these years of being dead have murdered my hunting skills.* He picked up the TV remote and flicked through the channels, trying to find something interesting to watch while he waited for Jamie to come home.

CHAPTER 55

$\mathcal{J}$amie wandered through the woods, barely paying any attention to where he was going.

Last night kept playing through his mind.

He was still in shock over Sam running out the way she did.

The night had come and gone, and so had most of the day, but he barely noticed the time pass. It wasn't until the sun was almost in setting position that he realised how long he had been wandering for.

I should go see her, he thought. *I should find out what happened. Find out what I've done wrong.* Jamie continued walking through the woods, but now with a better sense of where he was going. It took him about twenty minutes to get from where he'd found himself to the street that Sam lived on.

As her house came into view, he saw that she was walking towards him. He froze where he was standing, and she appeared to do the same. *She must have been just leaving to go somewhere and hadn't expected me to be here.*

"Sam?" He took a hesitant step in her direction. She folded her arms across her chest and took a breath. Then she marched towards Jamie, looking slightly irate. He took a cautious step back.

"What are you doing here?" she asked. Though it seemed like more of an accusation than a question. She was now less than an arm's length away, staring at him like she was trying to intimidate him.

Before Jamie had a chance to open his mouth to speak, Sam continued, "What the fuck gives you the right to be around me? What gives you the right to invite yourself into my life then mess it all up? Everything was perfectly fine before you came along. *I* was perfectly fine."

"Sam . . . I—"

"Who says you're allowed to make me cry?" she shouted. Jamie noticed her lips press together almost as if she were trying not to cry. "I *never* cry, who said you're allowed to do that?"

"I didn't mean to make you cry," Jamie said, feeling guilty. He felt his throat get tight. *I'm just upsetting her more by being here.* "Tell me what I did so that I can make it—"

"No!" Sam yelled in frustration. "Stop doing that."

"Doing what?"

"You know what! . . . Stop being nice to me! Stop liking me!" She looked like she wanted to either scream or burst into tears. Instead she just turned her back to him. "Just leave me alone. I was used to it being that way, so just leave me alone. I don't *need* you."

Jamie sighed. "Maybe *you* don't need me," he said. His voice sounded tired and sad. Jamie placed his hand on Sam's elbow, turning her around so that she had to look at him. "But did you ever stop to think that maybe *I* need you?"

He felt Sam shaking. That was the first time he noticed that there was something not right about her.

Her skin looked pale, she had circles under her eyes that were so dark they were visible through her make-up. Her eyes were red and bloodshot.

But not like she had been crying. More like blood was about to start leaking out of them.

"Oh my God!" Jamie stepped closer to her, filling the small space between them. Sam tried to move back, but he didn't let her. Jamie breathed in the air around her, it was dark and heavy, and felt as though it would suffocate you if you breathed it for too long. "Why didn't you tell me?"

She tried to pull her arm out of his hand, but she was too weak.

About three months ago she could floor me and keep me there and now she can't even push me away?

"Let me go!"

"How long?" Jamie shouted, the memory flooding back to him, just now realising what Sam had meant. "You asked that Faerie how long."

"Let me go," she whispered, her eyes welling up with tears.

"Sam . . . you're dying." Jamie said the words, feeling like he would cry. "What happened? What can I do to help? I won't let you die."

Sam pulled back again. This time Jamie let her go. "I don't want any help!" she yelled. "It's better this way. It *needs* to happen. So you just leave me alone!" Sam pointed to her house. "And move your fucking car away from my house! I'm sick of it being there all the time!"

Jamie looked towards the large black car that was parked across the road from her house in confusion. "What?"

Sam scoffed. "I know that's your car," she said. "It's been there forever . . . do you just sit around my house and stalk me twenty-four seven?"

"Sam . . . " Jamie put his hand on her arm and pulled her back. "I don't have a car."

She stared at him, her expression filled with confusion. "But the day we met, at the library, you pointed to *that* car and asked me if I wanted a ride home."

Jamie glanced towards the vehicle, now recognising it from that day. That night he had been so relieved she had declined his offer, that he hadn't stopped to wonder why there was a car in an otherwise empty car park, outside a completely empty building . . . and he also hadn't thought to check if there was anyone already in the car.

"I don't even know how to drive."

"But, you said —"

"Okay, listen. I will explain that to you later. Right now, let's focus on the fact that *that* is not my car. And it's been parking there for how long?"

Sam looked at Jamie, then back at the car, her eyes widening with fear. "A few months . . . I never see anyone get in or out, and you said it was yours so I never really thought about it."

He felt himself begin to worry, as it was the first time he had seen her wear such an expression.

Slowly she took a step forward.

Then another.

Jamie walked beside her, preparing himself for the possibility that he would have to kill anyone who stepped out of the car since Sam no longer had the strength to protect herself.

CHAPTER 56

$\mathcal{S}$am glared at the car as she approached it.

I can't believe I was stupid enough to think that Jamie was following me everywhere in a car. Vampires don't even need cars.

As she walked towards it she wondered how long it had really been following her. She only started to notice it after she told Jamie to leave her alone, but pretty much the only reason she noticed it at all was because she thought Jamie was driving it. It could have been following her all year and she wouldn't have realised.

"What are we going to do?" Jamie asked.

"I don't know," Sam replied.

She had been racking her brain for a useful suggestion for the past minute. But since her body had started deteriorating her mind hadn't been able to think as fast as it used to. "Um . . . I suppose we could knock on the window and find out who's there. I've got my dagger and a little Magic I can use and you've got your Vampireness. We can take them if we need to."

"Let me knock," Jamie said, "and stay behind me."

He moved himself in front of Sam, keeping his arm out to shield her. Sam let him as he was now physically stronger than her there was no point in arguing with the logic behind him going near the strange car first.

As they came close enough he reached out and knocked on the window, which was tinted so dark she couldn't even make out a silhouette behind it.

Sam jumped when she heard the door click on the other side of the car. "Someone's coming," she whispered to Jamie. He nodded and took three steps back, keeping her behind him the whole time.

Sam saw the top of someone's head over the other side of the vehicle. The hair was cut short, which made Sam immediately think that it was a man. She wrapped her hand around the hilt of her blade and squeezed it tightly, getting ready to use it if she had to.

The door in front of them swung open. Sam looked from behind Jamie at the man who was stepping out. He was youngish, with light mousy brown hair that was cut tight. He was dressed in a military uniform. He smiled at Sam as if she should recognise him . . . she didn't, but played along, forcing herself to smile back.

She looked at his eyes and immediately knew that something wasn't right.

The man who had gotten out of the car on the other side came around to where she and Jamie were standing. He was older than the other guy, but he was also wearing a uniform. Only his looked more official. As he stared at her, Sam noticed that he was carrying a large wooden chest in his hands.

Both of the men were looking at Sam strangely.

Almost as if they knew her and as if she was supposed to

know them.

Jamie stepped in front of Sam, completely blocking her from their line of sight. "Who are you, and what do you want?" he asked the men, though it sounded more like a demand than a question.

The older one stepped forward. "I am General Pike, this is Officer Smith. We are looking for a Miss Samantha Jacobs."

"What for?" Jamie asked.

"It's about your brother, Daniel," the younger one said directly to Sam.

Jamie looked to her for some clue as to what he should do or say next. "What about him?" she asked. Even though she was pretty sure what they were going to say to her.

"He's been killed," Officer Smith said, choking on his words as he spoke them, his eyes welling up as though he were about to cry.

Not a bad actor, Sam thought.

"Oh my God." Jamie looked at Sam with sympathy. "Sam, are you okay?"

Sam nodded. "He was my friend, you know," said the younger one.

"I know," she said as she looked him up and down. "I recognise your face." She lied to him because she knew from his expression that she was expected to recognise his face. That was the point of the whole show after all.

He smiled. Sam laughed internally. *He thinks I'm fooled.*

General Pike cleared his throat to get her attention. She looked at him. "We were asked to return his belongings to you."

Sam looked at the chest, wondering what tricks were inside it. She knew for a fact that it was nothing that belonged to Danny.

First off, why would he own a wooden chest and bring it

with him on deployment?

Secondly, why would these two bring it to her in person?

Thirdly, Danny didn't have anything of importance with him. All of his crap was in his room exactly where he left it when he ran away.

And finally, if all they had tracked her down for was to return 'Danny's' chest to her, why had they been stalking her for months?

Sam just nodded, trying her best to pull off a convincing look of grief—which was difficult because she knew they were lying and also because she was still angry at Danny and so couldn't even imagine being sad about his fake death. After a moment of Sam looking at the chest and not taking it, Jamie reached out and took it from the 'General'.

"Do you need help getting it inside?" Officer Smith asked, stepping forward.

"No," Sam replied quickly. *I am not gonna invite you in my home.* "That's okay."

"Alright then." He shrugged. "We'll leave you now."

General Pike walked back around to the other side of the car whilst Officer Smith climbed inside.

"When did it happen?" Sam asked Officer Smith just before he closed the car door.

"About a week ago," he replied, taking a moment before he clarified. "Last Thursday."

Sam nodded her head.

She walked towards the front door, with Jamie following close behind her. As she reached the porch she turned and watched the car drive away. Not taking her eyes off it until it was completely out of sight.

"Sam—"

"Calm down . . . he's not dead."

Jamie looked at her sympathetically, as if he thought she was in denial or something. Sam sighed irritably and rolled her eyes. She was so tired right now. She felt completely drained of everything, strength, energy, Magic.

Sam walked to the table in the hallway and opened the drawer where there were about a thousand unopened letters from Danny, each one sent to her weekly, on a Friday.

She picked up the envelope from last Friday, the day after he had supposedly died, and showed it to Jamie.

"This was sent to me last Friday . . . from Danny," she said as she opened the envelope and unfolded the letter inside to show Jamie the date on it.

He studied the letter, clearly confused. "But they said he died on Thursday."

Sam shook her head. "If Danny had died, I'd have been told about it straight away, by phone call or official letter or something, not a week later in person. The military has better shit to do than to send ranking officials door to door to do death notifications. And besides, he's fighting with humans in a human war. He's a lot stronger than a human, 'cause he's not one of them. He wouldn't die."

Jamie looked at the drawer as Sam put the letter and the envelope back inside with all of the others. "Sam, why are none of them opened? Haven't you read them?"

Sam closed the drawer and turned to look at Jamie. "That's personal," she said, folding her arms across her chest. "And I don't want to talk about it."

Jamie looked at her for a moment, then sighed. He peered down at the chest he was holding and changed the subject. "Okay, well if he's not dead . . . then what's this?"

"Exactly what I was wondering when they gave it to me." Sam walked through the hallway, with Jamie following her. She led the way to the kitchen and opened the back door. "Put it over there." She pointed down to the ground outside the door.

"What do you think it is?" Jamie asked as he placed the chest on the ground.

"I'm not sure. And I'm not gonna open it and find out."

Sam walked across the lawn to the tool shed by the back fence. "What are you doing?" he asked from the doorway.

"Digging a hole to put the chest in," she answered as she opened the door and took out a shovel. "I can't risk leaving it lying around in case someone tries to open it. I don't know what kind of evil is in there."

Jamie sighed. "Sam you can't dig. You're too weak for manual labour."

She ignored him, carrying the shovel to the back of the garden, where there were some flowerbeds that would be easy to dig up. She could always just put the flowers back when she was done and no one would ever know there was something there.

Jamie placed his hand on the shovel to keep Sam from digging.

"Let me do that," he said. "You go get some food or rest or something."

Sam hesitated for a moment, but decided to let Jamie do it. *It is past dinner time and I haven't had food yet.* "I'll be inside," she mumbled as she turned. She didn't want to talk to him anymore so she wasn't going to stand there and argue.

Even in her weakened state she could sense him watching her as she walked away.

CHAPTER 57

*J*amie hit the dirt back into place around the replanted flowers. It was dark now, the sky a shade of navy blue with black swirling clouds slowing floating across the sky. Completely blocking out the light of the moon.

He opened the tool shed and put the shovel back inside, casting a glance towards the kitchen window. The lights were on inside the house, but he couldn't see Sam from where he was. There was nothing but an empty kitchen.

As he closed the shed door, Jamie saw a shadow move across the lawn in the corner of his eye and jumped. He squinted to try focus on where he thought he had seen someone.

But there was nothing.

Just an empty garden.

For a moment, he just stood there and stared at the empty space, a thousand theories rushing through his brain all at once. Most of which were him listing off the many kinds of creatures that could be here in an attempt to attack Sam while she was weak and vulnerable. He stared, thinking that if there was something there he was bound to see it again.

But still, even after the countless moments he spent staring, he saw nothing. Jamie let a breath, shaking his head as if to shake away his paranoia. *It's probably just a cat*, he thought as he walked towards the back door.

Just before his hand reached the doorknob, there was a loud crash which sounded like it had come from the front of the house. Jamie froze where he was, his hand hovering above the handle. Slowly he turned to face where he had seen the shadow.

A cat could have knocked into some bins, he thought, willing his brain to believe that there were no threats around. But a feeling stirring in the pit of his stomach urged him forward. Somewhere in the back of his mind he knew that there was something more dangerous than a cat lurking around in the darkness.

Outside the front of the house, the streetlamps flickered on and off.

Jamie covered his eyes, turning his face away from the lights when they started to hurt them. That was when he noticed a pool of black liquid on the ground. Slowly, he walked towards it and knelt down beside it. He cautiously dipped a finger in the puddle, thinking it must be oil from the car that was parked there earlier.

The liquid didn't feel like liquid. It felt light, cold and dry when it should have felt heavy and sticky. He brought his hand up to his face to examine the substance. His finger was stained with black, but the closer he brought it to his face, the more the substance seemed to disappear. He stared at his hand, bewildered as the black 'liquid' turned to smoke and floated away.

He jumped with fright as he saw movement in his peripheral

vision. Jamie didn't bother to turn around. Instead he stretched out his senses. The only creatures he could sense were the humans safely tucked away in their houses and a few wandering cats. All of which were too far from him to be the cause of the movement.

He snapped his head to the side, hoping to catch a glimpse of whatever was there.

But there was nothing.

The street was empty of any signs of life.

He shook his head, thinking that his mind must be playing tricks on him.

As Jamie stood up, he swayed, suddenly feeling dizzy. The streetlamps flickered once more, before the light was sucked out of them. The next thing Jamie saw was what seemed like a black tidal wave of shadows, all coming towards him at a rapid pace.

He tried to run, but like in a nightmare he was stuck, unable to move forward. He was being held in place by some unseen force, and before he could think of a way to escape, the shadows took him over.

CHAPTER 58

$\mathcal{S}$am was sitting on the couch for well over an hour while Jamie buried the chest. Physical tasks had been taking more and more effort lately. After her eighteenth birthday her body had lasted longer than she'd expected in its deteriorating state, she had managed to keep her condition hidden for three months and it had been easy. But last week she had reached the final stages.

Her body was broken.

She was weak.

Her mortal vessel was no longer able to contain the amount of Power she had, and so it was tearing her apart from the inside. She knew that she didn't have more than a week left.

Three months ago she would have been happy about that, but now she wasn't so sure if death was really what she wanted.

She'd made a mistake.

She'd allowed herself to feel happiness when she knew it

would do nothing but make her reluctant to do what needed to be done.

She *needed* to die.

She knew that.

But Jamie . . . Sam tried her hardest not to think about him and how nice he was to her, how much he cared about her.

She had been more than ready to die.

At least she had been . . . until the point she had met Jamie and realised that she lo —

Sam jumped at the sound of the doorbell ringing.

She pushed herself off the couch and slowly walked towards the door. Opening it with trepidation at what she might find, only to discover Jamie on the other side, his clothes covered in dirt from digging outside. "What are you doing out here? The back door is open."

"I accidentally locked myself out," he said.

Sam looked at him curiously. There was something off about him, but she couldn't quite figure out what it was. She stepped aside to let him in.

He walked past her into the living room. Sam stared out at the streets which had not a trace of light — they were pitch black because for some reason all of the streetlamps had been switched off.

She jumped slightly at the sound of a high-pitched scream echoing somewhere far off in the distance.

"Did you hear that?" she asked, turning to Jamie. He shook his head slowly. Sam's heart pounded. *You know what that was,* her head whispered. *You're not safe.*

Sam ignored the voice and closed the door. She turned to Jamie, who was standing next to her, staring . . . again. Before Sam had a chance to tell him to stop, his mouth was on hers, and he was kissing her. Sam didn't push him away, mostly because she didn't really want him to stop.

But then he suddenly stopped himself and stood there, holding her face in front of his, a devious smile slowly spreading across his face. *Something is* very *wrong*, she thought. *That smile isn't his.*

"You've always seemed like the sort of person who's scared of nothing," he said, his voice quiet and malevolent. "But you're scared right now, aren't you?"

"What?" Sam asked in confusion. "I'm not scared."

"You are." Jamie grinned at her, showing all of his teeth. Then he moved his face so close to hers their noses were touching. He inhaled deeply. "I can smell it," he drawled, then lightly kissed her lips. "I can taste it."

Get away from him, her head yelled at her.

Sam ignored her thoughts and stayed where she was. Jamie would never hurt her. *He wouldn't.* "Most people who live in the dark learn to live there," he continued. "*They* embrace it . . . but not you. You don't want to live there because you're *scared* of the dark. You're *scared* of the Shadows."

Something's definitely *not right*, she thought, her mind starting to panic as her instincts urged her to run. "I'm not afraid of the dark," she said slowly, not sure why he would be saying any of this to her. " . . . Or of shadows."

"No?" he asked, as a flash shot across his eyes, and what looked like a black mist filled his irises. "What about now?"

Before Sam had a chance to work up the energy to defend herself, his mouth was on her neck. She felt a sharp pain pierce through her skin as she was filled with a burning ache, the sensation like fire in her veins as what remained of her Power fled her body.

And then she was paralyzed.

Her lips moving even though she could no longer speak . . .

And then, the world seemed to disappear.

CHAPTER 59

Jamie felt a shudder go through his entire body. Blurred shadows floated before his eyes. He closed them tightly, pinching the bridge of his nose to help rid himself of a building headache. He breathed in sharply, the scent of blood assailing his senses.

Slowly, he lowered his hand and opened his eyes, already knowing what he would see.

He clenched his jaw, holding back his screams as he gazed down at the lifeless body before him. Jamie reached his hand out and placed it against Sam's cheek.

Her skin was cold.

"Sam," he spoke, his voice barely able to make a sound. He moved his hand down from her face to her shoulder and firmly jerked her body. "Wake up!" he screamed. He moved closer to her, using both of his arms to lift her from the floor. Her head fell back, her neck unable to support its weight. He put one hand behind her head to try hold it up. "You have to wake up!"

he said, shaking her again. "You're not human . . . you can't die!"

Jamie looked down at Sam's unresponsive body, his hands shaking as his eyes darted around the room in confusion, trying to remember what had happened. Warm drops of blood fell onto his hand. He took it out from under Sam's head and looked at the crimson drops, slowly shifting his gaze to the wound they had come from.

He held his breath when he saw the tear in Sam's neck. Blood covered the whole left side, and spread up to her jaw line and down onto her t-shirt.

That was the first time Jamie noticed the taste in his mouth.

The taste of fresh blood — but not the taste of human blood.

He gently placed Sam down on the floor and used the hand not stained by her blood to wipe his mouth. He took his hand away from his face and looked at it. Then he brought his other hand up and stared at both of them in horror.

He was covered in blood.

Sam's blood.

Jamie let his hands fall down to his lap and looked at Sam, letting tears flow freely. "Sam," he whispered, moving towards her again, cradling her body in his lap. "I'm sorry," he sobbed, rocking her back and forth. "I'm so sorry." Jamie held her close, hugging her cold, lifeless corpse. He kissed her forehead and looked down at her face.

She was beautiful.

Even in death she was beautiful.

"I can fix you," he whispered, knowing she couldn't hear him but not caring. "I can fix you." He brought his arm up to his mouth and bit down hard, opening a wound on his wrist. Blood trickled down his arm as he brought it to Sam's lips.

He held it there hoping his blood would be able to heal her. But she wouldn't take it. "Drink," he whispered pressing his wrist closer, trying to get the blood to go down. "Drink it!" Jamie shook her again, hoping he could jerk her awake for long enough to make her drink just a little.

It was useless.

And in his heart he knew it.

He knew that she was dead, too far gone for him to bring her back.

He lay her down on the floor, wiping away his tears as an eerie calm settled within him.

He crossed her arms over her chest and fixed her head so that she looked like she was comfortable. He kissed her one last time before he stood up, and slowly walked away.

CHAPTER 60

Sam! . . . Sam! . . . " Jack shook her hard. "I will not let you die!" Jack hit her as hard as he could. Her head snapped to the side and her eyelids fluttered. She wasn't breathing. But he knew Sam, he knew the strength she had and the stubborn attitude that had pissed him off more than once.

She may have been weak, but every cell of her being was filled with Power.

If she wanted to wake up, she could.

If she wanted to live, she could.

She had the ability, she just refused to do anything to save herself.

"Say the spell!" he shouted at her. He knew that she could hear him, but she wasn't listening.

"You will *NOT* let us down, do you hear me? I won't let you!" He placed his hands on both of her shoulders and shook her violently. Her eyes were slightly open and the fingers on both of her hands twitched. "Your whole family died *for you!*

Don't you dare let them down Sam! You owe them!

"Everyone gave their lives to keep you safe! For fuck sake Sam, *I* died for you!" He shook her harder, refusing to let her slip away. "I gave my life for you and all I ever asked in return was that you live. So don't you *dare* make it so that I died for nothing!"

Sam gasped, and let air go into her lungs. "You *owe* me," he said and looked into her eyes. "Say the spell."

Sam blinked away tears. Jack knew that she didn't want to say it, but he couldn't just stay there and watch her die. Too many people had gone already. "Say it!" Sam jumped a little. He'd never really raised his voice to her in anger before, but right now it was necessary. It was the only way to get through to her.

Slowly she took a ragged breath, and spoke quietly,

"I will not shed a tear for life – "

She paused to get some more air, but hesitated before continuing. "Keep going," Jack snarled, encouraging her to go on. He could tell that she was weak and it was painful for her to speak, but seeing her suffering through some pain was a better option than watching her die.

"For death I will not cry
I am not scared to live
And I shall never die

I feel no pain of heart
I feel no pain of mind
My body may lie broken
But in my spirit find

The power at my centre
My will that keeps me strong
Even if this body dies
My soul will carry on . . . "

The last four words echoed throughout the room. A light shone around her, but Sam lost consciousness before she could see the effects the spell would have.

CHAPTER 61

*J*amie walked into a bar. He needed to drink something strong to help him forget. He closed his eyes to help his head to calm. But behind his lids all he could see was her face.

He could see her eyes, still full with colour, a beautiful vibrant bluish–purple, and they were watching him as if he had betrayed her.

He opened his eyes and looked around.

No longer able to bear the sight of her.

Jamie sat on his stool and wished he could go back and stop himself. He had no real recollection of what happened; the last thing he remembered was digging a hole behind Sam's house. But when he'd opened his eyes to find Sam dead in his arms, with her throat torn open and the taste of blood on his lips . . . it wasn't too difficult to figure it out.

He would have staked himself through the heart right there and then, but he didn't have the strength.

He just couldn't do it. Even though he felt death was all he deserved, his survival instincts got the better of him. He needed someone else to do it for him.

Jamie looked behind him as the woman walked past, trailing her fingers along his back as she went. She stopped at the door and turned to him. Jamie could smell her from where he was sitting.

Her scent was so irresistibly sweet.

He looked in her direction.

Their eyes met.

She smiled at him invitingly. As if she wanted him to leave with her.

Trying to convince him she wanted him, but Jamie already knew why she wanted *him* specifically and not someone else.

Jamie stood up and finished his drink in one go.

Then he followed the woman out of the bar.

EPILOGUE

ATHENS – PRESENT DAY

Atropos felt the world tremble as a vast circle of light flew outwards, encasing the entire earth in a shimmer of Power. Magic surged through the veins of time, calling back souls of the long dead.

Clotho's body jerked as the past flew forward, entangling itself in the present.

Lachesis closed her eyes and watched in her mind as present happenings wrote themselves onto her memories.

Atropos looked down and watched as thirteen cut threads started to glow before they mended themselves back into wholeness, and then wrapped around each other, entwining the souls of the people the threads belonged to. She dropped her scissors as a smile grew on her face.

She looked at her sisters as she declared, "The time of prophecy has begun."

<u>**AND SOME FINAL WORDS . . .**</u>

As this book is self published and I lack the advertising and marketing budget of more traditionally published books, my main form of advertising comes from you guys (the readers).

So please, if you liked, loved, hated, despised or felt/thought anything about this book at all, leave me a review and let me and others know what you thought.

Visit me online for book updates and some of my insane ramblings about life and stuff:

evilbunnybooks.com

For anyone who may be interested, this is
the birthmark on Sam's arm.

Enjoy . . .

The Immortal Souls: Magic & Chaos – Book 2
GUARDIAN VAMPIRE

Things are not right . . .

Something evil is happening, with Sam in a seemingly perpetual state of unconsciousness and Jack nowhere to be found, finding a solution rests on Jamie's shoulders.

But after drawing the attention of Vampire Hunters, how can he hope to survive and save the one person he cares about?